LILY'S STORY, BOOK ONE

HE *Loves* ME NOT

This is a work of fiction. Any resemblance it bears to reality is entirely coincidental.

Visit Christine's website: christinekersey.com

LILY'S STORY, BOOK ONE

HE *Loves* ME NOT

CHRISTINE KERSEY

Books by Christine Kersey

Lily's Story Series

He Loves Me Not (Lily's Story, Book 1)
Don't Look Back (Lily's Story, Book 2)
Love At Last (Lily's Story, Book 3)
Life Imperfect (Lily's Story, Book 4)

Parallel Trilogy

Gone (Parallel Trilogy, Book 1)
Imprisoned (Parallel Trilogy, Book 2)
Hunted (Parallel Trilogy, Book 3)
After (a parallel story)
The Other Morgan (a parallel story)

Over You — 2 book series

Over You
Second Chances (sequel to *Over You)*

Standalone Books

Suspicions
No Way Out

Chapter One

It was my first day of college at the University of Nevada, Reno—the beginning of a new chapter in my life. Excited to discover what lay in store for me, and eager to begin my future, I walked down the crowded hall looking for my classroom. At twenty years of age I was older than the average freshman, but that was okay. I felt just as young and inexperienced as any eighteen year old.

Not liking to draw attention to myself, I avoided eye contact with the other students. Out of habit, I reached up to adjust my glasses, but then remembered I'd traded them in for contact lenses. Worried I would be late for my first class, I hurried down the hall. It was hard enough to be alone in a new city—when I added my lack of familiarity with the campus and my poor sense of direction, the butterflies in my stomach became oversized moths.

Students sat on the floor of the hallway waiting for their classroom doors to open so they could flood in. Everyone seemed to know each other, which seemed to emphasize the fact that I didn't know a soul. I pushed down the sudden feeling of panic and continued walking, reminding myself that even though I'd just come through a very difficult time in my life, a new phase was about to begin. I straightened my back against the weight of my bulky backpack and withdrew a printout of my schedule from the front pocket of my jeans so I could double-check the room number I needed to find.

As I slowed my pace to scan my schedule, my long black hair fell into my face, and for the hundredth time I thought about chopping it all off. Just as I began tucking my hair behind my ear, I noticed a backpack lying in my path. Though I tried to avoid it, the strap seemed to wrap around my foot, and I began falling. Trying to catch myself, I flung my arms out and slammed into the back of another student.

"Whoa!" the man said as he turned around. He caught me before I crashed to the floor.

Blood rushed to my face and I thought I would die of embarrassment, but I forced my eyes to meet his. "I am so sorry. I guess I should watch where I'm going." He still held on to my arm—not that I minded—but I couldn't help glancing at his hand.

He let go. "Are you okay?"

I nodded.

"Where were you going in such a hurry anyway?"

"I really wasn't going that fast. I just, well, I was looking at my schedule . . . I wasn't sure where my class was and I guess . . . I . ." My voice trailed off and I stopped talking before I made myself look like more of an idiot.

"That's okay. Don't worry about it."

Relieved at his response, I smiled, and when he gazed at me, a blush rose on my cheeks.

He cleared his throat and reached for the schedule I still held in my hand. "Maybe I can help you find your class."

I let him take the piece of paper and watched him peruse my schedule, trying not to be distracted by his startling blue eyes or his blonde hair.

"Well, what do you know?" He glanced up from the schedule, catching me staring. "We have a class together."

"We do?" I reached for the piece of paper, self-conscious that he knew I'd been checking him out. "Which one?"

"Sociology. At eleven."

"That's cool," I said.

"What's your name?"

"It's Lily."

"Lily, huh?" He grinned again. "I'm Trevor."

"Hi," I said stupidly. It had been so long since I'd been in this kind of social situation, I felt awkward and didn't know the right thing to say. I finally said, “I’m still not sure where my next class is. Can you point me in the right direction?”

To my pleasure and dismay, he leaned close to me to look at the schedule I held in my hand. The subtle scent of his aftershave drifted into my nose, making me nearly flush again.

Well, I have to breathe. I didn't ask him to stand so close to me.

When he stepped back slightly, I was mortified to realize I'd almost leaned toward him to get one more sniff of his cologne.

“It looks like you’re almost there,” he said.

Trying to regain my composure, I nodded. “Okay.”

“Just go to the end of the hall and make a right.” He pointed in the direction I’d been heading. “Your class should be right around there.” He smiled at me. “Hey. I’ll save you a seat in our class.”

“That sounds great.” Pleased to have some help, and by such an attractive man, I smiled again. “Bye.” I started in the direction Trevor had shown me, forcing myself not to turn around to see if he was watching me.

In my Financial Accounting class I had a hard time paying attention to the professor. My mind kept drifting back to Trevor and how much I'd enjoyed our brief contact. Even though I’d dated a few boys in high school, I hadn’t done any dating recently and knew the few flirting skills I’d possessed had become rusty.

Visualizing how I would interact with Trevor when I saw him later that morning, I imagined myself as one of the characters in the romance novels I liked to read, and pictured myself saying something witty, which would of course charm him and make him fall for me instantly and completely.

Fifty minutes later it was time for my next class, but not yet time to see Trevor in Sociology. After placing my notebook in my backpack, I checked my schedule to see where my next class would be, then reached into the depths of my backpack for the campus map. I dug around for a moment, then realized I must have left it on my desk in my apartment. “Crap,” I muttered under my breath.

“Is everything okay?” the girl sitting next to me asked.

Startled to realize someone had heard me, I stopped digging in my backpack. "I was just looking for my campus map, but I'm not finding it. Maybe you can you tell me where this building is?"

She looked where I pointed on my schedule, then she unzipped a side pocket on her backpack and pulled out a campus map. She spread it out on the table and showed me where we were and where I needed to go.

"Thanks," I said.

"You can keep the map." She folded it and handed it to me. "I know my way around well enough that I don't really need it."

"Are you sure?"

"Positive."

I took it from her. "By the way, I'm Lily."

"Alyssa," she said.

I tucked the map into my backpack. "I appreciate your help."

"No problem." She smiled. "And don't worry. By the end of the week you'll know your way around really well."

We both stood and walked out the classroom door.

"I'll see you later," Alyssa said before walking away.

As my next class came to a close, I thought about Trevor, and when I remembered my romantic fantasies about him falling madly in love with me, my face burned with embarrassment.

What makes you think he's interested in you that way? He was just trying to be helpful.

Eight minutes later I stood at the entrance to the Sociology classroom. I didn't see Trevor anywhere and wondered if I should wait for him before going inside so we could sit together. After a couple of minutes I wondered if he would even be coming. With a sinking heart, I admitted that when he'd promised he would save me a seat, he really was just being kind.

He might not even have the class with you. He was probably trying to make you feel better about nearly knocking him over.

I lifted my heavy backpack from the floor, slung it over my shoulders, then walked into the classroom.

Chapter Two

The only empty seats were in the front row. The teacher smiled at me as I made my way to a chair, and it seemed as if everyone watched me. Heat raced up my face, and I tried to be as inconspicuous as possible as I unzipped my backpack and pulled out my Sociology book. While the teacher passed out the syllabus, I thought about Trevor not showing up, and felt stupid for agreeing to sit by him in the first place.

Once class was over, as I gathered my things, I glanced at the other students to see if Trevor was somehow there. He wasn't. I left the room, once again feeling gullible for believing he'd had any interest in me.

With an hour until my next class, I decided to take a break and have something to eat. Somehow I remembered where the student union was and found it without too much difficulty. I picked up a tray and gathered my lunch before paying and heading to an empty table to eat alone.

Halfway through my meal, I heard someone calling my name. It was Alyssa.

"Do you mind if I join you?" she asked. "Or are you going to do some studying?"

Pleased to see a friendly face, I smiled. "Not if I can help it."

"Are you getting around campus okay?" She sat at the table, then pulled a sack lunch out of her backpack.

"Yeah, actually. It's not too hard once you get your bearings."

"I knew you'd figure it out. I could tell you were smart."

I laughed. "Thanks." I picked up my fork and resumed eating. "How are your classes going? Do you think it'll be a tough semester?"

"As always." She rolled her eyes. "Only three semesters to go until I have my degree. Thinking of that keeps me going."

"Wow. I'm just starting. It seems like it will be forever before I finally finish."

"So you just graduated from high school?"

"No. I actually graduated two years ago."

"Oh. So you've been working for the past two years?"

I hesitated. "No. My dad had some health issues, so I took care of him. He passed away this past spring."

"I'm so sorry. That must've been tough."

I swallowed hard to keep a lump from forming in my throat.

"If you don't mind my asking," she said, "what kind of health problems did he have?"

I picked up my cup of soda and took a sip before setting it down. "I don't really want to talk about it right now."

"Sorry." She pulled out a napkin. "I can't help myself. I tend to be nosy."

"That's okay."

"What about your mom?" She asked. "Oops. There I go again. Just don't answer my questions if you don't want to."

"No, no. That's okay. She was killed by a drunk driver when I was young, so I don't remember much about her. It was just me and my dad for a long time."

"Oh." Alyssa paused to take a bite from her sandwich. "So where are you living?"

I told her the name of the apartment complex.

"That's a nice place. Do you have roommates?"

"Yeah, two. How many roommates do you have?" Glad for the change of subject, I put a forkful of salad into my mouth.

"Three. But at least I have my own room. I don't think I could stand sharing a room with someone else."

"Yeah, that would be hard for me too. I like my privacy." I finished my soda. "Well, I'd better get going. I don't want to be late for my next class."

"Okay. I'll see you later."

I dropped my tray off and went to find my Math class, happy to have made at least one friend.

By the time my last class finished, I was ready to go home and take a nap before starting on my assignments. I was surprised I had so much homework after the first day—mostly reading, but it would take a while to get through all the subjects.

As I walked home, I congratulated myself that I'd had the foresight to choose an apartment within walking distance of campus. Even though I had Dad's Honda Accord now, I wanted to save money where I could, and the price of gas seemed to keep going up. The money my father had left me had to be carefully managed to make it last as long as possible.

As I thought of my father, I smiled sadly, thankful he'd bought a life insurance policy when he did—he'd gotten sick shortly afterwards. That money was now my lifeline, enabling me to get my education so I could support myself.

I still had the house my father owned, but for sentimental reasons I couldn't sell it yet. Even though it took over an hour to drive to it, just knowing it was there and that I could go there anytime I wanted brought a feeling of comfort.

I stopped at the mailbox before walking up the stairs to my apartment. Once at my door, I inserted the key, but found the door already unlocked. I went in, expecting my roommates to be home, but they weren't. Even though we'd only been roommates for a few days, this wasn't the first time they'd left the door unlocked. And even though I'd been raised in a small town, my dad had originally come from a large city and had trained me to always lock the front door. Coming home to an unlocked and empty apartment made me uneasy—especially in Reno.

I locked the front door and went into my bedroom, then set my backpack on my bed. With a quick look around, I made sure all my belongings were still where they should be, then took the books from my backpack and set them on my desk in preparation for studying.

Glancing at the work before me, I decided I needed something to eat before beginning. I went into the kitchen, opened the refrigerator, then shook my head in frustration. Once again my chopped vegetables were gone.

Though I liked my roommates well enough, I wasn't used to living with anyone besides my dad. And for the last two years while I'd been taking care of him, I'd been in charge of everything at our house. Living with people who didn't respect me or my desires was becoming tiresome.

Maybe I should splurge and get my own place.

Fantasizing about having a place all to myself, I imagined coming home from somewhere and finding everything the way I'd left it—when I put food in the refrigerator, it would still be there when I next went to get it. But when I considered the cost of renting a place on my own, I knew I would regret it later if my money ran out and I couldn't finish school.

Maybe I could get a part-time job.

I shook my head as I looked through the cupboards for something to eat.

A job will cut into my study time and then it will take longer to finish school.

Giving up on finding anything to eat, I went to my room and closed the door, then plopped onto the bed. I sorted through the mail to see if anything interesting had come, but finding nothing for me, I set the few pieces of mail on my desk and lay down.

I thought about my day, smiling despite myself. I'd been so nervous to start classes that I'd hardly slept the night before. Things had gone better than I'd expected—I'd even met a few people. Though I knew I should socialize more, it wasn't something that came naturally to me.

I need to get out of my comfort zone, right, Dad?

I smiled at the memory of my father's advice. He'd told me many times that I needed to force myself to meet people, to join clubs, to socialize. He hadn't understood that I preferred to stay in my room and read a good book. That was a lot more fun for me than any party.

Excited voices from the living room seeped under my door, pulling me from my reverie. It sounded like my roommates, Michelle and Nicole. I rolled off the bed and went to see what was going on.

"I hope he's there," Nicole said. "He said he might go."

They turned as I entered the room. "What about you, Lily? Are you going Friday night?"

"Where?" I remembered my earlier annoyance with my missing snack and wondered if I should mention it.

"The dance, of course," Michelle said. "You know, the beginning of the school year dance. Maybe you'll meet some cute guys."

Trevor's face flashed into my mind. "I don't know yet. I haven't decided."

"You can come with us if you want," Michelle offered.

Warmed by their friendliness, I smiled. Nicole and Michelle had known each other before coming to the University and I couldn't help but feel a little left out of things when they were around. "Thank you. I'll let you know."

When the two girls began talking about what they were going to wear to the dance, I went back into my room to begin reading my assignments. I closed the door and tried to ignore the loneliness that washed over me. Even though they'd invited me to go with them, I didn't feel like I fit in with their group. They were all so outgoing and loved to socialize.

So unlike me.

I wondered if I would ever find someone I would feel completely comfortable with.

Someone who would love me exactly as I am.

Chapter Three

Before I knew it, Friday afternoon arrived and I had to make a decision about the dance. School had only begun that week, but I was already beginning to feel buried by all the work I had to do. Having high expectations of myself, I planned to spend a lot of time mastering the material being taught.

I hadn't seen Trevor on campus and wondered if I ever would. My Sociology class had only met twice so far, and when Trevor hadn’t shown up for the second class, I’d almost felt relieved—I could forget I'd ever met him. But in reality I knew I wouldn't forget, not after the strong magnetism I'd felt towards him.

Maybe I should go to the dance—just to see if he shows up. I can always come home if he's not there.

After doing a little digging, I found some clothes that made me feel confident and set them on the bed to put on after I’d eaten.

Excited now about going, I wasn't very hungry—my roommates had gone out to dinner with their friends and had left before I’d decided I was going. I fixed some pasta and a small green salad before taking a shower and pulling my long dark hair into a French twist.

Not wanting to be one of the first people at the dance, I waited until it had been going for nearly an hour before I left my apartment to walk to campus. There were a few other people out too, although no one I knew.

A short time later I entered the large room where couples swayed to the music. Slowly walking around the room, I watched the dancing couples, then stopped and leaned against a wall. Completely alone, I felt very self-conscious.

It was a mistake to come.

I turned to leave, but a large group of students walked by and I had to wait until they passed before I could make my way to the exit. Then someone tapped my shoulder and I turned to see Alyssa.

“Hey,” I said as my anxiety faded.

“Hi there, Lily.” She smiled. “I’ve been thinking about you. I’d hoped you’d be here. Do you have a date?”

I shook my head. “What about you?”

“Nope. But who wants to be tied down at one of these, right?”

I returned her smile. “I guess so, but I'm not planning on staying long. I just wanted to check it out.”

“Okay.” Alyssa took me by the arm. “Come with me. I have some friends you might like to meet.”

I allowed myself to be led to a small group of people sitting at a table. Alyssa introduced me and I tried to remember the names thrown my way. Everyone seemed very friendly and I felt better about coming.

Someone pulled a chair out for me and I found myself sitting next to a man I remembered being introduced as Justin. He smiled at me as I sat beside him.

“Hi, Lily. I’m Justin. Where are you from?” He leaned toward me as he spoke.

“Here in Nevada. In Lovelock.” I noticed his thick black hair and green eyes. “What about you? Where are you from?”

“Just here in Reno.”

Though I noticed how cute he looked when he smiled, I didn't experience the same intense attraction I'd had when I'd met Trevor. This realization brought relief. During the years I’d cared for my father I hadn’t had much opportunity to date, and now the idea of having to figure out relationships was a bit overwhelming.

“Tell me about yourself, Lily,” Justin said.

Suddenly self-conscious, I tried to steer the conversation away from myself. “I’m not that interesting. Tell me about you, Justin. What are you majoring in?”

“Computer science.”

Genuinely pleased, I smiled. “Really? My major is Information Systems.”

Justin grinned. “Cool. Maybe we'll have some classes together.”

“I doubt it. I have a long way to go yet. You’re probably way ahead of me.”

He picked up a drink and took a sip. “Do you want anything to drink?”

“Not right now, thanks.”

“You’re right though. I graduate next spring. But if you need help in any of your classes, I’m your man.” He grabbed my arm and stood. “Come on. Let's dance.”

Reluctantly I stood and allowed him to lead me to the dance floor.

I'm getting out of my comfort zone.

It was a fast song and I found myself having a good time. Then the song ended and I began to walk off the floor.

Justin took hold of my arm again. “Wait, Lily. How about one more?”

“Sure, why not?” Then a slow song began.

Justin pulled me into his arms and I swayed with him to the music, feeling slightly uncomfortable at being so close to him.

What's wrong with me? Why can't I just enjoy myself?

Even though a lot of women my age were experts at dating, I felt like a novice when it came to men. As Justin moved me around the dance floor I tried to relax and have a good time and found that the more I pretended to have fun, the more fun I actually had.

When the song ended, Justin led me back to the table, which was nearly empty. “Wait here. I'll get you something to drink.”

Alyssa smiled at me as I sat across from her. “I told you I had some friends you'd like to meet.”

My face flushed at the implied comment.

“Oh, you’re blushing,” Alyssa said. “I’m sorry. I didn’t mean to embarrass you.”

I watched Justin as he walked through the crowd, then I turned back to Alyssa. “You didn't embarrass me. It's just hot on the dance floor.”

"Well, anyway, Justin's a really nice guy. And I think he likes you."

I shook my head. "He just barely met me. He doesn't know anything about me."

"So? He's attracted to you. That's the first step." Alyssa glanced at the people dancing. "You should have seen his face when you guys were slow dancing. I've known Justin for a while. He doesn't get a stupid grin on his face like that too often."

I was flattered by Alyssa's comments, but I didn't really believe her. "I'm nothing special. Why would he be interested in me?"

"Listen to yourself. Do you ever look in the mirror?"

Self-conscious at the compliment, I tried to make a joke of it. "Of course I look in the mirror. How else am I going to get ready in the morning?"

Alyssa laughed. "Anyway, my point is you're a beautiful girl and guys are going to take notice. Surely you must be aware of that."

"I don't know. I never really paid much attention to that kind of thing. I've usually been too busy with other things." I frowned. "Who has time to worry about how they look?"

"Plenty of people."

Justin set a drink in front of me. "I hope you like Coke."

I nodded, acutely aware of Justin's attention. "Thank you." As I picked up my glass to take a drink, I heard my name, and when I turned to see who was speaking, I was shocked to see Trevor.

"Hi, Lily," he said with a smile. "Will you dance with me?"

I glanced at Justin, who was looking at the table, then back at Trevor. "Okay."

The song was just ending and the new one was a slow one.

Great. That's twice now.

When Trevor pulled me close, my heart began to pound, and as the scent of his cologne filled my senses, my heart quickened even more.

He pulled back slightly to look at me. "I'm sorry I didn't make it to class. Something came up and I had to leave."

"Oh," I said. "Is everything all right?"

"Yeah." He pulled me closer and whispered against my ear. "Now it is."

My breath caught in my throat. I didn't know what to say. Things were moving too fast tonight. Two men showing me so much attention was more than I was used to. I almost wished I hadn't come.

Don't be stupid. You're in the real world now. Not in that tiny town you used to live in.

The song ended much too soon and Trevor led me back to my table. "I'll see you on Monday." And he was gone.

"Who was that?" Alyssa asked. "He's cute."

"Where's Justin?" I replied.

"I don't know," she said. "Now answer my question."

"His name's Trevor. I met him Monday and he's in one of my classes." I drank my soda, suddenly thirsty.

"Well, he's really cute."

"What about you, Alyssa? Who do you like?"

She shook her head. "I haven't found anyone that interesting yet. I prefer to have lots of friends to a special boyfriend."

I considered her comment. "That sounds like a good idea."

Justin appeared next to the table. "Alyssa, how about a dance?"

I watched the two of them walk onto the dance floor and smiled as I watched them dance.

They're both really nice, and everyone is so friendly.

I relaxed as I sat alone, my back to the table. When I turned to grab my soda, I saw a folded piece of paper next to my drink. I picked it up, wondering where it came from, then glanced around to see if I could tell who'd put it there. Everyone was busy and no one seemed to be looking my way.

I unfolded the note and read it silently. *Stay away from him.*

What in the world?

I reread the message.

What is this supposed to mean? Is it meant for me?

My gaze darted around the room as I tried to figure out who'd put it there.

Unnerved now, and not having such a good time, I stuffed the note into my purse and gulped down the rest of my drink, then decided I wanted to go home.

Justin and Alyssa finished dancing and came back to the table.

I stood. “It was nice meeting you, Justin.”

“Are you leaving already?” Alyssa asked. “Are you okay? You look a little pale.”

I didn’t know either one of them well and felt weird about showing them the note. I thought they might think I’d made it up to get attention or something. “I'm fine. I'll see you Monday?”

“Would you like me to take you home, Lily?” Justin asked.

Normally I would have preferred to just go home on my own, but the note had spooked me and I was glad to have an escort. “Yes. That would be great.”

We walked out to his car and he opened the passenger door for me. “Where do you live?”

I told him and we were there in only a few minutes. He climbed out and opened the door for me.

“Thanks for the ride,” I said as I stepped out.

“Maybe I'll see you at school,” he said.

I looked into his green eyes as a small shiver of attraction coursed through me. “Yeah.”

“It was nice meeting you,” he said.

“Yes, I enjoyed meeting you too.” Reluctantly, I turned toward my apartment, then turned back. “Bye, Justin.”

“Bye, Lily.”

With a smile, I walked into the stairwell and hurried up the stairs. Once in my room, I peeked out the blinds and saw Justin getting into his car.

No one else was home yet and I was pleased to have the solitude. Although still disturbed by the note, I tried to push it to the back of my mind, wondering if it was even meant for me. I’d barely met Justin and had only talked to Trevor twice, so I didn’t see how anyone could believe there was something between me and either one of them.

Forcing thoughts of the note aside, I got ready for bed and analyzed my feelings after the night’s events.

Here I am, trying to concentrate on getting my education, and now I'm becoming attracted to two men.

Then I corrected myself.

No, not Justin. He's cute and everything, but I didn't really feel the pull I felt with Trevor.

The inner joy of a new crush swept over me, but just before I drifted off, the strange note pushed its way into my thoughts, and the happiness I'd felt moments before melted away as the words rang through my head.

Stay away from him.

Chapter Four

The next morning was Saturday and I slept late, then I spent a good chunk of the day finishing my assignments. When I was done, I indulged myself in reading a new romance novel I'd picked up from the library. As I read about the hero and heroine and their budding relationship, my mind went to Trevor and Justin. They were both good-looking, but I had a hard time believing either one was really interested in me.

In high school I hadn't gone on very many dates. I didn't know if it was because I was shy, or because the boys didn't find me attractive, but I was used to sitting home on the weekends. And then the last two years I'd been completely occupied with taking care of Dad, and had zero social life.

Comfortable in my own company, it didn't bother me to have no social life, although I couldn't help but fantasize about being swept off my feet like one of the heroines in the romance novels I loved to read.

I set the book down, then rested my head against the back of the chair and closed my eyes. In my mind I re-experienced the slow dances from the night before. The scent of Trevor's cologne seemed to fill my nostrils, making my heart pound. I imagined his arms around me and heard him whisper in my ear, then I pictured his face.

Could he be my Prince Charming?

Then I thought about Justin. I had to admit that I found his dark hair and green eyes alluring, and I'd thoroughly enjoyed his attention—plus Alyssa had told me she thought he liked me. But when I imagined his arms around me, it felt more like that of a big brother. Although I didn't have a brother—or a sister for that matter—I hadn't feel the same spark with Justin that I'd felt with Trevor.

Then I remembered why I'd left so abruptly. I grabbed my purse and dug around until I found the note. When I read it again, anxiety stabbed at my insides.

Is the note referring to Justin? That's who I spent the most time with. Why would anyone want me to stay away from him? I don't even know if I like him that way. And I spent less than five minutes with Trevor.

I shook my head.

It must be some kind of misunderstanding.

Determined to put the note out of my mind, I chose to believe it was some kind of mix-up.

On Monday morning as I walked toward my Sociology class and thought about seeing Trevor, a flock of butterflies bumped against my insides. And when I remembered what he'd said as he'd pulled me close at the dance, the butterflies beat their wings harder against my ribs.

Will he be here today? Or will something 'come up' again?

I was a few minutes early, so I sat on the floor, leaned against the wall, and watched the other students walk past. After pulling out my textbook, I reviewed what I'd read over the weekend, but after only a couple of minutes I sensed someone standing near me. I looked up to see who it was.

Trevor.

He was looking in another direction—apparently not noticing my head bent over my textbook.

Should I say something?

Panic pooled in my gut.

What if he saw me and just didn't want to say anything?

I mentally shook myself.

Get a grip. Speak up.

"Hi, Trevor," I said softly.

He turned in my direction. When he saw me, his face lit up and he immediately sat beside me. "Hey, Lily. How's it going? Are you ready for class?"

"Of course." My confidence grew at his positive response. "What about you? Did you do any of your reading yet?"

He shook his head as he smiled. "I wasn't here, remember? I didn't get the assignment."

I felt dumb for not thinking of that. "You could've gone ahead and read the first chapter."

"Yeah, right." His smile faded. "I have better things to do." He leaned closer to me, making my pulse race. "I'll bet you're a good student though. Do you study every night?"

I nodded, trying to ignore the erratic beating of my heart.

He leaned even closer and I could feel his breath on my face. It was warm and sweet. "Maybe you could help me if I get behind."

Trying to gain control of my emotions, I busied myself putting my textbook into my backpack. Without looking at him, I said, "I'd be happy to help you. Just let me know."

He leaned against the wall. "I'll need your phone number or address or something so I can get in touch with you."

"Okay." I gave him my cell phone number, which he typed into his phone. Then, reaching into a side pocket of my backpack, I pulled out a pencil and small notepad. "Let me write down my address for you."

He smirked. "Aren't you the organized one?"

I'd always been proud of my organizational skills—it was one of the few talents I knew I had. Feeling more self-assured that he'd noticed something I was good at, I handed him the slip of paper with my address.

He took it from me and looked it over. "I know a few people who live in those apartments. How do you like it there?"

"It's okay. My roommates are pretty nice, although I don't see them all that often. They're always going somewhere. How about you? Where do you live?"

"Me?" His eyebrows rose. "I can't tell you."

I laughed. "Why not?"

He wasn't smiling. "I'm kind of between places. I'm staying with some friends this week. I don't know where I'll be next week."

“Oh. That's not good.”

His smile was back. “It's no big deal. Keeps things interesting.” He stood. “It looks like we can go in now.”

I followed him into the classroom, wondering why he was between places, but when he sat by me I forgot all about his housing problems as I tried to think of something clever to say. Before I could come up with something, a female voice called Trevor’s name. I turned toward the voice and saw the back of Trevor’s head. He was looking at the owner of the voice—a gorgeous girl with auburn hair and flawless skin. Though I tried not to stare, I couldn’t help but notice how skilled she seemed at flirting. Trevor completely ignored me, transfixed with her.

My gaze shifted to my textbook as my shoulders slumped. There was no way I could compete with this girl or others like her. I resigned myself to admiring Trevor from afar.

The professor began the class and out of the corner of my eye I saw Trevor finally turn away from the girl and pay attention to the lecture. Though I tried to take notes on the lecture, I was totally distracted by the interplay between Trevor and the auburn-haired girl. Every time the professor turned her back to write on the white board, Trevor and the girl whispered to each other.

At the end of the lecture I looked at my notes and saw no more than ten words, and what was written made absolutely no sense. When the teacher dismissed us, I stalled in gathering my things, hoping Trevor and the girl would leave before me.

Sure enough, Trevor stood to leave when the girl did.

“See you later, Lily,” he said to me.

Surprised he remembered I was there, I lifted my gaze from my backpack and met his eyes. He had a friendly grin on his face, and when our eyes met, he winked at me.

I had no idea what that meant, but forced a smile onto my face as I tried to hide the jealousy that sliced through me. “See ya.”

I zipped my backpack and silently counted to ten before leaving the room, hoping Trevor and his friend would be long gone. Stepping into the hall, I glanced in both directions and didn’t see them anywhere.

I finished my classes and headed home, disappointed with myself that I was getting so distracted by a man I had no hope of dating. I vowed that I would push him out of my mind and focus on my studies. After all, I only had so much money to pay for school—I couldn't afford to waste it. My thoughts went to my sweet father. When he'd died suddenly of a heart attack it had been difficult for me. Since my mother had been killed by a drunk driver when I'd been just eight years old, my father and I had become very close. And though taking care of my father had consumed my life for two years, the suddenness of his death had only made me feel worse, and I was still struggling to accept his passing.

As I reflected on one of the most life-shaping experiences of my life, I realized that, in a very tragic way, that experience was preparing me for the rest of my life.

You never know what's around the corner.

Trepidation washed over me at the thought.

Chapter Five

The next afternoon when I answered the knocking at my door, I was shocked to find Trevor standing there.

"I was hoping you could help me with the questions we have to do for our class," he said with a smile.

I almost told him to ask the auburn-haired girl for help, but knew that would be counter-productive. Instead I said, "Sure." Then opened the door wider. "Come on in." As he lifted his backpack from the ground, his biceps flexed. Trying to distract myself from the way I was drawn to him, I asked, "Which ones have you done so far?"

He laughed. "None yet. I thought we could do them together."

"Have you even looked at the questions?" I asked as I sat on the couch. "Or were you just assuming I'd do them for you?" I smiled when I said it, but I was only half-joking. I had to admit I was a little irritated that he'd ignored me during class, but was coming to me for help now.

"What kind of a guy do you think I am?" He asked with a smile. "I was hoping we could study and get to know each other at the same time."

His words soothed my bruised ego. Flattered by his unexpected attention, I didn't know how to respond. I didn't have much practice with flirting and I didn't think I was very good at it—unlike the auburn-haired girl from class. I stood abruptly. "I'll be right back." I went into my bedroom and closed the door.

Standing in front of my mirror, I took a deep breath, then ran a comb through my hair.

He might actually be interested in you, Lily. Just relax and be yourself.

After glancing at myself one last time, I went into the living room.

“Everything all right?” he asked. His book was open on the coffee table, the questions were next to it, and a blank sheet of paper lay beside that.

“Yes, and I see you're all ready to work.”

He smirked. “Yes, Miss Jamison. Your student is ready.”

“Very funny,” I said, though I liked the way he teased me. “I assume you've actually read the chapter?”

“Not exactly. I prefer to just find the answers as I need them.” He read the first question before flipping through the chapter and spotting the answer. “See? Here we go.”

“Okay, whatever.” I watched him write down the answer. “What are you majoring in, anyway?”

He looked up from the sheet of paper. “Business management. If things go the way I hope, I’ll graduate two years from next spring.”

“Really? That's not too bad. So how old are you anyway?”

“Twenty-three. I’ve been putting myself through school, so it’s taking a while to finish.”

“Well, I think it’s great that you’re doing that.”

He smiled at me, then bent back over his paper as I watched him work. A moment later he looked at me. “Aren't you going to do your homework?”

I smiled, and in a non-boasting voice said, “I've already done it.”

His vivid blue eyes bore into mine. “I like that in a woman.”

The intensity of his gaze unnerved me. “What's that?”

“You get things done.” He smiled with obvious approval. “You don't mess around.”

My confidence soared at his words. “That's why I'm here. To get my degree.”

He nodded. “Good for you. I'll bet you're going to get it done, too.”

An hour later he closed his book, finished with the assignment. “Do you want to grab something to eat?”

I considered the offer. I'd really enjoyed spending the afternoon with him—in fact, I didn't want him to leave—but I still had other homework to do and didn't want to get sidetracked by his attention. Besides, I didn’t want him to think I was so anxious to be with him that I would drop everything just because he threw out a last minute invitation. “Thanks for the offer, but I still have a lot of work to do before tomorrow.”

He smiled, hiding any disappointment he might have felt. “Okay. I'll see you in class.”

I closed the door behind him, wondering if he’d been let down by my refusal or if the invitation had only been a way to thank me for my time. The fact that he’d ignored me in class and just come to see me so I could help him made me think it was the latter. That thought brought a prick of regret because I found myself more and more attracted to the blond man with the penetrating blue eyes.

He seemed to have a lot of secrets hidden behind those eyes and I was curious to discover what they were.

The next day when I got to Sociology class I didn’t see Trevor, though the auburn-haired girl was present. About five minutes after class started I heard a student come in. I turned, and when I saw Trevor sliding into a seat in the back of the room, my heart leapt. When he looked directly at me and smiled, my heart went into a gallop. I smiled back, then turned and stared at my notes, trying without success to wipe the smile from my face.

Once class was over, I took my time gathering my things, waiting to see if Trevor would approach me. As I zipped my backpack, he still hadn’t come over to where I sat. Disappointment cascaded over me, and I stood and turned to leave. He still sat at his desk, but the auburn-haired girl had joined him. She was sitting in the desk in front of his, turned to face him.

I would have to walk right past them to leave the room.

Gathering my courage, I walked toward the door, ignoring him as I neared his desk. Though I felt his gaze on me, I kept my eyes on the exit. A moment later, as I passed his desk, I heard him say, “I’ve gotta go, Amanda." I walked out the door and into the hall. A moment later I heard him call out, "Lily, wait up."

Anticipation surged through me as I stopped and turned toward him, letting him catch up. Trying to act like it was nothing special that he'd sought me out, inside my heart throbbed. "Hey, Trevor. Glad to see you made it to class."

He smiled as he reached me, and we began walking down the hall. "Yeah, I got stuck at work. But at least I made it."

I wanted to ask him about Amanda, the auburn-haired girl, and what their relationship was, but didn't have the courage.

"So Lily, I was wondering if you were doing anything later."

His question was completely unexpected and it took me a moment to respond. "Uh, just studying."

"Do you think you can pull yourself away long enough to grab some dinner with me?"

I swallowed. "Sure, I guess so."

He looked offended. "You don't have to."

Feeling stupid and inexperienced, I said, "No, no. I want to."

"Okay then." He grinned. "I'll pick you up at six."

I smiled back, relieved he wasn't mad. "Okay."

"See you then." He turned and went the other direction.

For a moment I stood in place, watching him go, amazed he'd asked me on an actual date.

Maybe his invitation yesterday afternoon had been sincere.

Chapter Six

That evening he took me to a local Mexican restaurant. We chatted about inconsequential things for a while, then he asked me about my family.

"It's just me now," I said, trying to keep the sadness at my father's passing at bay.

"Really? What happened to your parents?"

I explained how my mother had died when I was young and how my father had gotten sick and I'd cared for him until he'd passed away recently.

"Wow. And you don't have any siblings or aunts and uncles or anything?"

When he put it that way, loneliness swept over me, and I had to swallow hard to push the lump down my throat. "No."

"I really admire you, Lily. Being completely on your own and getting your education." He paused. "That must be tough. I'm surprised you're not working though. I mean, school's not cheap."

Feeling proud at his acknowledgment of my independence, I opened up a bit more. "I was fortunate that my father had a life insurance policy so I'm able to use that to pay for everything."

"Well, that's great. I'm sure that helps a lot."

"It does. I couldn't get by without it."

He nodded. "I hope the food comes soon. I'm starved."

"Me too."

While we waited for our food to arrive, Trevor had the waiter bring him some wine. After it was poured and the waiter left, Trevor looked at me and said, “I know you’re not twenty-one yet, but do you want some of my wine?”

“No thanks.”

“Not a wine drinker, huh?”

“You know how I told you my mom died when I was young?”

He nodded.

“Well, she was killed by a drunk driver. Because of that, my dad completely stopped drinking and I guess I just adopted his attitude toward alcohol.”

He looked kind of shocked. “So you don’t drink at all?”

“Yeah.”

“How do you feel about other people drinking?”

I hesitated. “I haven’t thought about it much before, but I suppose it doesn’t bother me if other people drink in moderation. I do have a problem with people drinking to excess. And I especially get upset if someone drinks and drives.”

Once our food arrived, we talked some more and I noticed he barely touched his wine. He told me he worked at an auto-body shop, helping out from time to time, but that wasn’t what he wanted to do for the rest of his life.

When he took me home, we walked to my front door, but I didn’t invite him in.

“I had a good time, Lily. I hope we can do this again sometime.”

“Thank you. I had fun too.” I wasn’t sure what the protocol was at this point in the date, so I just stood there, waiting for him to take the lead. When he stepped closer to me, my breath caught. His blue eyes seemed to look right into my soul and I leaned toward him. His hand slid to the back of my neck, then he gently pulled me to him. When our lips met, feelings exploded inside me—warmth, longing, desire. I'd never experienced those feelings in my life, and after too little time he pulled away, his hand still on my neck, my gaze locked with his.

He smiled, then released me. “I’d guess I’d better go.”

I didn’t want him to go.

“I’ll see you later,” he said.

“Bye, Trevor.”

I watched him walk to his car, then I went into the apartment. I touched my mouth and felt his hand at the back of my neck, pulling me close. I peeked through the blinds and watched his older model blue Camaro pull away from the curb.

My attraction to him worried me because I feared he was just a player. Even so, I knew I was falling for him.

I didn't see or hear from Trevor the next day and we didn't have class together. I wondered if he was at work. I didn't know exactly where he worked, just that he worked with cars.

When he didn't contact me over the weekend, I doubted the vibe I'd gotten from him—that he liked me. Even though I tried to push him out of my mind, I found it hard to not think about him. When I was able to turn my thoughts away from him, I worked on my assignments and read my romance novels.

The next time we had class, I got there after Trevor did, and as I walked into the room, Amanda, the auburn-haired girl, slipped into the desk next to his. Even though I knew I had no claims on Trevor, possessiveness rushed through me, nearly choking me. Turning away from them, I found a seat in the back row. As I pulled out my notebook, I looked their way. Trevor turned in my direction and gave a subtle shrug of his shoulders, which I hoped meant he'd been saving the seat for me but Amanda had gotten there first.

Feeling marginally better, I listened to the lecture, although my eyes kept straying to Trevor and Amanda and noticing every single time Trevor gave her the slightest bit of attention. As I looked at her radiant smile, I could almost feel myself shrinking into invisibility.

The professor droned on and my mind began to wander. I imagined Trevor and Amanda spending the weekend together, hand in hand, laughing. As it seemed more hopeless that Trevor would be my Prince Charming, my head pounded.

Once class was mercifully over, I quickly gathered my things and left before I had to face him.

Chapter Seven

Alyssa called that evening.

"How are you?" I asked as I sat on the couch.

"Good. Hey, I was wondering if you wanted to meet me on the quad for lunch tomorrow."

I agreed, and after chatting for a few minutes, we hung up. We'd eaten lunch together several times and were becoming good friends.

With my roommates out it was quiet and I was glad I'd be able to concentrate as I worked on homework. To make sure I wouldn't be interrupted, I set my phone to mute before placing it on the coffee table, then picked up my Econ textbook and began reading.

I was nearly finished reading the chapter when there was a knock on the apartment door.

"Hey, Lily," Trevor said with a smile when I answered the door.

Before I had a chance to think, I asked, "What are you doing here?"

His smile vanished. "I thought you'd be happy to see me."

Briefly closing my eyes and shaking my head, I sighed. "You confuse me."

"What do you mean?"

I was hesitant to share my feelings.

Am I supposed to be coy and pretend like I haven't noticed him flirting with Amanda, or is it okay for me to tell him how I really feel—that I'd sensed a connection when he kissed me and I thought he'd felt the same way? Then again, I've only been on one date with him. Why do I think he owes me an explanation?

"Nothing," I said. "Never mind."

His smile was back. "Okay then. Have you done your homework for class yet?"

"Actually, no. I was going to do it tomorrow."

"Do you want to work on it together?"

Maybe I should enjoy his company as a friend, if that's all we'll ever be.

"Sure," I said. "Come on in."

He sat on the couch and unloaded his study materials from his backpack.

"I need to grab my notes," I said. "I'll be right back."

"Okay."

I went into my bedroom and pulled out my notebook, then grabbed some paper and a pencil. I heard Trevor's voice in the other room—it sounded like he'd answered his phone. Jealousy flared inside me as I imagined Amanda calling him and asking him to come over. Shaking my head and frowning, I rebuked myself for thinking I had any claim on him. Then, taking a deep breath, I went into the living room.

Expecting to see him chatting on his phone, I was surprised to find him reviewing the questions we needed to answer. The thought that he'd told Amanda he was busy boosted my mood.

We focused on the assignment and had it done within an hour. A moment later his phone chimed a text. He read the message and frowned, then put his phone in his pocket. "I'm sorry. I've gotta go. I need to go into work for a while."

I tried to hide my disappointment. "Okay. I understand."

He seemed preoccupied as he stood to leave, and to my dismay, he didn't even try to kiss me. I knew we weren't on a date or anything, but I'd still been hoping that we could recreate the moment we'd had when he'd kissed me goodnight after our date.

I walked him to the door and he said goodbye with hardly a backward glance. I closed the door and went to the couch, then picked up my Econ book to finish reading, trying to regain the concentration I'd had before Trevor had shown up.

"Justin is really interested in you, Lily," Alyssa said as we sat on the grass. "I've never seen him like a girl so much."

"What are you talking about? I hardly ever see him. And he's never called me."

Alyssa sipped her drink, then shook her head. "He told me he tried to call you last night but some guy answered so he thought he had the wrong number."

"What?" I set my sandwich down.

"I gave him your number. I'm sorry."

"No, that's okay, but I wonder if he dialed wrong."

"I don't think so. He called me back after he tried calling you and made sure he had the right number."

I thought about Trevor taking a call the night before when I'd been getting my notes.

Could he have answered my phone?

I pulled my phone out of my pocket and looked at the call history, but didn't see any numbers I didn't recognize. "What's Justin's number?" Alyssa told me and I verified that it wasn't in my call log. "That's really weird. It doesn't look like he tried to call me."

"Well anyway, I know he thinks you're cute and wants to ask you out." She paused to take a bite of her lunch, then asked, "So what's going on with this Trevor guy?"

"I kind of like him, but mostly we just do homework together."

"So nothing serious there?"

A smile curved the corners of my mouth.

"What?" she asked.

Trying to wipe the smile from my face, I shook my head. "Nothing. I actually think he likes this girl in our Sociology class."

Alyssa took a drink, then set her cup on the grass. "Hmm. Well, you certainly seem to have feelings for him. What do you know about him?"

"We haven't spent a lot of time together, but I know he has a part-time job working with cars, and he's majoring in business."

"Where's he from?"

"His family's in Las Vegas."

"Okay. Anything else?"

As I considered what I knew about Trevor, I realized I didn't know very much about him—he never seemed to share much about himself. All I knew was that I was very attracted to him.

I plucked at the blades of grass near my feet. "I can't explain it, Alyssa. There's just something about him that draws me in."

Sipping her drink, she just raised her eyebrows.

A few minutes later Justin appeared and plopped down next to us, a little closer to me than to Alyssa.

"Hey, Justin," I said.

He smiled in my direction. "How's it going, Lily?"

"Good. Keeping busy with homework. You know how it is."

He smiled. "Yeah." He paused, then said, "I was, uh, wondering if you'd like to go out with me sometime."

Pleased by his invitation, I said, "Sure."

"You don't think Trevor will mind?"

"He's not my boyfriend, Justin." *Unfortunately.*

"Oh." He paused. "How about this Friday night then?"

"That sounds good."

He stood. "I'll see you ladies later." He smiled at me one last time before walking away.

"Whoa!" Alyssa said, apparently finding her voice at last. "I told you he really likes you."

"So he asked me out. That doesn't mean he's in love with me."

"He's a really great guy. You could do much worse." She arched an eyebrow.

"Are you trying to imply something about Trevor?"

"I'm just saying."

Irritation sparked inside me, and I began gathering my things. "You don't even know Trevor. He's a great guy, too."

"Whatever you say. But I know Justin and I know he's a great guy." Alyssa reached out and touched my arm. "Look. I care about you and I don't want you to make any mistakes you might regret, that's all."

Her sincerity soothed my annoyance, and I smiled warmly. "I know and I do appreciate your concern. But I don't think Trevor's all that interested in me anyway."

Chapter Eight

On Thursday afternoon I was in my room with my door shut, doing math homework, when I heard a knock at the front door. Focused on a difficult problem, I didn't want to stop just then, so I ignored the loud knocking. People were always stopping by for my roommates, Michelle and Nicole, so I assumed it was for one of them.

The knocking stopped and I turned my attention back to my assignment. But then a knock sounded on my bedroom door. I knew I was the only one home and I thought the front door had been locked. A shiver of fear raised goose bumps on my arms.

"Who is it?" I called out with a shaky voice.

"It's me, Trevor. Are you okay?"

Excitement, relief, and irritation surged through me as I opened my door. "What are you doing here? How did you get in?"

He smiled. "I'm sorry if I scared you. I saw your car parked outside, and when you didn't answer the door, I got worried."

Flustered by his unexpected appearance, I said, "How did you get in? Wasn't the front door locked?"

He looked toward my desk. "No." Then he met my gaze. "What are you working on?"

Wanting to believe him, I went to the desk and looked at my assignment. "It's math." I turned toward him and frowned. "I'm having trouble with this problem."

"Sit down and I'll see if I can help you for once. I'm pretty good at math."

I slid into my chair and showed him what I'd done so far. He stood behind me, and as he leaned over me, I tried to concentrate on the paper in front of me.

He pointed to one of my calculations. “Here's the problem. You skipped a step right here.”

Trying to breathe normally despite his proximity, I erased my error and corrected it. He stayed where he was, his warm breath tickling my neck.

“I really like you, Lily,” he said in a husky voice as he leaned closer.

Shocked, yet thrilled, to hear him say what I'd been dreaming of, my pulse skyrocketed as his lips brushed against the side of my neck. Then his lips moved to the curve of my cheek. Everything felt surreal and it seemed as if things were moving too fast. “Trevor,” I said, turning toward him, but it only came out as a whisper.

Dazzling blue eyes bore into mine as longing surged through me. His face came closer, and our lips met for a lingering kiss. I closed my eyes, my heart racing. When our lips parted, he knelt next to my chair, putting him on the same level as me. Placing one hand behind my neck and the other around my waist, he gently pulled me toward him. As his lips neared mine, I gazed into his blue eyes, and when our lips met, his eyelids fluttered closed. Somehow that was more intoxicating then when they were open—it was as if I could see how much he enjoyed kissing me. His tongue probed my mouth and waves of desire washed over me as I wrapped my arms around his neck and kissed him back.

He pulled me out of the chair and it seemed as if I had no control over my body’s movement. We stood together, our mouths entangled, but after a moment his mouth released mine. I gazed into his eyes, captivated by his smile. Taking my hand in his, he led me to my bed, then he sat on my comforter and pulled me onto his lap.

As he gently stroked my face, panic flooded me as I realized what he was expecting. I stood abruptly, shaking my head from side to side. He stood next to me and tried to pull me into his arms, but I pushed him away and ran into the living room. I stood in the middle of the floor, waiting to see what would happen next.

Trevor was by my side in seconds. “What’s wrong, Lily?” After a moment, he led me to the couch.

I sat on the cushions as he sat beside me and took my hand. I didn't meet his eyes, staring at my lap instead. Finally I looked up and met his gaze. “I’m sorry, Trevor.”

“For what? You didn’t do anything wrong.”

“I just can’t do what you want me to do.”

He stared at me for a moment, apparently at a loss for words. “That’s okay. We don’t have to right now. I can wait until you’re ready.”

Trying to gather the courage to tell him what was on my mind, I bit my lip. This was completely new territory for me and I was scared that what I was about to say would push him out of my life forever. “That’s just it, though. I’m not going to be ready any time soon.”

Confusion played across his face.

“I know it’s no big deal for most people to sleep around,” I said. “But a long time ago I made the decision that I was going to wait until my wedding night to . . . you know.” This was harder than I thought and I held my breath, waiting for him to walk out of my life.

“Oh.” He stood up.

My breath came out in a rush as I accepted that my choice was going to be the cause of me losing him. He walked toward the door, but to my surprise, he turned around and walked across the room. I realized he wasn’t going to leave, but that he was pacing as he gathered his thoughts. Giddy with relief, I smiled.

He stopped walking and sat next to me again, taking my hand in his. I watched his face, worried about what he was thinking.

“Lily, even though I don’t completely understand, I respect your decision.” He brushed a stray hair away from my face. “I’m sorry I put you in that position. If I’d known how you felt, I never would have done that. Let me make it up to you. Let me take you out tomorrow night.”

Exhilarated by his reaction, I immediately agreed.

A smile lit his face. “Great.”

Still unnerved by what had happened, I said, “Maybe it's best if you leave now.”

"Sure, I understand. I'll pick you up tomorrow at five."

I nodded and walked him to the door. This time I made sure the door was locked before going back into my room. I pulled up the calendar app on my phone so I could post the information about my date with Trevor.

As if I'd forget.

A moment later I was horrified to see I already had a date that night. With Justin. "Oh no," I moaned.

Now what am I going to do? Friday's tomorrow. I need to decide right away.

I tried calling Alyssa but just got her voice mail.

I agreed to the date with Justin first, but I really want to go out with Trevor.

My stomach churned as I tried to decide what to do—no matter what, someone would be unhappy. After a few minutes I came to a decision and made the call. When I got voicemail, I left a message.

"I'm so sorry," I said. "I'm going to have to cancel our date for tomorrow night. Please, let's do it another time." I ended the call and fervently hoped that he would ask me out again.

Chapter Nine

As I got ready for my night out, Michelle, my roommate, was getting ready for a date of her own.

Only Nicole wasn't going out that night and she was moping around the apartment. "It's just not fair," she was saying. "Why does everyone get to have fun but me? I'm a nice person."

"Of course you are," Michelle soothed. "And I'm sorry Rick cancelled on you, but sometimes that's how it works out."

"Yeah, yeah." Nicole dropped onto the couch and turned on the television.

I tried to keep from smiling as Nicole continued to complain. Nicole had been out every weekend that semester so I had trouble feeling sorry for her. This was only my second actual date since I'd been there and I wasn't going to let anyone spoil my good mood.

When the doorbell rang, Nicole ran to open it. "It's for you, Lily."

As I walked toward the door, I thought about the message I'd left the day before to cancel one of my dates and felt guilty—until I saw who was at the door. "Trevor! What are you doing here? Didn't you get my message?"

He handed me an arrangement of flowers as a smile filled his face. "Sure I did. But I didn't think you meant it." He leaned close and whispered. "Not after what happened."

Though my face flushed, I was angry he hadn't followed my wishes. "I'm sorry, but when I agreed to go out with you I'd forgotten I'd already committed to go out with a friend of mine."

"Can't you cancel it?" he asked, not moving from the landing.

"I can't do that. When I make an agreement, I keep it."

"Oh." He seemed to be getting the message. "All right then. I'm busy tomorrow night. How about next Friday?"

Relieved that he understood, I agreed to go out with him the following week.

"You can keep the flowers," he said as he turned and walked away.

I closed the door behind him to the stares of my roommates.

"Gee, Lily," Nicole said, a smirk on her face. "I didn't know you had to fight them off."

"Ha, ha." I went into the kitchen to put the flowers in a vase. A short time later the doorbell rang again and I dashed back into the living room. "You guys, please don't say anything about Trevor, okay?"

"Okay, whatever," Nicole called out as she opened the door. "Big surprise, Lily. It's for you."

I ignored Nicole's comment and stepped out the door as I greeted Justin.

"You look beautiful," he said.

"Thank you. You look good, too."

He took me to a nice restaurant and then to a movie. I had a good time and told Justin so as he walked me to my door.

"Let's do it again," he said. "What about next week?"

I'd enjoyed myself, but I didn't want him to get the wrong impression. I thought of him as a good friend, not a boyfriend. Besides, I remembered my date with Trevor for the following Friday night—I wasn't going to make that mistake twice. "I can't next week, but I think it would be fun if a group of us did something together."

He frowned. "Oh. I see. A group activity." Then he became serious. "Tell me, Lily, do you have any interest in me at all?"

Surprised by his honesty, I knew he deserved the same. "I really like you, Justin. But as a friend."

"The old 'just friends' thing. Great." He began to turn away. "I had a fun time tonight. I'll see you around." He began walking down the stairs.

"Bye, Justin," I called after him, feeling terrible somehow that I wasn't attracted to him like he was to me.

Later, as I lay in bed waiting for sleep to overtake me, I thought about Justin. I agreed with Alyssa that he was a really great guy, and I wished I was attracted to him like I was with Trevor, but I couldn't force those feelings.

Either I'm attracted to someone or I'm not. I can't choose who I fall in love with. Can I?

Over the next week I didn't hear from or see Trevor at all. He didn't even come to class. Disturbed by his lack of communication, I feared my rejection of him the previous Friday night had bothered him more than he'd let on.

Rather than worry about Trevor and his feelings though, I concentrated on my studies. Things were going well in my classes so far—I thought I was getting high grades and I was pleased with my progress.

Even more importantly, I hadn't gotten any more strange notes, which only confirmed my assumption that it had been put on the table next to me by mistake.

Obviously someone had gotten me confused with someone else. Surely no one would feel threatened by me.

Chapter Ten

Friday night arrived and I still hadn't heard from Trevor. I hoped our date was still on, although I was uncertain. Michelle and Nicole were gone for the weekend and I relished having the place to myself. I took a long, hot shower and took my time getting ready for a date I wasn't sure was even going to happen.

By seven o'clock I was becoming convinced that Trevor wouldn't be showing up. Upset and disappointed, I tried to use the time to get ahead of the next week's assignments, although my thoughts strayed to Trevor.

How could he do this to me? I thought he really liked me. He even said as much.

At eleven o'clock my phone chimed a message. Grabbing my phone from the nightstand, I read the message and frowned. It was from Trevor.

Sorry about tonight. Something came up and this is the first chance I've had to let you know.

I deleted the message without replying.

The next day I ran several errands and didn't get home until late in the afternoon, but when I arrived at my apartment, I found a note addressed to me stuck in the door. I pulled it free and went into the apartment.

I dropped my packages on the counter and unfolded the slip of paper. It read, *Lily, if you'll still have me, I'd like to take you out tonight. I'll come by at six. I'll understand if you don't answer the door. Trevor.*

Checking the time, I saw I only had an hour to decide and get ready. I pictured his handsome face, blond hair and blue eyes, and knew I would be ready by six. Quickly putting away my groceries and other items, I hurried into the bathroom to freshen my make-up.

Half expecting him to be a no-show again, I was almost surprised to hear the doorbell ring at six o'clock sharp. I tried to slow my pounding heart as I walked to the door.

He held a large bouquet of long-stemmed white roses. “These are for you.”

I was pleased by the gesture, then recalled that he’d brought flowers on the night I’d had the date with Justin. “Do you bring flowers for every date?”

Offering me a half-smile, he shook his head. “I'm not that rich. I'm just trying to make up for last night. I feel really bad about that.”

Remembering the way I’d sat around waiting for him, and the distress I’d felt the previous evening, made me a bit grouchy. “You sure have things 'come up' a lot, don't you?”

“Ouch. I guess I deserved that.”

I took the flowers from his hand and opened the door wider. “Come in while I put these in a vase.”

He shut the door behind him as he entered and followed me into the kitchen. “It looks good in here. Are your roommates gone or something?”

I smiled to myself at his observation. It was true. Things were much neater with my roommates gone. They were sloppy and careless —another thing that drove me nuts about sharing an apartment. The idea of having my own place was becoming more and more appealing. “Yeah, they're taking an early vacation down to Vegas.”

“Why didn't you go? That sounds like fun.” He leaned against the spotless counter and watched me.

I filled the vase with water and set it on the table. “I wasn't invited, but I don't have time anyway. I have three tests next week.” I smiled at him. “You know how that goes.”

His eyebrows pulled together. “Do we have a test in Sociology?”

“If you ever bothered coming to class, you'd know that we do.”

“It's not that I want to miss class, it’s just that I had some things I needed to take care of.” He folded his arms across his chest. “Some of us have to work, you know.”

The remark stung and I walked away from him and toward the front door. My hand on the doorknob, I turned back to face him. “We all deal with our circumstances the best we can.”

He stared at me for a moment. “Wait a minute. Did you think I was implying something about you? Because I wasn't. How insensitive do you think I am?”

I wondered if I'd made an assumption about what he’d meant. “What did you mean then?” I walked to the couch and sat.

He sat beside me, touching my leg with his. “You’re lucky your father left you some money so you don’t have to work while you go to school.” He paused. “I know you don't have anybody and I really admire you for all you're accomplishing.”

Tears sprang to my eyes at his words. It hurt to be reminded of my father's death and the fact that I had no family.

He wiped a tear from my cheek. “Don't cry, Lily. I'm here for you.” He gently stroked my face. “I'd do anything for you. Don't you realize that?” He lifted my chin to make sure I was looking him in the eye. “I really care about you.”

His words surprised me, especially after he’d pretty much ignored me all week. And even though I really liked him, I wasn't ready to share my feelings with him. Instead I leaned into him and let him hold me and comfort me. His strong arms wrapped around me and I melted a little at how good it felt to be in his embrace.

Eventually he pulled away from me. “We should probably get going. I made a reservation.”

Reluctantly I stood and followed him out the front door and to his car. He held the passenger door open for me before getting in on the driver's side.

The restaurant was nice and I enjoyed myself. Trevor didn't mention his feelings again until he took me home. I invited him into the apartment and we sat on the couch.

"I know we've only known each other for a couple of months, Lily, but the more I've gotten to know you the more I've grown to like you."

I wasn't sure what to say. Things had gone from uncertain to Trevor professing his affection much too quickly. Only twenty-four hours before I'd been wondering if he remembered our date.

He held my hand in his. "Don't you want to say anything?"

"It's just that, well, I'm not sure how I feel yet." At the look of disappointment on his face, I hurried to explain. "I mean, I do care for you, Trevor. But I don't feel like I really know you yet. For example, you say you want to get your degree, but you don't come to class half the time."

He drew back. "I can't control my schedule. I have to work when I'm needed."

"Can't it wait until after classes though? I thought you wanted to do well."

He looked beyond my shoulder before meeting my gaze. "I do want to do well, but Rob's schedule can't always work around mine. I do the best I can."

"Rob's your boss?"

"Yeah."

I pulled my hand free from his grasp. "What kind of work do you do for him anyway?"

He stiffened slightly, then sighed. "You know, body work, repairs, that kind of thing."

I nodded. "So, your major's business management. What do you plan to do with that degree?"

"I don't know yet what I'm going to do with my degree. It just seemed like the thing to go for. Speaking of work, I need to work early tomorrow, so I'd better get going."

The abrupt end to our conversation threw me off balance and I didn't know what to say. But I did have one more question that had been on my mind. "What about Amanda?"

"Amanda?" he asked.

"You know, that girl in our Sociology class who's always flirting with you."

"Oh. You don't have to worry about her. I've known her for a while. We're just friends."

Somehow I didn't feel reassured, but when he stood and held his hand out to me, I took it. When we were both standing he pulled me close and held me tight, then he leaned toward my ear and whispered. "I do care about you, Lily, and I'll prove it to you."

A shiver of anticipation worked its way up my spine. Captivated by him, I wanted him to be the man I'd always dreamed of. We walked to the door and he gave me a lingering kiss. When he pulled back, he said, "How about if I take you out tomorrow afternoon?"

Pushing aside my worries, I smiled. "That sounds great."

"Okay. I'll come by around two o'clock."

The next afternoon, right on time, Trevor was at my door. The dark blue shirt he wore emphasized his tanned skin and vivid blue eyes, and my pulse quickened at the sight of him.

"Ready to go?" he asked, a wide smile on his face.

"Yes." I stepped out the door and locked it behind me. "Where are you taking me?"

"Do you like to miniature golf?"

"I've only done it a few times, but I liked it."

"Good, because that's where we're going."

A few minutes later we pulled up to the local miniature golf place. After we got out of the car, Trevor took my hand as he led me to the counter. The warmth of his hand in mine only strengthened the attraction I felt towards him.

We had a good time as we golfed through all the holes. Trevor did a lot better than me—even getting two holes-in-one—but the main thing I enjoyed was Trevor taking my hand as we walked from one hole to the next.

When we finished the round of golf, we turned in our golf clubs and went into the arcade. Trevor bought some tokens and we played several different games. My favorite was Skee Ball. When we ran out of tokens, we took our tickets to the counter where Trevor told me to pick out a prize. We had enough for me to get a small stuffed bear.

"Let's get something to eat," he said, taking my hand after I tucked the bear into my purse.

When we got in line to buy our food, he stood behind me and put his arms around me. My heart did a flip at his nearness, but when his warm breath brushed by my ear and he whispered, "I'm hungrier for you than for any food," I nearly stopped breathing.

"Can I help you?" the girl at the counter asked us.

Forcing myself to focus on the menu instead of how close Trevor stood to me, I ordered a burger and a Sprite. Trevor ordered his food, and once it was ready, he carried the tray with both our orders to a table. I scooted into the booth and he slid in next to me.

We were halfway done with our meal when Alyssa and Justin stopped next to our table.

"Hi, Lily," Alyssa said.

"Hello," I said, feeling awkward to have Justin there. "Are you guys going miniature golfing?"

"Yeah." Alyssa turned her gaze to Trevor. "I don't believe we've met. I'm a friend of Lily's. Alyssa."

"Hey," Trevor said.

"Oh sorry," I said, embarrassed I hadn't done the introductions. "And this is Justin Radford."

Justin held his hand out and Trevor shook it. "Nice to meet you. I'm a friend of Lily's too."

"Oh. How are you?" Trevor said.

"Good," Justin said.

"So, how long have you known each other?" Trevor asked Justin.

The question sounded innocent enough, but I when I detected a hint of jealousy in Trevor's voice, a thrill went through me. Especially after the way I'd felt when Trevor had given Amanda so much attention.

"Just since the beginning of the semester," Justin answered.

Trevor nodded in response. "That's great."

“I guess we’d better get started on our game,” Justin said. “It was nice meeting you.”

“You too,” Trevor said.

Alyssa smiled in our direction, then followed Justin out the door.

Uncomfortable having Trevor and Justin in the same room, I was glad they hadn’t stayed to chat. After the date I’d had with Justin and his obvious disappointment that I didn't have more than a friendly interest in him, I felt self-conscious around him.

Chapter Eleven

The next day at school I ate lunch with Alyssa. "I think things might be getting serious with Trevor," I told her.

"Oh?"

"The other night he told me that he really likes me." I couldn't get the smile off of my face.

She didn't return my smile. "I see."

My smile vanished. "What's wrong? Why aren't you happy for me?"

Alyssa sighed. "I am happy for you, but I know it will devastate Justin. That's all."

"He seemed fine to me."

"That's because you're blind to his feelings." Alyssa frowned, then took a bite of her sandwich.

I didn't respond as I thought about Justin and Trevor. They were both nice guys, but it was Trevor that I liked. No matter how great Alyssa thought Justin was, I couldn't make myself feel something for him that I felt for Trevor.

That afternoon Trevor came over to study with me. We spent an hour working, then decided to take a break.

"By the way," he asked as he put his books in his backpack. "What's the deal with that Justin guy?"

"What do you mean?"

"I mean, he acted like he'd known you your whole life, but he's only known you a couple of months."

I sensed Trevor's jealousy again, but this time it didn't thrill me. It bothered me. "I don't know. He's just a friend, that's all."

"Have you ever gone out with him?"

The question seemed out of place and I didn't want to answer it. "What difference would that make?"

"Is that a yes or a no?"

"It's a none of your business. I can go out with whomever I want. You and I haven't made any commitments to each other."

Trevor seemed taken aback by my response. "Maybe we should make a commitment then. Or are you okay with me dating other women?"

That wasn't the response I'd expected, and the thought of Trevor with another woman, especially Amanda, pained me deeply. As I pictured them together, my stomach churned. I jumped up from the couch and went into the kitchen, grabbing a glass out of the cupboard and filling it with water.

He followed me to the kitchen. "What's wrong?"

I glanced at him and was surprised to see triumph on his face.

"Now you know how I feel," he said, reaching out to stroke my back. "The thought of you dating another man makes me crazy."

"I'm sorry, Trevor. I guess I hadn't thought about that before." I hesitated, but only for a moment. "And just so you know, I did go out with Justin once. But really, he's just a friend. Even if he wants to be more than that."

Trevor's eyebrows bunched. "He wants to be more? How do you know?"

I immediately realized I shouldn't have mentioned that. "Never mind. It's not important."

He placed his hands on my shoulders. "It's important to me. How do you know he feels that way? Did he tell you that?"

Not understanding why it was so important to Trevor to know, I decided to be honest. "Yes. But I told him I don't feel the same."

"Lily, I don't want you to be alone with him."

I pushed Trevor's hands from my shoulders. "Why on earth not? He's just a friend."

Trevor's expression became more intense. "Please, just trust me."

He suddenly pulled me into a tight embrace. "I care so much about you. I can't stand the thought of losing you."

"Losing me?" I said against his shoulder. Then I imagined what it would be like if he was no longer in my life—if I were never to see him again. It felt like someone was digging a knife right into my heart. Agony and sadness gripped me, and I admitted the truth to myself. Then I decided to say it out loud.

I pulled back from him and gazed into his blue eyes. "I think I'm falling in love with you, Trevor."

"Really?"

"Yes," I said, worried that I'd admitted my feelings too soon.

"Oh, Lily." He cradled my face in his hands and his eyes sparkled as they gazed into mine. "I love you too."

He pressed his lips to mine and I thought I was going to explode with happiness. In my wildest dreams I hadn't imagined him falling in love with me.

He pulled back and smiled at me.

This is just like my romance novels. I've found my Prince Charming.

Joy suffused me.

Just then my roommates burst through the front door and the mood was broken.

Nicole looked at our faces. "What's going on? What are you guys up to?"

Beyond annoyed at my lack of privacy, I shook my head. "Nothing, Nicole. How was your weekend?"

Nicole began telling us about the great time they had until Michelle interrupted. "I'm starving, Nicole. Let's get something to eat."

"All right, all right."

They left a short time later, leaving us alone once again. "As much as I'd like to stay," Trevor said, "I need to get going. I promised Rob I'd come down to his shop to help for a little while this evening."

My newfound happiness enveloped me. "I'll see you in class tomorrow, won't I? Remember, we have a test."

"Great." He grimaced. "Thanks for reminding me."

I laughed. "No problem."

Trevor leaned toward me and my breath caught. A moment later our lips met and I didn't want our kiss to end. He pulled away first, but kept his hands on my shoulders. "I've really got to go. I'll call you later."

He left the apartment and I watched him walk down the stairs.

The next day after class I found a note addressed to me stuck in the front door. Hoping it was from Trevor, I yanked it out and hurried into my room before unfolding it.

Maybe I didn't make myself clear. Stay away from Trevor or you'll be very, very sorry.

My heart hammered in my chest as I reread the words printed plainly on the slip of paper.

What is going on? Why would someone want me to stay away from Trevor? Should I tell him about it? What would he say? Would he know anything about it?

The ringing of my cell phone jerked me out of my thoughts and I dug it out of my purse. "Hello?"

There was no response.

"Who's there?" I demanded as fear seeped into my bones.

There was silence and I knew the call had ended. I looked at the Caller ID but it just said Unknown.

Putting my phone in my pocket, I sat on my bed and tried to think of who could have sent the note. Was the caller also the note sender? Who could it be?

My cell phone rang again, startling me. When I saw Trevor's name on the Caller ID, I let out a breath of relief.

I was on the verge of tears, and it came through in my voice. "Trevor?"

"What's wrong, sweetie?"

The obvious concern in his voice touched me, and my heart blossomed with love for him. Even so, I wasn't sure if I should mention the note—why let some anonymous note decide my life for me? "Nothing. I'm just tired. Are you coming over today?"

"That's why I'm calling. I'm not going to be able to come over. Rob needs me to work."

Sharp disappointment stabbed at my insides. "I was looking forward to seeing you this afternoon."

"At least we saw each other in class today."

I rolled my eyes, dejection and fear ruling my emotions. "Whoopee, we got to say hi before taking the test."

"Hey, now. I'm disappointed, too." He paused. "It might be kind of late, but maybe I can come by tonight. How would that be?"

The idea immediately brightened my mood. "That would be great. Please try."

"I will. And Lily?"

"Yes?" I asked, a smile on my face.

"I love you."

Joy saturated me. "I love you, too."

After ending the call, I tore the note into tiny pieces before flushing it down the toilet. "I won't let you ruin my happiness," I said to the empty room.

Chapter Twelve

I didn't know if Trevor would be coming that night, but I made sure I looked my best, just in case. After finding the note in my door, I felt a stronger need to be with Trevor—to be reassured that he loved me and that we should be together.

Michelle and Nicole had gone to a study group, so I had the place to myself.

When a knock came at the door at seven o'clock, a thrill went through me at the prospect of seeing Trevor. I ran to the door and flung it open. Disappointment crashed through me when I saw it wasn't him, but the disappointment quickly fled when I saw it was Alyssa.

I invited her in and we sat in the living room.

"Were you expecting someone else, Lily? Perhaps a certain blond man I know of?"

"Is it that obvious?" I laughed quietly. "He said he might come over tonight."

"Where is he?" Disapproval was clear in her tone.

I ignored her criticism. "He's working tonight. He wasn't even sure if he'd be able to come by, but he said he'd try."

She crossed her arms as she gazed at me. "I can't believe you, Lily. I thought you were here to get your education, but now you're waiting around for a man to come see you when he has time. Where's your self-respect?"

Annoyed by her comments, I said, "I have plenty of self-respect. I've also fallen in love with a man who loves me too."

Her eyes widened. "What? Did he say that?"

Remembering the sound of Trevor's voice on the phone the night before when he'd told me he loved me, I couldn't hold back a smile. "Just last night, in fact."

"What about Justin?"

"What about him? I don't have feelings like that for him. He's only a friend."

Alyssa stared at me. "But you haven't given him a fair chance. He's so much better for you than Trevor."

"How do you know that? You don't even know Trevor. And as nice as Justin is, neither you nor anyone else can make me have feelings for him that don't exist. In fact, if you think he's so great, why aren't you dating him?"

Alyssa stared at me, the idea obviously never occurring to her before. "It's not like that with him. He's just a good friend."

I smiled victoriously. "That's exactly how I feel!"

She was quiet a moment. "Okay, I see what you mean. I just don't want you to rush in to anything. I've seen some girls do that and then regret it."

"We're not engaged, Alyssa," I said as I tucked my feet underneath me.

"Thank goodness," she said under her breath.

I ignored the remark. "All I know is that he loves me and I love him. We want to be together all the time."

"I just don't want you to write Justin off completely yet."

Wanting to turn the conversation in another direction, I said, "I wouldn't worry too much anyway. Someone out there doesn't want me to be with Trevor anymore than you do."

Alyssa stared at me. "What are you talking about?"

I told her about the note I'd received at the dance and the one I'd found just that afternoon.

"Let me see it," she demanded.

I shook my head. "I can't. I got rid of it."

Alyssa jumped up and walked towards the kitchen. "Is it in the trash in here? I'll get it out."

"No, no. I flushed it down the toilet."

She turned around. "Why'd you do that? Did you tell Trevor?"

I shook my head again. "No. I haven't had a chance. But I'm not sure I want to tell him. It's too bizarre, don't you think?"

"It is pretty weird," she said as she came back into the living room. "No doubt about it. But I think you should tell him. Communication is very important in a relationship."

"I'll think about it."

Alyssa nodded. "Good. Look, I'd better get going. I have an assignment due in the morning."

I walked her to the door.

"I didn't mean to upset you," she said. "I hope you know I'll support you, no matter what."

I smiled warmly. "Thank you. And thanks for being my friend."

A short time after Alyssa left, I remembered an assignment I needed to complete. With my emotions in such turmoil, I'd forgotten all about the project. I went into my bedroom and pulled out my notebook, and after reviewing my notes, I set to work. Not stopping until I was done, I didn't realize how much time had passed. Glancing at the clock, I saw it was nearly nine o'clock.

Michelle and Nicole should be home anytime. And if Trevor's coming, it should be soon.

At the thought, the doorbell sounded. I shoved my books aside and raced to the door, hoping it would be Trevor this time. It was.

When I opened the door, his face lit up, and I went into his arms. The strength of his embrace brought a sense of security, and I didn't want him to ever let me go. He held me for several moments before finally pulling back.

"That's a nice welcome," he said as he smiled at me.

Now that I'd declared my love for him, it seemed as if my love grew every time I was with him. The feeling was wonderful.

"Come in," I said as I led the way to the couch. "Are you tired? Can I get you some water or something?"

"Water would be great. Thanks."

I hurried to the kitchen and poured him a large glass of ice water before bringing it back to him, then I snuggled against him as he drank nearly all of it.

“I’m pretty tired, but at least I got paid tonight,” he said. “Now I can pay my share of the rent.”

Soon after telling me he was homeless, he’d found a cheap apartment to share with some other men. I’d been relieved when he'd found a permanent place to stay.

“So, Rob's keeping you pretty busy at his shop?” I asked, pulling away from him.

“Where're you going?” he asked as he pulled me close to him again.

I happily rested my head on his shoulder as he put his arm around me.

“And yes, he is keeping me busy. But the busier I am, the more money I can make.”

Just enjoying being near him, I didn’t respond.

“You're quiet tonight.” He stroked my arm. “Is it getting past your bedtime?”

I laughed softly. “No, it's not my bedtime for a while yet.” The conversation I'd had with Alyssa flooded my mind and I remembered my promise to consider telling him about the note.

As I mentally composed the words I wanted to say, the whole note incident sounded silly, unimportant, almost childish. Was it something I really wanted to mention? I hesitated to bring it up.

“Penny for your thoughts,” he said.

“Nowadays, a penny won't cut it. It'll take at least a dollar.”

“Okay then, a dollar for your thoughts.”

I sat up straight again, determined to talk about my concerns. “Trevor, I found a note on the door today.”

He turned his body to face me. “Okay. Who was it from?” A dark look came over him. “It was from Justin, wasn't it?”

“No, no,” I answered quickly. “That's the problem. I don't know who it was from.”

He seemed to relax. “What did it say?”

I hesitated, feeling slightly foolish and embarrassed. “It said 'Maybe I didn't make myself clear. Stay away from Trevor or you'll be very, very sorry.'"

"What?" He moved to the edge of the couch, then turned and looked at me. "Are you sure?"

That wasn't the response I'd expected. I'd thought he'd brush it off and I could forget about it. "Yes, I'm positive."

"Can I see it?"

Embarrassed now by my decision to flush it away, I told him what I'd done with it.

"That was dumb, Lily. You should've kept it."

Embarrassed by his comment, I said, "I'm sorry. I know now that I shouldn't have thrown it away, but it's too late to change that." Tears stung my eyes and I blinked several times. "Excuse me." I rushed into the kitchen as I tried to hold back the tears, then grabbed a tissue and blew my nose.

A moment later Trevor stood behind me and wrapped his arms around me, pressing himself against my back. "I'm not mad at you, Lily. I'm sorry I said that was dumb. It just kind of freaked me out."

I turned into him and let him cocoon me in his arms. Getting my emotions under control, I asked, "What do you think it's all about?"

"I have no idea."

"I'm really tired all of sudden, Trevor. I think it *is* getting to be my bedtime."

"I can take a hint," he smiled. "I'm pretty tired myself. I'll see you tomorrow." We walked toward the door together. "And make sure to lock up after I leave."

I smiled. "I will, but I can't guarantee my roommates will lock the door after they come in."

His expression turned more serious. "Make sure they do, okay?"

I didn't like the intensity in his voice. "Okay."

He pressed a kiss to my lips before walking out the door.

After he left, I turned the locks on the door and sat in front of the television, resigned to waiting until Michelle and Nicole got back to make sure they would lock up as well.

Why did Trevor get so serious? Does he know something he's not sharing?

Chapter Thirteen

Nearly an hour later my roommates returned. I turned off the television show I'd been watching and stood to speak to them.

"Lily, you're still up," Michelle said. "Is everything okay?"

With a tentative smile, I said, "Actually, no. I need to talk to you about something."

"I'm really tired," Nicole said. "Can't it wait?"

"No, it can't," I said.

"Okay. What is it?" Michelle asked.

"It's simple, really. I just need you to make sure you lock the door when you leave, okay?"

"Is that all?" asked Nicole. "I usually do. I only forget once in a while. It's not that big a deal."

"I know. But my boyfriend," I paused, realizing it was the first time I'd called Trevor that. I liked the sound of it.

"Yeah, your boyfriend?" Nicole prompted. "What about him?"

I relished the confirmation Nicole gave in also calling Trevor my boyfriend. "He said we need to make sure we lock the door." I didn't want to explain about the note if I could help it, and hoped that would be explanation enough.

Nicole laughed. "Who is he to tell us what to do? He's not my boyfriend."

"Please," I said. "Just do it. I can't get into it right now, but it's very important that we don't leave the door unlocked."

Obviously trying to calm the situation, Michelle turned to Nicole and said, "Of course we'll make sure to lock the door. It's a good idea anyway." She turned back to me. "Is everything all right?"

I tried to hide my concern with a smile. "Yes, everything's fine. Thank you, Michelle."

Michelle purposefully walked to the apartment door and turned the lock. "There. Now I'm going to bed."

All three of us headed to our rooms for the night.

For the next week Michelle and Nicole were very conscientious about locking the door when they left, and I appreciated their effort.

I spent more time with Trevor than I should have, and when I received a sixty-two percent on my math test, I was shocked and distressed. With the test in my hands, I silently berated myself for slacking off so much in my schoolwork.

I'd better be careful or I might end up failing my classes. I love Trevor and I want to be with him every free moment, but I have to keep up with my assignments.

In disgust, I stuffed the exam into my backpack before heading to the parking lot, climbing into my car, and driving home.

Upset over my poor performance on the math test, at first the unlocked apartment door didn't register as unusual. Then I realized no one else was home. Fear jolted through me as I quickly glanced around the living room. Everything seemed fine there, so I walked carefully toward my room and stared at my closed door.

Will I find everything okay in there as well?

I turned the knob and slowly pushed the door open.

At first everything did seem fine, but as I began unloading my backpack, I noticed a few items out of place. Being the organized and neat woman that I was, it quickly became apparent that someone had been there and had gone through my things.

Gathering my nerve, I flung open my closet to make sure no one was lurking inside. Then I peeked under my bed. All was clear. I ran from the room and made a quick check of Michelle's room, then Nicole's. They were both in their normal messy state, but no one was in them.

I went back to my own room, then quickly took a mental inventory of my things to ascertain if anything was missing. Nothing was, but I did find a new item added to my belongings. It was a picture of Trevor—a photograph that had been sliced in half with only Trevor left. In the picture, laughter filled Trevor's face, and an arm snaked around his waist. The owner of the arm had been cut out of the picture, but I could make out nail polish on the nails and an amethyst ring on the hand nestled tightly against Trevor's waist. There was also a date stamp in the corner. It was dated nine months before.

I flipped the photo over to see if there was anything written there. Nothing. I thrust the photo into my back pocket.

"How strange." I spoke out loud, wondering what the message was supposed to be.

Does Trevor have a jealous ex-girlfriend in the wings? Someone who doesn't want to see him with anyone else? Does he know what kind of person she is and that's why he's concerned about me locking my doors?

A shiver of fear rolled up my spine. The photo had been left in my dresser drawer. This person, whomever he or she was, had been in my room and had had access to my private things.

The realization made me feel violated and angry—angry with the intruder, but also angry with my roommates for carelessly leaving the door unlocked.

Deciding some chocolate might make me feel better, I went to the kitchen to have a few of my favorite cookies—ones I'd hidden. I opened the cupboard and reached into the very back, groping for the cookies, but didn't find them. In desperation, I pulled out the dishes and stuck my head into the cupboard. The cookies were gone.

That's it. That's the last straw. I can't stand living here anymore. First my roommates can't manage to lock the door when they leave, putting me in danger from some deranged ex-girlfriend of Trevor's, and then they eat my food.

I stood, then stared at the wall as my mind churned.

I'm going to look for my own place. I don't care how much it costs

—I have to think of my safety and my sanity.

I went into my bedroom and shut the door. All the difficulties of the day—the bad grade on the test, the missing cookies, and most especially the photo in my dresser—added up to frustration and helplessness. My throat thickened with unshed tears as loneliness welled up in my heart.

"Trevor, I need you," I said out loud, my voice breaking. I knew he was working this afternoon, but my desire to have him near was overwhelming. I hadn't been to Rob's shop before, but I decided this was as good a time as any.

He'd told me where it was, but I couldn't remember what he'd said. All I remembered was the name—*Rob's Auto Body*—which I entered into the GPS app on my phone. A moment later the directions appeared. I grabbed my purse and headed out the door, making sure to lock it behind me.

Ten minutes later I pulled up to the shop. When I saw Trevor's blue 1968 Camaro parked around the back, comfort swept over me. Just knowing he was near made me feel better. I climbed out of my car and went through the front door.

A man in blue coveralls and a hat with the shop's name emblazoned across the front came to the counter. "Can I help you, miss?"

I noticed the name 'Rob' on the front of his coveralls and assumed he was Trevor's boss. "I'm looking for Trevor Caldwell. I'm Lily."

The man's face broke into a smile. "Oh, so you're the one who's distracting Trevor from his work. I'll tell him you're here."

The man walked through another door and several minutes later Trevor came through. He wore his own set of coveralls, although there was no name on his. When he saw me, his face lit up, and he immediately came around the counter. "I'd give you a hug, but I'm kinda dirty."

I shook my head and closed my eyes. "That's okay." When he was near, I felt safe and loved, even if I couldn't be in his arms.

"What are you doing here?" he asked. "Not that I mind, but you've never come before. Is everything okay?"

My eyes filled with tears, which annoyed me.

"Hey, what's wrong, honey?"

I silently reached into my back pocket and pulled out the half photograph. "I found this in my dresser drawer this afternoon." I held out the picture.

He took it from me and stared at it a few moments before handing it back. He didn't say anything, just looked at me.

"Well?" I demanded.

"Well, what? I didn't put it there."

"Can you explain it? You're in the picture. Whose arm is around you? Surely you must know that."

He looked away. "I honestly don't know who it is."

I pointed to the date in the corner. "It wasn't taken that long ago."

He looked at the date, then met my gaze. "I'm sorry. It really doesn't look familiar."

Releasing a deep sigh, I shook my head, then in a strained voice, said, "I don't believe you, Trevor."

His nostrils flared. "Fine. Don't believe me. But I'm telling you the truth. I don't know who that is or where it was taken."

I stared at him, speechless.

"Look," he said with a frown. "I need to get back to work."

Biting my lip to keep the tears from starting afresh, I shook my head as I turned away from him and walked out the door. As I opened my car door, I glanced toward the shop, hoping he would come running out with an explanation.

But he didn't, and I drove slowly home, devastated by his lack of trust in me.

Why won't he tell me about the picture? What is he hiding?

Chapter Fourteen

I stared at my tear-streaked face in the bathroom mirror.

The one person I thought I could count on has failed me.

An image of Trevor's face as he refused to tell me what he knew filled my mind, and I squeezed my eyes closed, forcing down the disappointment that threatened to overwhelm me. I took several deep breaths until I'd gotten my emotions under control, then I splashed cold water on my face, toweled my skin dry, and went into the kitchen to take two aspirin.

Maybe Alyssa's right. Maybe Trevor's wrong for me.

That thought was immediately replaced by another.

No. I love him. And he loves me. He'll tell me the truth if I give him time.

I stared at the kitchen cabinets as a question pushed its way into my brain.

How much time will he need?

The headache that had bloomed inside my skull throbbed, and I swallowed two aspirin and gulped down the glass of water. Then, not wanting to think about Trevor any longer, I went into my bedroom, pulled out one of my textbooks, and began a reading assignment. Ten minutes later I'd reread the same paragraph over and over without taking in a word. I gave up and put the book back on my desk.

Maybe I should go online and look for a new place to live.

A few moments later I'd pulled up the school's website and navigated to the housing section. It didn't take long to find some places that seemed promising. I called the numbers listed in the ads and arranged to look at two of them right away.

The idea of having my own place excited me and I left the apartment to check them out.

The first one was in a basement and wasn't too bad, except that I would have to share the kitchen with the other tenants. I didn't like that idea—that was part of the problem I was having already.

The second unit held more promise. It was also in a basement, but it was a one bedroom apartment with its own kitchen. It was a walkout basement, so I would have my own entrance. And it came furnished.

"I like it," I told the woman showing me the place.

"I've had several people express an interest," the woman said as she adjusted one of the curlers in her hair. "But it's available now and they can't move in for a couple more weeks. What about you?"

"I can move in right away." I hoped that would give me an edge. I'd already paid rent through the end of the month, and I would have to find someone to take over my rental contract, but it was worth the loss of money to get this place. It seemed perfect.

"Okay. Just fill out this application and I'll give you a call when I decide."

"Can I fill it out now?" I didn't want to let the place get away.

The woman studied my face. "Are you a student?"

"Yes, I am. And I promise, I'm very responsible."

The woman smiled for the first time. "Okay, then. Go ahead and fill it out."

I quickly filled in the information before handing it back to the woman. "When do you think you'll know if I'm chosen?"

"I'm losing money on it every day it's empty. I'll call by tomorrow."

"Great!" I said, trying to think positively. "I have classes in the morning, but you can leave a message on my cell phone."

The woman smiled. "I'll let you know."

I thanked her before driving home.

When I walked into the apartment and found Michelle and Nicole arguing about whose turn it was to clean the bathroom, I became even more excited at the idea of having my own place.

"Hey, guys?" I started.

They looked at me in surprise, apparently not hearing me come in. “Yeah?” Nicole said.

“I just wanted to let you know I'm moving out.”

That got their attention. “How come?” Michelle asked. “Are you and Trevor getting married or something?”

The mention of Trevor’s name brought a sharp sting to my heart. “No, I’ve just decided to get my own place. No offense, but I prefer living on my own.”

“Okay. Have you found another place yet?”

“Possibly. I'll find out tomorrow. My share of the rent's paid up till the end of the month. Do you know of anyone who could take over my contract?”

Michelle paused. “I might know someone. I’ll check with her and let you know.”

I smiled. “Great.” Then I went to my room for another attempt at my reading assignment. This time I was able to concentrate.

“The place is yours if you want it,” the landlady of the basement apartment said in the message she left on my phone the next day.

Elated, I deleted her message, then listened to the next one.

“Lily,” Trevor said. “I need to talk to you. When can we get together?”

With the two messages one after the other, and still upset with him for his refusal to tell me about the picture a stranger had left in my dresser, a wicked thought came to me.

What would he do if I moved and didn't tell him where I went?

The idea tantalized me. I had so few belongings, it would only take an hour to pack up and move it all to my new place.

As I packed my clothes into my suitcase, and the rest of my things into a couple of boxes, I thought about Trevor and his refusal to tell me about the picture.

How dare he compromise my safety by not telling me who was in the picture? Someone broke into my home and violated my privacy. He needs to learn a lesson in how it feels to be betrayed by someone he thought he trusted.

I shoved the last of my things into the box.

I won't tell him where I am—just for a few days. It's Thursday and we won't have class until Monday, so he probably won't run into me until then.

The idea gave me grim satisfaction.

That will teach him to value me.

As I pictured his face and imagined how he might feel in not knowing where I'd gone, guilt lanced through me. But I snuffed it out by remembering how I'd felt when I'd discovered someone had been in my room—a stranger who clearly knew Trevor.

With a final look around my room, I mentally said good-bye, then I lugged my belongings to my car and drove to my new place—my very own place.

The woman had said she would leave the key under the doormat and come by later to collect the first month's rent and have me sign the paperwork.

Carrying my suitcase, I walked across the stone steps to my front door where I found the key under the mat as promised. It didn't take long to bring in all of my things, and once I'd finished, I securely shut the door behind me and locked it, feeling safe in my new place knowing I wouldn't have to depend on anyone else to keep things the way I wanted them.

My home would stay the way I desired.

With a smile on my face, I pulled the string next to the window, collapsing the blinds upwards and letting the sun shine in. Because it was a walkout basement, the front window was full-sized. A large tree took up most of the front yard, and even though the leaves were mostly gone, it was still lovely.

With my suitcase in hand, I went into my bedroom and set my sole piece of luggage on the bed, then glanced at the old, scratched-up dresser and night stand, then looked inside the closet.

Decent enough storage space. I smiled. *And it's all mine.*

With the house built on a slope, the only window in the bedroom had a deep window well that didn't let in much light. Regardless, the room was pleasant enough, and I decided I would brighten up the space by purchasing matching bedding and curtains.

I went into the living room and took a closer look around. A small desk sat along one wall, an ugly but comfortable couch was along another, and an old, but tiny, television rested on a cart. I didn't watch much TV, so I wasn't concerned about the poor TV.

A compact side table with a lamp was positioned beside the couch. I walked over to the lamp and turned it on.

Not very bright. I'll have to get a higher wattage bulb.

I took my notepad and pen out of my backpack and started to list the things I needed to buy. Though it would take some of my precious reserves to get the items I wanted, I was determined to make the place how I liked it. To make it my home.

It was my only home.

As I stood in the middle of the room, I thought about the upcoming Thanksgiving holiday and knew I'd be spending it here. I had nowhere else to go, and I had absolutely no family to spend it with. I was completely on my own. The thought made me inexplicably sad.

There was Dad's house in Lovelock, but without him there, it was just a building. Eventually I would sell it, but I wasn't ready to do that yet.

I was so grateful to my father for teaching me how to take care of myself, even though I'd had to learn those skills at an early age. While still in high school, I'd done all I could to make his life easier—he'd always come home from work so tired. At first I'd thought it wasn't fair that I had to do it all, but eventually I'd come to appreciate my independence. And then, once my father had become unable to take care of himself, my skills had been critical.

Pushing the sad thoughts aside, I went into the kitchen to see what I could find. The sink was chipped in a couple of places, and the oven needed to be cleaned, but there was plenty of counter space. I opened the cupboards, but they were completely empty. The dishes in the apartment I'd shared had all belonged to Michelle and Nicole—all of the things from my father's house were still in Lovelock.

There was a phone jack in the kitchen but no phone. Since I had my cell phone, there was no reason to get a land line, although I would need to get an Internet connection set up. As I was adding items to my list, a knock sounded at the door. Startled, I wondered who it could be until I remembered that the landlady was supposed to come by.

I hurried to the door and looked out the peephole. It was the woman from the day before. Maureen was her name, I recalled. I opened the door for her.

"I see you got my message," Maureen said, dressed in sweats, but no curlers in her hair this time.

"Yes, please come in." Maureen stepped through the door and I shut it behind her.

"I have the lease for you to sign." She held out a piece of paper.

I read it over, signed it, then wrote a check for the deposit and first month's rent.

"Thank you, Lily." Maureen smiled warmly. "If you have any trouble, my number's on your copy of the lease agreement. The phone line's working, but if you want a land line you'll need to put it in your name. The rest of the utilities are included in the rent.

"Okay. I was just going to use my cell phone, but that's good to know. Thank you."

Maureen left a moment later, and contentment in having my own place cascaded over me.

Checking to make sure the refrigerator was plugged in, I jotted down a few more things I needed to buy, then grabbed my purse and headed out the door, locking it behind me, secure in the knowledge that when I returned everything would be as I'd left it.

Chapter Fifteen

At the nearby super store I walked up and down the aisles looking for just the right things. Though I knew this would be an expensive shopping trip, I was prepared to spend the money necessary to make my place a real home.

After finding a comforter and decorative pillows for my bed, I picked out a slip cover for the couch, then filled my grocery cart with food for my empty kitchen. The rows of kitchen implements reminded me that I needed to drive to Lovelock very soon to collect the dishes, pots, and other kitchen items that I'd stored there before moving to Reno.

With my trunk full, I headed home, excited to get things organized in my new place. As I neared my apartment, a car similar to Trevor's passed me, forcing my thoughts to him. I'd been so busy getting my new place ready that I'd managed to keep him out of my head. But now, guilt at not telling him I'd moved stabbed at my heart, and I knew I would be telling him my whereabouts sooner than I'd planned.

By the time I'd finished my errands and gotten home, the sun had set, but I brought everything inside, then settled on the couch to catch my breath. I hadn't wanted to talk to anyone—okay, maybe I just hadn't wanted to talk to Trevor—so I'd left my cell phone off all day. But now, as I turned it on, I found several texts from Trevor.

For the briefest moment I considered calling him to tell him I'd moved, but then I decided to make him wait.

He probably doesn't even realize I'm gone. He wouldn't know unless Michelle or Nicole told him.

With lingering anger for the way he'd behaved, I read his texts. They were all the same—telling me he wanted to talk to me. I deleted them without replying, then I called Michelle and let her know I'd moved out. When she told me she'd found someone to take over my contract, I smiled, glad I had one less issue to deal with.

Needing something productive to do, I put my new comforter and decorative pillows on the bed, then stood back and admired the way my room was shaping up.

It didn't take long to unpack my clothing—I didn't have much—but when I was done I spread my toiletries around the bathroom, thrilled not to have to share space anymore. It seemed luxurious to have all the storage to myself.

Too tired to do any more that night, I got ready for bed, then read in bed for a while before finally turning off the light on the night stand and going to sleep.

The next day, Friday, I only had one class and was able to spend the balance of the day making my apartment just right.

The slipcover went on the couch, and the desk was stocked with my school supplies. I took out my math book, prepared to begin working on my latest assignment, but before I'd even started on the first problem, my mind filled with thoughts of Trevor. My anger at him had seeped away, and I realized I wanted to share my joy in my new place with him. Even if his response to the picture I'd found in my dresser had upset me, I wasn't one to hold a grudge.

I called his phone, but got his voice mail. "It's Lily. I wanted to let you know that I moved to a new place. My own place. Give me a call if you want." I ended the call, anxious now for him to call me back.

With no idea how long it would be until he called back, I set to work on my math assignment. When my cell phone rang, I was nearly done, and I dropped my pencil before grabbing my phone.

"Lily," Trevor said, his voice intense. "I was worried sick. I went by your apartment last night and found out you'd moved. They didn't know where you'd gone and I was afraid you weren't going to tell me."

Hearing the tension in his voice, I felt dreadful for not calling him sooner. If the situation had been reversed, I would have been beside myself if he'd moved and hadn't told me where he'd gone. "I'm sorry, Trevor. I really am. Please forgive me."

"Where are you? Can I come see you?"

"Of course you can." I gave him my address and he promised he'd be there shortly.

Expecting him any minute, I hurried into the bathroom to make sure I looked presentable. The doorbell rang just as I was coming out of the bathroom.

With a wide smile on my face, I flung open the front door.

Trevor stormed inside, then turned to me with a frown. "How could you do that to me? I was so worried about you."

My smile faded as I closed the door.

He stepped close to me, then dragged me against him. "I didn't know what had happened to you. I haven't even eaten since last night." He pulled back, gazed into my eyes, and with a soft voice, said, "I love you. Don't you know that?"

The intensity of his emotions shocked me. "I'm sorry, Trevor. I guess I needed a little space. You know, time to myself."

"That was selfish of you."

Heat rushed to my face. "I'm really, really sorry. I didn't think—"

"No, you didn't," he cut in. "That's the problem. You only thought of yourself."

Is that true? Was I only thinking of myself?

I looked away from him, my shoulders hunched.

He glanced around the room. "This place is pretty nice." He paused. "Lily?"

I lifted my gaze to meet his.

His eyes narrowed. "How long were you thinking about moving?"

This was a question I could answer without feeling guilty. "Before Wednesday it had only been a vague wish." I hesitated. "That's when I found that strange picture in my bedroom. The one you apparently know nothing about." I paused to see how he would react, but he didn't.

"After that, and your refusal to tell me anything about it, I knew I needed to get out, to make a change. So here I am."

"That's a pretty big change."

Talking about the picture reminded me why I'd moved in the first place, and the shame I'd initially felt at his accusations of selfishness evaporated. With a tone of self-satisfaction, I said, "I can do whatever I want. I don't have to answer to anyone. Least of all to you."

His nostrils flared. "You're right. You don't have to answer to me. And I don't have to answer to you either. But do you really want it that way? I thought we loved each other." His voice dropped to a whisper. "At least, I love you."

Embarrassed by my childish attitude, I wrapped my arms around his waist and lay my head against his shoulder. "I do love you, Trevor. I guess I just needed to assert my independence."

He pulled away, lifted my chin, and after gazing into my eyes, he pressed his lips to mine.

Love for him surged through me, and I wrapped my arms around his neck. A moment later he broke our kiss and smiled at me, then took my hand and led me to the couch. With extreme gentleness, he pressed my shoulders so that I would sit, then he knelt in front of me, reached into his pocket, and pulled out a small velvet box.

Stunned, I watched his face as he opened the box and held it out to me.

"Lily, will you give me the great pleasure of becoming my wife?"

Chapter Sixteen

I stared at the gorgeous diamond ring nestled on the bed of black velvet, then looked into Trevor's handsome face. Earnestness shone from his vivid blue eyes. I so wanted to make him happy, but his proposal was completely unexpected. He knelt in front of me, waiting for an answer, and I tried to form one. "Trevor," I whispered. Then I spoke louder. "I don't know what to say."

"Say yes," he said with a grin, then he lifted the ring from the box and slipped it onto my left ring finger. It fit perfectly.

I admired it for a moment before speaking. "I do love you. Very much. I'm just not sure that I'm ready to get married. I have to think about it."

"At least that's not a 'no'," he said, still smiling. "Hang on to the ring while you're deciding."

Relieved that he was accepting my answer so readily, I smiled. "Okay."

He moved to sit beside me on the couch.

"Rob must be paying you pretty well for you to afford such a beautiful ring," I said as I admired the ring some more.

Trevor didn't answer. Instead, he lifted my left hand and kissed my palm. "I'd do anything for you, Lily."

Touched by his words, I didn't know what to say. "Tomorrow I need to drive to Lovelock to pick up some things from my dad's house. Do you want to come?"

"I wish I could, but I promised Rob I'd work."

Disappointed he couldn't come, I said, "That's okay. It shouldn't take too long anyway."

A while later we went out for dinner, and when we were done, Trevor brought me back to my place, but didn't stay.

Lying in my bed on the second night in my own apartment, I thought about Trevor's proposal. Before I could even consider agreeing to marry him, I needed to learn so much more about him.

Early the next morning I got ready for the day, anxious to drive to the small town where I'd grown up, and gather the things I needed for my apartment. Finished dressing, I opened my jewelry box and picked out a pair of earrings. The diamond engagement ring caught my attention. After a slight hesitation, I slipped it on my left ring finger and went to the front window.

Tilting the diamond this way and that, I admired the way the ring sparkled in the rays of sunlight that streamed in. A sudden bright glint made me squeeze my eyes closed, and in that brief moment I pondered what I was considering. My heart stuttered with an ominous feeling, but I shut it off and continued admiring the stunning ring.

I haven't committed to anything yet.

With a resolute tug, I slid the beautiful ring off of my finger and set it on the windowsill where it continued to reflect the sun's rays.

I just promised him I'd think about it.

And think about it I did—all the way to Lovelock. The drive took over an hour, but it was a lovely day and I enjoyed the trip.

Knowing the ring must have cost a small fortune, I'd decided to wear it, and every time it caught my eye, I smiled, despite my uncertainty that I would be keeping it.

I need to have a serious talk with Trevor to get the questions in my mind answered satisfactorily. But not yet. It can wait a few days.

Once I'd reached my destination, it felt strange to walk into the house where I'd spent most of my life. Dad's presence seemed to be everywhere, making me miss him more than usual. I walked from room to room, enjoying the good memories. Finally, I went into the kitchen and unloaded all of the items I wanted to take to my new place, including my mother's china. Once the table was covered with dinnerware and cooking implements, I went into the garage and found several cardboard boxes that were lying flat—left over from when I'd packed up before moving to Reno.

I dragged the broken-down boxes into the kitchen, unfolded them and used packing tape to hold them in the right shape, then packed up the items I'd placed on the table, carefully wrapping fragile items in newspaper. Two hours later I'd loaded everything into my car. On impulse, I went back into the house and pulled out two boxes that held our Christmas decorations. I had just enough room in my car to take them with me.

Even though I'd grown up in this town, with my father gone there was no one special to me there—the few girls I'd known in high school had mostly moved away. I headed toward Reno without a backward glance, and once home, I set right to work unpacking my kitchen and getting things just right.

When I finished, I fixed myself a mug of hot chocolate and curled up on my couch to catch up on some reading.

Finals weren't very far away. Still, I had to get through Thanksgiving first. Thinking about the traditional Thanksgiving meal and making all the fixings for Trevor and myself excited me.

Maybe I'll even invite Alyssa.

But even as the notion entered my mind, I tossed it aside.

Alyssa would sit across from Trevor and judge him the whole time.

I shook my head.

No, I'll just invite Trevor. We'll have our own private dinner.

I smiled at the thought.

I have so much to be thankful for. I'm doing well this semester, I'm healthy, I have my own place, and I have Trevor. I never even considered falling in love, certainly not right after getting here.

With my recent flurry of activity, I realized I hadn't told Alyssa I'd moved. Smiling to myself, I dialed her phone.

"I haven't heard from you since Wednesday's class," she said. "Is everything okay?"

"Everything's great. In fact, that's why I'm calling."

"Uh oh," she said. "Does this involve Trevor?"

Slightly annoyed at her reaction to the possibility of good news involving Trevor, I sighed. "No, it doesn't. I've moved. That's all."

"What? Serious?"

Laughing, I said, "Yes. I moved on Thursday. My very own place. I love it!"

"Wow, that was kind of sudden. What brought it on?"

I explained about the door being unlocked and the picture I'd found in my dresser.

"Shouldn't you call the police?"

"What for? Nothing was taken, no threats were made. Just a strange picture." I wondered if the police should get involved, but didn't like the idea.

"Certainly Trevor thinks the police should be called." Disapproval of the whole situation was evident in her voice.

I shook my head. "No, he never mentioned that."

"What was his explanation?"

I didn't answer as a flush crept up my cheeks.

"He *did* have one," Alyssa said. "Didn't he?"

For some reason I felt the need to defend Trevor, but I didn't want to dwell on my lack of information. "He doesn't know who it could be. Now let's talk about something else for a while. Like, how's Justin doing? I haven't heard from him in ages."

"Lily, something about this whole thing is very weird. You must realize that." When I didn't reply, she went on. "Fine. I'll drop it for now, but you'd better let me know if anything else like that happens. Will you promise me that at least?"

Rolling my eyes, I promised.

"And as far as Justin," Alyssa said, "I wouldn't worry too much about him. I think he's found a new prospect."

"Really?" I said. "Good for him."

"It is good for him. I think he's given up on you."

I didn't want to talk about Justin anymore. "I'd better get going. All the time I spent moving in has really cut into my study time, and I was already behind."

"Okay. I'll see you in class."

After hanging up the phone, I considered Justin and his 'new prospect'. I was happy for him, but also a little disappointed he'd given up on me so easily.

Well, there was no point in him pursuing me. Not when I'm with Trevor now.

I spent the rest of the day trying to catch up on assignments due the following week. Trevor hadn't said he'd come by, but I hoped he would. I pushed thoughts of his proposal out of my mind, not ready to go there. It was such an important decision, and it was easier not to consider it at all.

Besides, I need to learn a whole lot more about Trevor before I make that kind of commitment. Like, does he want to have children? How many? Does he want his wife to be a stay-at-home mom or a working mom? Where does he want to live after graduation? What does he plan to do for a career?

Though I knew it might be awkward to pepper him with all of my questions, I also knew that if we were going to be married, I would need to have those questions answered. I knew I would have to improve my communication skills with him.

If he comes by tonight, we'll sit down and talk about some of these things.

As the evening wore on, I began to wonder if he would show up. Deciding not to wait around, I drove to the grocery store to get the rest of the staples necessary to run a home.

Trevor never came by and I took a novel to bed with me, enjoying reading for pleasure instead of for an assignment.

Chapter Seventeen

The sun shone brightly on Thanksgiving morning, and when I woke, excitement cascaded over me. I'd invited Trevor to spend the day with me, and he'd been as enthusiastic about the idea as I'd been.

Lately I'd worn the engagement ring when I was home by myself, but for this day I'd decided to leave it off—I didn't want Trevor to get the wrong idea. After placing it in one corner of my jewelry box, I went into the kitchen and prepared the turkey to go in the oven. I'd bought the smallest one I could find, and I placed it in the oven before starting to chop up vegetables for a veggie tray.

Trevor had been working a lot lately and I hadn't had a chance to have a serious talk with him yet. Today I would have him all to myself, uninterrupted, for an extended period of time. Today I would get the answers to my questions.

When Trevor arrived just before noon, I threw my arms around his neck, and he slid one arm around my waist. In his other hand he held a lovely bouquet of flowers.

"I love when you greet me like that," he murmured in my ear.

Pulling back slightly, I raised an eyebrow. "Then I guess you need to come over more often."

"You know I would if I could." He held out the flowers. "These are for you."

"Thank you. They're beautiful." Impressed with his thoughtfulness, I took the arrangement and carried it into the kitchen where I placed it in a vase, then I turned to him. "I know you come over when you can."

He drew me into his arms. “That’s right.” Using one finger, he tilted my chin upwards, then he pressed his lips to mine. After a lingering kiss, he said, “I would definitely prefer to do that than to work, but I’ve gotta pay the bills somehow.”

I laughed. “Like my Dad used to say, ‘Another day, another dollar.’”

“Exactly.” His gaze went to the dish I’d been making. “Do you need help with that?”

“No. I’m almost done.”

“What is it?”

I laughed. “Can’t you tell?”

With a small frown, he said, “No.” Then he looked apologetic. “Sorry.”

“No reason to apologize. It’s a sweet potato casserole, but I like to cook it in the crock-pot so that I can keep the oven free for other dishes.”

He nodded with obvious approval. “Clever.”

“Thanks.” Once I’d started the casserole cooking in the crock-pot, I took the veggie tray out of the refrigerator. “Let’s sit on the couch.”

“Okay.” He reached for the tray. “Let me carry that for you.”

Pleased that he was being considerate, I handed it over, then followed him to the couch where we sat side by side.

We chatted about our week as we munched on the vegetables, but then he turned serious.

“In my family we have a tradition of telling what we're thankful for,” he said. “Did yours do that?”

“Yes,” I said with a smile. “But we usually waited until we were at the dinner table.”

“We did too, but I'd like to share my thoughts with you now, if that's okay.”

I nodded and waited for him to begin.

Taking my hand gently in his, he gazed into my eyes. “I'm thankful for you, Lily. I can't believe how happy I've been since I met you. You're everything I've always imagined the perfect woman would be. That's why I want to spend the rest of my life with you.” His voice quieted. "Have you decided yet?"

Worried that he wouldn't like what I had to say, my stomach churned. "Oh, Trevor, I love you, too. So much. But . . ."

He let go of my hand. "But, what?" He dragged his hands through his hair. "Please don't tell me no."

I scooted closer to him. "I'm not saying no. I haven't decided yet. That's all."

He released a breath of air, and then a smile slowly curved his mouth. "Oh, is that all? I can deal with that, I guess. And I don't want to pressure you, but do you have any idea when you might make a decision? I can hardly stand the uncertainty."

Holding back a sigh, I pushed my hair behind my ear. "Give me another week. Does that sound reasonable to you?"

"Yes, it does." He pulled me into his arms, and when I lay my head against his chest, I heard the steady rhythm of his heartbeat. The closeness of his body warmed me, but after a few moments I sat up, ready to begin the conversation I'd been putting off.

Just as I opened my mouth to speak, my cell phone rang. I glanced toward the coffee table where my phone continued to ring.

"Aren't you going to get that?" Trevor asked.

Resigned to the interruption, I picked up my phone and saw the call was from Alyssa, who was at her parents' house for the holiday. "Hello?"

"Hi, Lily. Happy Thanksgiving."

"Thanks, Alyssa. Same to you."

We chatted for a minute, and I tried to keep the rest of the conversation brief. "Okay, I'll see you on Monday," I said before hanging up.

The mood with Trevor broken, I decided to wait for another opening before talking to him about my concerns.

We enjoyed a relaxing afternoon as we waited for the turkey to finish cooking, and when it was ready, Trevor helped me get everything finished and then he set the tiny table. There were only two chairs and so little room on the table that we had to leave most of the food on the counter.

"This is delicious, Lily," Trevor said, his mouth nearly full. He swallowed his food before continuing. "I had no idea you were such a great cook. My mom can't cook at all, and my dad isn't much better, so Thanksgiving was usually pretty interesting."

"You've never told me much about your family, Trevor. All I remember you telling me is that you have two older brothers. And of course that you're from Las Vegas."

"What else do you want to know?" he asked as he helped himself to some more sweet potatoes.

"I don't know. How about, what do your parents do for a living?"

"My dad was a high school math teacher and my mom's a housewife. My dad's retired now. I was kind of unexpected and they had me late in life. They're in their sixties now."

"That's something we have in common. My parents were older when they had me, although I don't have any brothers or sisters."

"It must've been hard for you to take care of your father for so long. Especially without anyone to help you."

"It was. But it was a gradual thing. At first he just seemed forgetful and I had to remind him about a lot of things. But eventually it became clear that there was something more wrong with him."

"Why didn't you just put him in a home or something?"

"I couldn't do that to him. Ever since my mother died, he'd always put me first. I felt I needed to do the same for him."

"I don't know if I could've done that. I love my parents and everything, but I just don't know if I could make that kind of sacrifice."

I didn't want to talk about my father anymore—thinking about him saddened me. "Speaking of your parents," I said instead, "weren't they upset that you didn't come home for Thanksgiving?"

He took another bite of turkey before answering. "I guess so. I was planning on coming home for Christmas though."

"Oh." I hesitated. "Have you told them about me?"

His face lit up at the question. "Yeah, of course. They're dying to meet you." He began buttering a roll, but stopped and looked at me. "Hey! Why don't you come home with me for Christmas? That would be perfect."

The idea had its appeal. After all, I had nowhere else to go. I'd been planning on staying here by myself, so the thought of spending Christmas with Trevor's family sounded much better. "Yes, I'd like that."

"Sweet," Trevor said as a wide smile curved his mouth.

Seeing how happy my answer made him, I was doubly glad I'd accepted his invitation.

Chapter Eighteen

When we were too stuffed to eat another bite, we cleared the dishes.

"I know what I'll be having for dinner for the next week," I said with a laugh.

"You can always send some home with me," he said as he helped me put the leftovers in plastic containers. "I'd be happy to take any extra food off of your hands."

"Good. Take as much as you'd like."

Once the dishes were washed, Trevor suggested we take a walk. "I need to burn off some of those calories," he said.

I admired his muscular body, then I nodded. "Yeah, you don't want to let yourself go."

Laughing, he took my hand and led me out the front door.

The day was crisp but clear as we strolled down the street. It was a quiet neighborhood and we enjoyed the peacefulness that surrounded us, walking for nearly an hour before turning back.

By the time we arrived back at my apartment, it was getting dark. "Are you ready for pie and ice cream," I asked. "Or do you want to wait a while?"

"I'm always ready to eat. Just let me know when you're ready." He sprawled on the couch.

I perched next to him, then laughed. "Are you comfortable?" I shoved his legs over to make room.

"Sorry," he said as he scooted over. When I sat beside him, he began rubbing my back.

"Mmm, that feels good. Slaving over a hot stove makes my back tired sometimes."

"Just wait until we're married," he said, "I don't expect you to do all of the cooking. I like to cook sometimes."

I turned to face him. "Really? That's nice to know."

With a smug smile, he asked, "Does that mean you'll marry me?"

I laughed. "Oh yeah, that just clinched it."

He leaned close to me. "Will you, Lily? Please tell me you will."

Knowing this was my second opportunity to question him, and hoping for no interruptions, I plunged ahead. "Trevor, there are some things I need to know about you before I can make a decision. Serious things."

"Okay, I can understand that."

"Will you be honest with me?"

His forehead wrinkled. "I'll be as honest as I can."

"I've made kind of a mental list of questions, but I hope this doesn't sound like an interrogation."

"Okay. I'm ready, I guess."

I smiled, glad to finally resolve questions I'd had. "How do you feel about children? Like, do you want to have them?"

"Yeah, sure. I guess so. Honestly, I hadn't really thought about it."

"Well, I do want to have children someday. And I want to make sure we're on the same page when it comes to important things like that."

"I'm sorry, Lily. I just haven't thought that far ahead."

"Okay. I guess I understand that. But what about your future? Like, what do you plan on doing with your degree? Have you thought about career goals?"

He let out an audible sigh as he drew away from me. "Do we really have to go into this now?"

"It's been bothering me, Trevor. I need to know the kind of man I'm considering marrying."

At the mention of the word marriage, he nodded. "Okay. Eventually I'd like to open my own auto-body shop."

Now we're getting somewhere. Now's the time to get the answer

I've been most concerned about.

I pulled the picture that I'd found in my dresser out of my pocket and handed it to him. "What do you know about this picture?"

He studied the image of himself with a disembodied hand wrapped around his waist. "Fine. I suppose you deserve to know all my deep, dark secrets."

I laughed nervously, wondering if I really wanted to know the truth. I loved him right now. Would the truth destroy that?

He leaned against the couch cushions and was quiet as he stared at the picture. "I was telling you the truth before. I really don't remember the picture being taken." He glanced at me before studying the picture again. "I'm pretty sure that was one of the days I got drunk."

My heart raced, and I didn't say a word.

Trevor closed his eyes as if he didn't want to face me directly in his confession. "Rob and me, sometimes we like to have a few beers after work, party a little. That's why I haven't come by after work most nights. I knew you'd be able to tell."

Wanting to give him the benefit of the doubt, I asked, "Why didn't you tell me this sooner?"

His eyes opened and he gazed at me. "What? And take a chance on losing you? I know how you feel about drinking. You wouldn't have given me the time of day if you'd known this before." He leaned toward me and took my hand in his. "I love you so much, Lily. I couldn't take a chance on losing you."

"You'll stop partying now though, right?"

He stared at me for a moment. "Yeah, of course."

His hesitation worried me. "Remember last week when you gave me the ring?"

"Like I could forget," he said with a smile.

"Well, I remember you saying you'd do anything for me." I gazed at him. "Do you recall saying that?"

He shrugged his shoulders. "I guess so. Where's this leading?"

"You must realize that there's no way I'd marry a man who parties." My voice softened. "You do realize that, don't you?"

His smile turned bitter. "I do now."

One should never make assumptions.

His lips pressed together in a grimace.

It's a good thing I decided to discuss this now, rather than blindly agreeing to marry him.

Then his eyes went cold. "And by now you must realize that I'm not the man you thought I was." He stood abruptly. "I'll see you around."

Before I could stop him, he rushed out the door and into the night.

I stared at the front door, stunned by how quickly things had changed.

Chapter Nineteen

Crowds of people filled the mall two days after Thanksgiving—and I hated crowds. Nevertheless, after moping around the apartment waiting to hear from Trevor for the past two days, I'd decided it was time to get out, and with the hope that Christmas shopping would pull me out of my funk, I'd decided to brave the throng.

To my dismay, as I passed the food court, Justin walked in my direction holding hands with a beautiful woman.

At least some people aren't alone.

Self-pity flooded me, and I had to take several deep breaths to keep from bursting into tears.

Knowing there was no way to avoid him, I arranged a cheerful expression on my face and headed in his direction."Hey, Justin."

"Lily, how are you?" he said as he and his lady friend stopped in front of me. "How was your Thanksgiving?"

With a tenuous smile, I said, "It was great."

He turned to the woman at his side. "Pamela, I'd like you to meet a friend of mine. Lily Jamison."

"Nice to meet you," she said.

The three of us chatted until I couldn't stand the small talk any longer. "I'd better get going," I said. "It was nice meeting you, Pamela."

They walked away, and barely holding onto my composure, I headed toward the exit. It wasn't the idea that Justin had a new girlfriend that upset me, but rather the combination of that and the fact that not only did Justin not want me anymore, but neither did Trevor.

On autopilot, I drove home as thoughts of Trevor intruded on my mind.

Is he partying with Rob right now?

An image of him getting drunk popped into my head, bringing on a sense of discouragement that we could ever work out our differences.

Once home, I sat at my desk and dug out the only picture I had of Trevor—the one someone had left in my drawer, the one with another woman's arm around his waist. I stared at his handsome face.

He said he was drunk in this picture, but he doesn't look drunk to me.

I frowned.

Then again, I haven't really been around people who are drunk, so it's not like I have a clue what to look for.

The note someone had left at my apartment door came to mind, and as I recalled the message, I spoke out loud. "You were right, whoever you are. I am very, very sorry I didn't stay away from Trevor."

After taking one last look at his picture, I thrust it back into my desk and slammed the drawer shut. Emotionally exhausted, I lay on my bed and took a long nap.

Pounding on my front door jerked me out of my slumber. Groggy from my nap, it took me a minute to get up and trudge to the door, but when I looked out the peephole, no one was there. A tingle of apprehension tickled my neck.

Fully awake now, I peered out the front window toward the front door, hoping to catch a glimpse of whoever had knocked. As I stood there for several moments waiting for the knocker to walk past, a few snowflakes drifted past.

I loved the peaceful silence of falling snow and drew my sweater closer around me in anticipation of the colder days.

I guess whoever it was left before I made it to the door.

With a shrug, I went into the kitchen and made a mug of hot chocolate, adding a dollop of whipped cream on top. Then, when I realized that I'd bought the whipped cream for Trevor and me to put on our pie on Thanksgiving Day, sadness engulfed me.

I opened the refrigerator to put the whipped cream away and saw the pies I'd baked, untouched on the shelf.

I sighed softly, then sipped my hot chocolate. But when it nearly scalded my mouth, I set it on the counter to let it cool, then went to the front door and pulled it open, almost expecting someone to still be there. No one was there, but when I opened the door, a small envelope fell to the ground.

The person who knocked on my door must have stuck it there.

I picked it up, forgetting about my hot chocolate, then carried the envelope to the couch. I ripped open the envelope and pulled out the single sheet of paper.

Lily,

I need to think some things over, but I want you to know that you are on my mind. I'll be gone for a while. I'm sorry.

I still love you,

Trevor

I stared at his handwriting, then mentally scolded myself.

He was here just a little while before. Why wasn't I faster in answering the door? Then I could have seen him face to face.

I reread the note, then set it on the scarred coffee table, my mind on Trevor.

Where will he go to think things over? Wherever it is, I hope he finds the answers he's looking for.

Needing someone to talk to, I called Alyssa and asked her to come over.

"So that's the ring, huh?" she asked as she examined the diamond Trevor had given me.

"Yes. It's gorgeous, don't you think?" Despite my worry and fear that my relationship with Trevor was over, I smiled.

"It's nice I suppose," Alyssa said before handing it back to me. "Justin said he ran into you at the mall today. Did you meet his new lady love?"

I nodded, thinking Pamela was lucky to have him. "How serious are they?"

"From what he says, they're getting pretty serious." She laughed. "I think the guy's ready for marriage."

I laughed with her.

Alyssa leaned against the cushions. "Now, let's talk about you and Trevor. That *is* why you invited me over, is it not?"

Sighing, I nodded. "I'm not sure where things are going with him. When he told me he likes to party, we had a big fight and he stormed off." I shook my head. "But today he left this note." I handed it to her and she read it over.

"Hmm."

"What's that supposed to mean?"

She frowned. "I can see how much you love him, Lily, and it's clear your feelings run deep. But you need to look beyond those feelings. Like my mother has always told me, you need to think to the future and your children and think about the kind of man you're considering marrying." Her voice softened. "Think how important it is to have a good husband."

"I know all that," I said with a shake of my head. "But I don't know what I'm supposed to do when I've fallen in love with a man who's perfect except for one small weakness." Then a thought occurred to me that brought me sudden hope. "Who knows, maybe he'll come home from his little excursion a changed man."

"For your sake, I hope so," Alyssa said. "But you have to be realistic. If he didn't enjoy partying, he wouldn't be doing it."

I knew she spoke the truth. I also knew habits could be hard to change, but that they *could* be changed.

Chapter Twenty

All week long I waited to hear from Trevor, but didn’t get so much as a text.

Finals were coming up, and my stress level increased by the day. I wasn't sure if I was prepared for my exams, and I was pretty certain Trevor wasn't ready for his—assuming he even showed up.

Trying to focus on my reason for being in Reno, I pushed thoughts of Trevor out of my head and concentrated on school. I planned on getting all A's, but knew I’d have to work hard to make that happen.

Finals week arrived before I knew it and Trevor still hadn't come to class or to my apartment. On the day of my last exam I got to class early to review my materials, worried on Trevor’s behalf because he hadn't been in class for our Sociology final.

Pushing thoughts of him aside, I took my last test and drove home, relieved to have school over for a few weeks. Though I didn’t have plans for the break, I looked forward to having time to relax. Alyssa had invited me to spend time with her family, but I’d declined, preferring to spend the time alone.

I dug out the boxes I’d brought from the house in Lovelock, opened the lids, and gazed at the Christmas decorations. Memories flooded me—good memories of my father and Christmases past.

I'm going to make my home as warm and inviting as Dad's was.

To bring that wish to fruition, I knew what I needed to do. After putting on a warm coat, I grabbed my purse and left my apartment. The thin layer of snow crunched beneath my feet as I walked to my car, but the roads were clear and in a few minutes I arrived at a small Christmas tree lot.

I chose a four-foot fir tree—something small enough to handle myself and not too big for my collection of ornaments. The lot worker helped me load it into my trunk, then without too much effort, I managed to drag it into my cozy home. I set it up in a corner, plugged my iPod into my player, and turned on my Christmas music playlist. As I listened to my favorite songs, I put up my meager collection of Christmas decorations.

Once done, I looked at the festive room but decided it needed one more thing to make it perfect—a fresh Christmas wreath.

They had wreaths at the Christmas tree lot.

After a quick trip, I'd picked one up, then headed home. To my utter pleasure and surprise, when I arrived at my apartment, I saw Trevor's car parked at the curb. I hadn't seen him since Thanksgiving, yet he'd been on my mind constantly. The wreath forgotten, I raced down the stone steps where I found him knocking on my door. "Trevor!"

He turned at my voice, his face lighting up. "You're home. I thought I'd missed you."

I threw myself into his arms, not realizing until that moment how desperately I'd yearned to have him near.

He held me tight, burying his face in my long dark hair. "Lily," he murmured. "I've missed you."

After several moments I pulled back, a huge smile on my face. "It's freezing out here. Let's get inside."

"I've missed this place these last couple of weeks," he said once we were standing in my living room. "It looks great. Reminds me of home."

"Thanks." I beamed. "Do you want some hot chocolate?"

"Sure, that sounds good."

He followed me into the kitchen and leaned against the counter while I fixed both of us a mug, then we took our drinks and sat on the couch.

"You got my note?" he asked.

"Yes. Are you just now getting back? That was a long trip." I blew on my drink to cool it.

"Actually, I got back earlier this week, but I had finals to take."

"I didn't see you in Sociology class. Did you take that one?"

"Yeah, the professor let me take it during one of her other sections."

I set my mug on the coffee table. "So you got them all done?"

"Just barely. My grades aren't going to be as good this semester, unfortunately."

"That's too bad."

"It's my own fault," he said, then he sipped his chocolate. "If I hadn't worked so many hours, I wouldn't have missed as much class."

We were both quiet for a moment, lost in our own thoughts.

"Look," he began, setting his empty mug on the table. "We need to talk."

Afraid of where the conversation might go, my heart rate skyrocketed.

He smiled as he took my left hand in his. "I notice you're wearing the ring."

Blushing, I said, "You caught me. I guess I just needed something to help me feel near you."

He stroked my hand. "Hey, it's fine with me." He looked at me with undisguised hope. "Does this mean you've decided?"

I hesitated briefly. "No, it doesn't. After what happened on Thanksgiving, things were left up in the air."

"Yeah, that's kind of what I figured." Still holding my hand, he said, "I've been doing a lot of thinking and I've come to a decision."

I stilled, waiting to hear what he had to say.

"I'm going to do everything within my power to be what you want me to be."

Somehow I didn't feel the joy I would have expected to feel at those words. "That's great, Trevor. Really it is."

His smile dimmed. "You don't sound too excited." He stood up and his lips pinched together. "I just can't please you, can I?" He stared at me. "First I leave town to think about what I can do to win you over—messing up my grades in the process. Then when I tell you I'll change, you seem less than excited. What's the deal?"

"I understand why you're angry," I began, but paused when he scowled at me. "I *am* happy that you're willing to change, but I want you to do it for the right reasons. Don't do it for me. Do it for yourself. Do it because you know that's the life you want to live."

"Oh, I get it. You think I need to grow up. Is that it?"

My eyes widened as my eyebrows drew together. "Is that such a bad thing, Trevor?"

Why can't he see how important it is to consider the consequences of his actions? How his drinking could affect more than him?

Then a new question filled my mind

Or is that part of my attraction to him? The fact that he's a bit of a rebel, that he doesn't seem to care what anyone else thinks.

Vivid blue eyes crackling, he said, "Lily, I think you've led a sheltered life. For your information, everything isn't always black and white. There are a lot of grays in this world and I think it's time you realized that."

"You know," I said as I lifted my chin, "a person can be aware of the grays in life and still make smart choices."

He shook his head and turned away before facing me again. "This conversation is going nowhere. You seem to think things have to be done your way or not at all. That doesn't work for me." He looked just beyond my shoulder, as if weighing his next words, then he met my gaze. "I don't know what your father brought you up to expect in a husband, but maybe I'm not it." His voice dropped. "I just don't know if we're right for each other."

I flinched at his pronouncement, but defensive thoughts tumbled into my mind.

He doesn't understand my point at all. What makes him think he knows so much about me? He doesn't know me as well as he seems to think he does.

Before he could say anything more, I leapt from the couch, yanked the ring off my finger, and shoved it into his hand. "You're exactly right, Trevor, so here's your ring back. I'll see you around." With that, I dashed to the door, threw it open, then without making eye contact, I waited to see what he would do.

At first he didn't move, just stared at my implacable face. But when it became clear I wasn't going to change my mind, he stalked out the door and to his car.

The moment he was out of sight, I softly closed the door, then stared at the spot where he'd been only moments before.

All of a sudden, it hit me.

I just ended it with him. Completely.

I sank to the floor, my back to the door, and moaned, "What have I done?"

Chapter Twenty-One

The next morning I didn't wake until nearly noon—I'd been up most of the night rehashing my encounter with Trevor. Even after a nights' sleep nothing had been resolved, and I fervently wished I could go back and handle our conversation differently.

It's all my fault. He was willing to change and I just threw it back in his face. What is wrong with me? Why couldn't I be glad for his willingness to change? Can't I be pleased?

My stomach churned.

Will he be able to forgive my selfish behavior?

Completely miserable, I considered calling him, but was too ashamed by my behavior. Stewing over what to do, I made myself a late breakfast, then, not able to stand the torture any longer, I decided to call him.

I'll invite him over so we can talk.

The decision made, I was able to eat with a bit of an appetite—until I mentally rehearsed what I wanted to say. Nothing sounded quite right and I wondered if calling him would be such a good idea after all.

My need to at least try to talk to Trevor overrode my reticence, and I dialed his cell phone.

I'd been so concerned about what I would say that I hadn't considered that he wouldn't answer. The phone rang and rang, and when I heard his voice mail, I hung up.

Before despair could overcome me, I called Alyssa and told her all that had happened.

"I can't say I'm completely sorry you guys broke up," she said.

"But I *am* sorry you're feeling so bad. Why don't we get together tomorrow? Girl's day out?"

The idea appealed to me. I needed to get away from my problems for a while. "Sure, why not? We could have some lunch, do some shopping, maybe go to a movie." The more I thought about it, the more I liked it.

"I'll pick you up bright and early," she said.

"That was a delicious lunch," I said as Alyssa and I left the restaurant. "I haven't eaten that well in quite a while."

"You need to get out more," she said, hooking her arm through mine. "Now, how about a little shopping before we go see that movie?"

"Sounds great!" I said as we walked toward her car.

Several hours later Alyssa dropped me off at my apartment. I turned up the heat on my way to the bedroom, then changed out of my jeans and sweater before pulling on a comfortable pair of sweats. I'd checked my phone for texts from Trevor throughout the day, but there had been nothing.

Has he even thought about me today?

Sadness threatened to overwhelm me, and I considered trying to call him, but still embarrassed by the things I'd said to him when he'd been trying so hard to please me, I couldn't bring myself to do it.

Still full from lunch, I settled down with a novel and tried to forget my problems, but I found it hard to focus. Then I remembered my journal. I hadn't written in it in months, but I'd always enjoyed reading the passages from the past.

I set my book down, then went to my desk and quickly found it. I carried it back to the couch before opening to my last entry.

I've decided to leave Lovelock and go to the University of Nevada, Reno. It has a good Information Systems program and that's something I'm interested in. I leave tomorrow. Without Dad here I don't think I'll miss this place too much.

That night seemed so long ago now, although it had been less than four months. And as I considered all that had happened to me since that night, I knew I should write down everything while it was fresh in my mind.

I grabbed a pen, then I began writing, expressing my feelings about Trevor. I covered several pages, and as I reread my entry, something became very clear. I realized how very much I loved him and that I would accept him, imperfections and all.

The important thing is that he's willing to try to change. I'm not perfect either, and I know I can be hard to please, but he's willing to overlook that. I love him and I know that my love can help him be a better person. As long as we love each other, what else matters? That is, if he still wants me.

I closed my journal and got ready for bed, disheartened by the course my relationship with Trevor had taken.

I wanted to make things right.

That night I had a dream.

I ran up and down the halls at school, opening and closing classroom doors, searching, searching.

"Trevor," I called out. "Where are you?"

No one seemed to be around, but eventually I ran into a man that looked like Trevor's boss, Rob.

Frantic to find Trevor, I pulled on Rob's arm. "Have you seen Trevor?"

The man yanked his arm away, a look of irritation on his face. As he walked away, I sank to my knees, engulfed by desolation.

I woke abruptly, the feelings from my dream flowing over me. Pulling the blankets close around me, I shivered, but I had one overriding feeling.

I need him.

Chapter Twenty-Two

Before I went to Trevor’s apartment, I wanted to buy him a Christmas gift. When I’d gone shopping with Alyssa the day before, we’d concentrated on buying presents for her large extended family. I only needed to buy gifts for two people—Alyssa and Trevor. I hadn't become close to anyone else and knew my Christmas was going to be lonesome indeed. Trevor had invited me to spend Christmas with him and his family, but I didn't know if he would want to do that now. In fact, I wasn't sure when he was leaving for Vegas to be with his family. For all I knew he was already there, getting together with an old girlfriend.

The thought made my heart pound with jealousy.

Once at the mall it didn't take long to find something for Alyssa—a pair of earrings she’d admired the day before. I had them wrapped so I could drop them by on my way home before she left to spend the holidays with her family.

Figuring out what to get for Trevor was harder.

He’s seems to really like the Denver Broncos.

After searching through many stores, I settled on a team jacket. It cost a lot more than I'd wanted to spend, but I knew he'd love it, and I wanted to get him something that would show him I was thinking about him.

As I walked down the mall, I saw a booth that wrapped gifts and stopped to have Trevor’s gift wrapped. I bought a card at another store and decided to drop by his apartment after going to Alyssa's place, hopeful I would catch him home.

"Are you sure you don't want to come with me to my family's house?" Alyssa asked when I stopped by with her gift.

"No, really. I'll be fine by myself." I pushed a reassuring smile onto my face.

Alyssa handed me a colorfully wrapped gift. "Here's your Christmas present."

"Thank you. You're so thoughtful."

She smiled warmly. "Have a Merry Christmas, will you?"

"Don't worry. I'll be fine."

As I drove to Trevor's apartment it occurred to me that this would be the first time I'd been there, and I realized I'd never met his roommates.

I hope he won't be angry that I'm stopping by unannounced.

It took a few minutes to find the right apartment, and by the time I stood on his porch, I'd begun shivering from the cold—what little sun that had managed to push through the clouds earlier had nearly disappeared.

A tall, slender redhead answered my knock. "Can I help you?"

I stared at the woman.

Is she visiting Trevor?

"Is this Trevor Caldwell's apartment?" I asked.

The woman smirked. "Yeah, he lives here. But he's not home." She eyed the package in my arms. "Is that for him?"

Suddenly unsure if I should leave it for him, I didn't reply.

"Well, is it? You can leave it for him if you want."

"Beth, who's at the door?" a voice shouted from somewhere inside.

The redhead turned to look over her shoulder. "Some girl for Trevor."

A dark-haired man came to the door and looked me up and down. "You must be Lily." He grinned.

"How did you know?" I asked.

"Trevor is always talking about you. No one else comes here looking for him."

Relief swept over me. "Do you know where he is?"

He shook his head. "Sorry. Can't help you there. And I don't know when he'll be back." He paused. "Maybe he's at work. I don't know his schedule."

"Oh," I said, then wondered if he could answer one question I had. "Do you know when he's going to Vegas?"

"Vegas? Why would he go there?" The man seemed genuinely puzzled.

My eyebrows drew together. "To see his family?"

"His family's all dead," he said, a half-smile on his face. "They were murdered when he was in high school."

Astounded, I just stared at the man. "I didn't know," I finally whispered, then I turned away from the door.

"If you see him, tell him he got another package," the man called after me.

I walked back to my car in a daze.

As I drove home I considered going to see Trevor at work, but after what his roommate had told me, I knew I couldn't face him yet.

Why would he tell me his family lives in Vegas? And invite me there for Christmas?

It was completely dark when I got home, and as I walked toward my door, a shiver of fear slid up my spine. I hadn't thought I'd get home so late and hadn't left the porch light on. With my key in hand, I felt around the door lock to find where the key needed to be inserted. After a moment I found it, and when the locks released, I shoved the door open and hastily flipped on all the lights.

With a quick glance around, I realized everything was as I'd left it. I sighed, relieved to be home. I set the gift from Alyssa under the gaily decorated Christmas tree, then placed the one I'd gotten for Trevor next to it. Only two, but the brightly wrapped packages cheered up the room.

After eating a light dinner, I curled up with a novel on the couch. The heroine in the story was having family issues, and as I thought about families, my mind went to Trevor's family and what his roommate had revealed that afternoon.

Did he even know what he was talking about? Maybe Trevor just told him that, although I can't imagine why he would. Maybe I should call him.

I shook my head.

No, his roommate will tell him I came by. It's up to him now.

My mind made up, I went back to my book, but after rereading the same paragraph repeatedly, I knew trying to concentrate was useless.

I set the book beside me on the couch.

Last night I promised myself I'd make things right. But that was before I knew Trevor might have lied to me about his family.

With my eyebrows bunched, I stared at the wall.

There's no way to know until I ask him.

I grabbed my purse and dug out my cell phone, then with my fingers trembling slightly, I called Trevor's number. It rang several times, and when I was about to hang up, I heard his voice.

"Trevor!" I said, surprised at how thrilled I was to hear his voice.

"Yeah? Who's this?" His voice sounded sleepy.

"It's me. Lily. Are you okay?"

"What? Oh, Lily, I didn't recognize your voice. You caught me sleeping. Why are you calling? I thought you didn't want to have anything to do with me."

I pushed my hair out of my face as I tried to think of what to say. "I . . . I was wrong. I need to talk to you. Can you come over?"

"Right now?"

"Yes. It's not that late."

Why is he hesitant to see me? Is he sleeping off a hangover?

"Uh, yeah, sure," he said after a moment. "I'll be there as soon as I can."

Chapter Twenty-Three

An hour later I crossed my arms as I looked out the front window —again.

Where is he? It only takes a few minutes to drive over here. Is he even going to show up?

Then a new idea came to mind.

Maybe he's trying to punish me for hurting him the other day.

Forcing myself away from the window, I went into the kitchen and drank a glass of water. A few minutes later the doorbell rang.

The tenseness in my muscles seeped away as I hurried to the door, and a moment later, as I gazed at him standing on my porch, I had to use all of my self-restraint not to fling myself into his arms.

With a calmness I didn't feel, I said, "Come in, Trevor." He smiled at me as he stepped into the living room. "I was starting to wonder if you were going to show up."

His smile grew. "Like I told you on the phone, I'd been sleeping. I wanted to take a shower." He leaned toward me and whispered in my ear. "I wanted to smell good for you."

Longing pulsed through me, and when he led me to the couch, pulled me onto his lap, then pressed his lips to mine, I responded eagerly. But after a few moments I remembered that all was not well, and still breathless, I disengaged my mouth from his.

"Wait a minute, Trevor."

His heavy-lidded eyes met mine. "What's wrong?"

I slid off his lap and moved to the other end of the couch. "We need to talk."

"Why can't we talk over here?" He patted his lap.

He didn't seem to be himself, and I wondered if my earlier suspicion was accurate, and that he'd been drinking.

"I feel more comfortable over here," I said, watching him closely. His voice sounded normal enough, but he wasn't usually so blatant about wanting to be physical—especially when he knew how important it was to me to wait until marriage to be intimate.

Despite my concern, I pressed ahead. "I wanted to apologize for the other day. I didn't mean to be so rude and throw you out. I was just upset."

With a disarming smile, he said, "That's okay, Lily. I understand. But now what? Where do we go from here?"

His vivid blue eyes, combined with his killer smile, drew me to him, and I forced myself to focus on our conversation. "I don't have all the answers."

"You don't?" he said with a laugh. "And here I thought you did."

His comment hurt my feelings, and I decided to go on the offensive. "Have you been drinking?"

"No." He shook his head. "No, I decided I wasn't going to do that anymore, don't you remember? I told you the other day." His eyes hardened. "You know, the day you kicked me out of your life."

So that's it. He's still angry with me.

I sighed, and decided to change direction. "I have a gift for you." I pointed to the package under the tree.

His gaze went to the present, then he looked at me. "I heard you came by my place earlier."

"Yes I did." The memory of his roommate's comment about Trevor's family flashed through my mind. "I met your roommate, and when I asked him when you were going to Vegas, he told me something very odd."

"What was that?"

As he gazed at me, I found it hard to look away, and even harder to say the bizarre words I'd been told.

"What did he say, Lily? Tell me."

I blinked, breaking his mesmerizing stare, then took a deep breath.

"He said your family had been murdered when you were in high school."

Of all the reactions I'd expected, hysterical laughter was not one of them.

"Oh, Lily!" he laughed. "I can't believe you fell for that!"

Feeling extremely foolish, my face flushed deeply. I'd believed his roommate. My embarrassment turned to anger. "Why would he say such an awful thing? That's just creepy."

His laughter died down to brief chuckles. "That's because he *is* creepy."

"Why do you room with him then?"

Trevor reached over to stroke my arm, but I pushed his hand away, still feeling stupid for believing such a ridiculous comment.

"Hey, don't feel bad. Bronson does that to everyone. Kind of a test."

"A test for what? To see if they're as bizarre as he is? Did you pass his test?"

He smiled. "When I first moved in, he told me that the last guy who lived in my room killed himself, right there in that room. For a couple of weeks I'd get freaked out every time I walked into the room —until the guy who was supposed to be dead showed up to collect some money he was owed."

Glad I wasn't the only one who'd fallen for Bronson's weird practical jokes, I smiled.

"Besides," he said, moving closer to me. "Why would I invite you to come to my parents' house for Christmas if they weren't there? Now that would be really strange."

"That's exactly what I'd been wondering." My embarrassment over, I scooted closer to him.

"So," he said, "are you still planning on coming down to Vegas for Christmas?"

"I hadn't planned on it. After the other day I assumed the invitation had been revoked."

"I'd really like you to come. And I've already told my parents you're coming."

His body heat radiated toward me, warming not only my body, but also my heart. “Let me think about it. When are you heading down there?”

“My flight’s in three days.”

“Ooh. It will be expensive to buy a ticket with such short notice.” I grimaced. “That is if I can even get a flight.”

With a gentle hand, he stroked the curve of my cheek. “If it's the money you're worried about, I'll pay for your ticket. I don't care about the money. I just want you with me.”

Touched by his obvious desire to spend time with me, I felt loved and cared for, and I leaned in for a kiss.

We talked for a while, and when he got up to leave, I walked him to the door. “I'll let you know tomorrow what I decide. Is that all right?”

“Yes.”

I smiled as I watched him walk toward his car.

Chapter Twenty-Four

After sleeping on Trevor's invitation, I awoke with the desire to spend Christmas with Trevor and his family. Once the decision had been made, I dialed Trevor's number, but when he didn't answer, I drove to his apartment to see if he was there.

Bronson answered the door.

"Is Trevor home?" I asked.

"I think he just got out of the shower."

Remembering my feelings of foolishness from the day before, I said, "Hey, I'm sorry about your car."

His eyes widened. "What?"

"Oh, whoops. I thought Trevor told you."

Alarm filled his face. "What are you talking about?"

Grimacing as if I'd made a terrible faux pas, I said, "He told me last night that he saw your car in the parking lot and that it was pretty banged up."

The alarm turned to pure panic, and he raced past me.

I tried not to laugh too hard.

He'd left the door open, and I called, "Trevor? Trevor, it's Lily."

I heard a door open, then Trevor came strolling toward me, barefoot. Jeans hugged his narrow hips, and as he pulled a t-shirt over his head, I caught a glimpse of his washboard abs.

"Lily," he said with a smile. Then confusion descended over his face as he glanced around. "Where's Bronson?"

A giggle burst from my mouth, then I told him what I'd done.

Trevor laughed. "He so deserved that."

"Tell me about it."

"I have to leave for work in a second, but do you want to come in?"

"Sure." The moment I stepped inside, I could tell this was a bachelor pad—there were no feminine touches whatsoever. Dishes overflowed the kitchen sink, an empty pizza box sat on the coffee table, and the place had a closed-in smell.

"Sorry about the mess," Trevor said.

"That's okay," I said, although I was thinking I didn't want to be there too long.

"What brought you by today?"

The mess around me forgotten, I smiled. "I'd like to go with you to Vegas."

"Really?" His voice was filled with enthusiasm. "That's great! I can buy your ticket right now!"

At his tone, my smile grew. "Do you think there are any seats left on your flight?"

"There's only one way to find out." He grabbed a laptop off of the coffee table and booted it up.

The front door burst open, and Bronson stormed inside, his eyes tight with fury as he glared at me. "That was *not* funny."

"Chill out," Trevor said. "It was just a joke."

Bronson's gaze shifted to Trevor. "Were you in on it?"

Trevor glanced at me, then smiled at Bronson. "Of course. And after what you told Lily about me yesterday, you deserved it."

The anger seeped out of Bronson's face, and a half-smile turned up his mouth. "Maybe." Then his gaze shifted to me. "You're pretty gullible."

Trevor put his arm around my shoulders. "It's called being trusting, dude."

I leaned against him, glad he had my back.

"Now, beat it," Trevor said to him. "We're busy."

Bronson frowned and shook his head. "Whatever." But he left us alone.

A moment later Trevor said, "It looks like they have one seat left on my flight. I don't know if we'll be able to sit together, but we'll be on the same flight."

"That's great," I said. "I was sure the flight would be full."

He typed in his credit card number, then turned to me with a grin. "It's full now."

My heart leapt with anticipation as I thought about going on this trip with Trevor. We would be able to spend so much time together. "You're sure your mom doesn't mind me coming?"

"Believe me, she's thrilled I have a girl I want to bring home. My parents have been hoping I'd find a nice girl for a long time. I think they were starting to give up hope."

His words warmed me, made me feel special. "I've never been to Vegas. I'm really looking forward to it."

A short time later we walked out to the parking lot together, and before Trevor left for work, he gave me a lingering kiss.

"I can hardly wait for our trip."

"Me too," I said as love cascaded over me.

Two days later we flew to Vegas, and as the plane approached the airport, I saw that it was sunny and clear. The pilot announced that the temperature was a pleasant fifty-three degrees.

As we deplaned, I held tightly to Trevor's hand, anxious about meeting his parents. They were supposed to pick us up and I was afraid they wouldn't like me. It was very important to me that they approve of me. My parents were no longer around and I knew that whomever I married, that man's parents would become replacements for my parents—at least that was my hope. Especially my future mother-in-law. I really looked forward to having a mother.

"There they are," Trevor said, squeezing my hand reassuringly.

I tried to pick out his parents in the crowd, and when I saw a man and woman looking our way, and saw their friendly smiles, my body relaxed.

Trevor pulled me toward the couple and I felt the warmth in their eyes.

"Dad, Mom, I'd like you to meet Lily," Trevor said, smiling broadly. "Lily, these are my parents, John and Marcy Caldwell."

"It's nice to meet you both," I said, holding out my hand.

John shook it, but Marcy stepped forward and pulled me into an affectionate embrace. "It's so wonderful to meet you at last, Lily," Marcy said as she released me.

"Thank you," I said, a little overwhelmed by the woman's attention.

Trevor laughed. "Don't mind her. I told you she's ecstatic I'm finally bringing a woman home to meet her."

Marcy laughed along with him. "I'm sorry, Lily, but it's true. Please excuse me."

"No, no. It's fine." I was just glad they were happy to meet me.

We collected our luggage and followed the Caldwell's out to their car, and as we drove to Trevor's childhood home, I listened to the family banter, enjoying the warmth they had for each other.

Growing up, it had only been myself and my father, so our drives had usually been fairly quiet.

"Are Scott and Chris coming?" Trevor asked.

"Yes, they are. We'll have a houseful," Marcy said.

"You know you'll love it, dear," John said.

Marcy chuckled. "Yes, I will. All my boys together."

A short time later we pulled into the driveway of their modest home.

"You'll be in the guest room, Lily," Marcy said.

I followed her down a short hall to a small bedroom, while Trevor carried my suitcase and set it on the floor.

"I'll let you get settled," Marcy said. "I'm going to put lunch together."

"Thank you."

Trevor took my hand. "Let me give you the tour."

Any discomfort I'd felt at being in a strange place with people I'd just met was alleviated in the warmth of Trevor's hand. He showed me where the bathroom was and then showed me his old bedroom. "This is where I'll be staying, in case you need anything." He kissed me lightly on the lips.

It looked the way I imagined a teenaged boy's room would look. Blue walls with posters of different rock groups taped to the walls, a bedspread with dark stripes, and a television on the dresser.

"Nice," I said.

"Thanks. It was a good place to live." He smiled at me. "Of course I like having my own place a whole lot better."

I nodded. "I know exactly what you mean. There's nothing quite like being completely on your own."

Over the next few days Trevor showed me around his old haunts and I felt like I was getting to know him better and better. And growing to love him more. His parents were accepting of me and made me feel very much a part of the family.

"So when are your brothers coming?" I asked him as we took a walk.

"They only live about an hour from here, so they'll just come on Christmas day."

I was looking forward to meeting the rest of Trevor's family—there was a distinct possibility that they would one day be my family as well, and I was excited to get to know Trevor's sisters-in-law. I'd never had brothers or sisters and was delighted at the idea.

"I've been meaning to tell you, Trevor, your Mom's a great cook. I don't know what you were talking about when you said she couldn't cook."

"Yeah, I noticed too. Maybe she's been taking cooking lessons since I've been gone." He grinned.

"Or maybe you were exaggerating just a bit."

I reached out to punch him on the arm but he grabbed my wrist and pulled me close, burying his face in my hair. "Lily, Lily," he murmured. "I love you so much. When will you say you'll marry me?"

His words warmed my heart. "Oh, Trevor, I love you, too. And I promise, I'll give you an answer soon. Please be patient with me."

He looked into my eyes as a gentle smile turned up the corners of his mouth. "I'm trying to be patient. I really am."

Then and there I gave myself a deadline.

I'll decide by Christmas.

That gave me two days.

In my heart I wanted so badly to say yes, but I knew it was a decision I had to be sure about. Over the next two days I thought about marrying Trevor constantly, mentally listing the pros and cons. My biggest worry was his tendency to want to drink excessively and maybe use drugs.

But he'd promised he would stop and I desperately wanted to believe him. And I loved him so much.

Finally, after much deep thought and introspection, I decided to accept his proposal.

Chapter Twenty-Five

On Christmas morning I woke earlier than normal, more keyed up than I'd been in a long time. Besides meeting the rest of Trevor's family, today was the day I would give Trevor my answer. I quickly showered and dressed, then went into the kitchen to see if I could help Marcy with anything.

"I've got it all under control," she said. "For now at least. But later I probably will need some help."

Trevor came out a short time later, already showered and ready for the day. He wrapped his arms around me. "Merry Christmas," he said in my ear.

Knowing I would be telling him that I would accept his proposal of marriage later that day, I thrilled at his presence. "Merry Christmas to you, too." I smiled at him and he kissed me softly on the lips.

After breakfast we went into the living room to open presents. Just as I'd hoped, Trevor loved the Broncos jacket I'd given him. He handed me a gift and I carefully unwrapped the paper. It was the latest eReader.

"Trevor, it's perfect," I said, leaning over and giving him a hug. "But it's so expensive," I whispered in his ear.

He grinned at me. "You're worth it."

John reached under the tree and pulled out a small gift. "Here, Lily. This one's for you."

"Oh." I took it from his hand, pleasantly surprised that they'd given me a gift. It was a gift card for books to load onto my eReader. "Thank you, John. Thank you, Marcy. I love to read, so this is perfect." I looked under the tree for the gifts that I'd bought for them once I'd decided to come and handed one to Marcy and the other to John.

A ceramic dog for Marcy to set on a bookshelf, and a Denver Broncos book for John.

"These are perfect, Lily," said Marcy.

John nodded as he chuckled. "I guess Trevor told you how much of a Broncos fan I am."

"That's right. And he told me that you like anything to do with dogs, Marcy."

"I'm so glad you could come, Lily," Marcy said. "I've really enjoyed getting to know you."

Her words meant more to me than she knew. I looked over at Trevor. "I'm glad I came, too."

He took my hand in his.

"Why don't you kids take off for a while?" Marcy said. "Scott and Chris won't be here with their families for another hour or so."

"Okay, Mom," Trevor said, then he helped me stand.

As we headed out the front door, I smiled at the lovely day—sunny and clear and pleasantly cool.

"It's a good idea to enjoy some peace before all the kids get here," Trevor said, leading me down the driveway.

"How many kids do they have?" I tried to calm my heart, knowing this walk would be the best opportunity to tell Trevor my decision.

"Scott has three and Chris has two. But sometimes when they're all together it can seem more like a dozen."

"I can hardly wait." I meant it, too. It had always been so quiet at my house on Christmas that I was looking forward to the commotion a family would bring.

We walked in silence, hand in hand, for several minutes. As we approached an elementary school, I led Trevor to a small bench that was near a playground. Other than a pair of boys riding new bikes on the path, we were alone.

"Trevor, I need to talk to you. Let's sit down."

He followed me to the bench and looked at me expectantly.

"I've come to a decision on your proposal." I watched his face, and was not disappointed at the hope I saw in his eyes. "I would love to marry you."

His eyes glistened. "Really? Do you mean it?"

"Yes," I whispered. "I mean it."

"Oh, Lily, this is the best Christmas present I could have ever wished for." He slid his arms around me and pulled me to him. "I love you."

"I love you, too," I said, pressing my face into his neck.

Security and warmth spread over me as I snuggled in his arms.

Chapter Twenty-Six

We agreed to wait until after Christmas dinner to announce our engagement to his family, but as I looked at the perpetual grin on Trevor's face, I wasn't sure he'd be able to keep our secret that long.

Trevor had been right about his nieces and nephews—there was a lot of commotion with them around. I met Scott and Chris and their wives and everyone had been kind to me. I hadn't had much of a chance to visit with any of them—they were kept busy with their rambunctious children.

I helped Marcy get the finishing touches ready for dinner, and when everyone found his place at the table, I thought of the contrast this meal and large group of people was to Thanksgiving when Trevor and I'd been by ourselves.

When everyone had finished eating, Trevor stood. "I have an announcement to make."

All eyes were on him as he reached down to me and helped me to my feet to stand by his side.

I felt extremely self-conscious as everyone's attention shifted to me. I looked at Trevor, waiting for him to take the lead.

"Lily and I are getting married," Trevor said.

"Congratulations, little brother," Scott said, standing to shake Trevor's hand.

Marcy came over to us and hugged me. "I'm so happy." Tears shimmered in her eyes.

After several minutes everyone settled back down.

"Have you thought about when the wedding will be or where?"

Marcy asked.

I looked at Trevor then back at Marcy. "We haven't gotten that far."

"I'd like to get married as soon as possible," Trevor said, a grin on his face.

I was pretty sure why he said that, but I was also pretty sure no one else had a clue. Everyone's eyes swiveled in my direction and I wondered if they thought I was pregnant. The idea was the definition of ironic.

When I said nothing, Trevor laughed, and everyone's attention shifted back to him. "But I guess there's really no hurry."

Everyone seemed confused, but I wasn't about to say anything.

"Well," Marcy said, breaking the silence, "I suppose we can discuss the details later."

We finished off the meal with pie and ice cream, then I helped Marcy clean up. I enjoyed the time I spent chatting with her and getting to know her better, but after a while she sent me away and told me to spend time with my fiancé. The sound of the word exhilarated me.

I found Trevor with his dad and brothers watching a football game in the living room. When he saw me come in he motioned for me to sit by him. There wasn't much room on the couch, so he pulled me onto his lap and nuzzled my ear. Waves of desire raced through me and I turned to face him, meeting his lips in a kiss.

"None of that in here, you two," Chris said, laughing.

I laughed too, embarrassed to have been noticed, but I loved the feeling of being part of the group.

After a few minutes, Trevor whispered, "I've had enough football."

He helped me from his lap and then he stood, and taking my hand, led me down the hall to the room where I was staying. He closed the door then sat on the bed and patted the spot next to him.

I sat beside him with a smile.

He reached into his pocket and pulled something out. "This is why I wanted to come in here." He took my left hand and slid the diamond ring onto my finger.

The diamond sparkled, and now that I knew we were going to be married, peace and contentment settled over me as I gazed at the gorgeous ring. "It's just as beautiful as when I first saw it."

He opened his arms and I eagerly went into them. "Do you have any idea how happy I am right now?" he murmured next to my ear.

I smiled against his shoulder. "I think I have an idea." Then I pulled back. "Do you think your parents think I'm pregnant?"

"Why would they think that?" He looked perplexed.

I laughed. "Well, when you said you wanted to get married right away, I could almost see the wheels turning in their heads. I mean, why else would you want to get married so fast?"

"I guess you're right." He grinned. "But I'll bet you know why I'm anxious to get married." He smirked at me. "Unless you're willing to change your mind." His hands cradled my face as he pressed his lips to mine.

I responded eagerly.

One of his hands slid around my back while the other gently held my neck, then his lips moved away from my mouth to my jaw. He tilted my head back and pressed tiny kisses along my neck, and when I moaned, his lips formed a smile against my skin.

Feeling like things were getting out of hand, I gently pushed him away. "Stop it, Trevor."

"Come on, Lily. We're engaged now. What's the problem?"

I didn't like the pressure he was putting on me. My hormones were just as powerful as his, but it was important to me to wait until marriage before giving that part of myself away. "The problem is, you're not respecting my boundaries."

He turned away with a loud sigh, then he turned back to me. "You're just being old-fashioned."

"I know some people might look at it that way, but that doesn't change the fact that I want to save that part of myself until my wedding night." I hoped he would understand.

He shook his head, clearly irritated. "I know it's a cliché," he began, "but men have needs. And right now I have a strong need for you." His voice dropped to whisper. "Please, Lily."

I felt terribly guilty for denying him, which made me angry. I wasn't doing anything wrong. In fact, his pressure on me was wrong. "No," I said.

A bright flash of fury darkened his eyes, but he got it under control as he said through nearly clenched teeth, "I shouldn't have to beg."

A small feeling of fear tickled the back of my neck. "And you won't have to, as soon as we're married."

He sighed, and his face calmed. "Okay. Let's set a date then. And let's make it soon."

The tension in the room dissipated. "What did you have in mind?"

"Well, we are in Vegas. We could get married today."

My mouth fell open. I'd barely decided to marry him—I didn't know if I was ready to actually make it legal that day. Plus I wanted the full experience, not some quickie wedding. "Trevor, I know you don't want to wait, but I promise we'll have the wedding soon. There's planning involved."

"Why can't we just elope? The results will be the same whether we have a big wedding or a quick one."

I sighed. "Don't you know that every girl fantasizes about her big day? I don't want to be denied that experience."

"Fine," he said, clearly not thrilled. "I guess I can wait a little longer." Then he looked at me with intensity. "But Lily, you need to know that this is not easy for me."

A small smile turned up the corners of my mouth, and I reached out and stroked his face. "Trevor, the fact that you're respecting my wishes on this shows me how much you love me and it makes me love you even more."

That brought a smile to his face and he pulled me into a warm embrace. "I do love you and I'd do anything for you."

Relief swept over me that he wasn't angry any longer, and I reveled in the love I felt from him.

"Thank you for bringing me to meet your family," I said as we sat on my couch. I snuggled up to Trevor's side and he put his arm around me. “I really like them.”

“They like you, too.”

“Do you really think so?”

He ran his fingers through my long, dark hair. “Trust me, they like you. They're happy we're getting married. By the way, when are we going to set a date?”

Now that I'd accepted his proposal, I enjoyed fantasizing about our special day. “I know you want to do it soon and I agree.” I tilted my face to his and kissed him with longing. He cradled my face in his hands as his lips met mine with urgency.

He pulled back. “Good.” His voice was husky. “Because if you want me to respect your wishes, we need to get this thing going.”

“Okay, do you want to talk about it now?”

“Unfortunately, Rob needs me to come in.”

“Why now?”

“Since I took all that time off to go to Vegas he needs me to help him catch up. I promised him I’d come in. What about tomorrow night? Can we talk about it then?”

“Okay. I’m meeting Alyssa for lunch, and then I’m going to buy my books for next semester since school starts in a week. But if you're coming over, I'll make sure to be home.”

He kissed me before standing and putting on his jacket. “I'll plan on it, then.”

I walked him to the door and gave him one last kiss before he left. Once alone, I unpacked my suitcase and admired the ring on my finger.

Now that we were engaged I didn't plan on taking it off ever again.

Chapter Twenty-Seven

"I can't believe you're officially engaged," Alyssa said before taking a bite of her salad.

I sat across from her at the restaurant, nearly beaming with my good news. "And all those things you hear about in-laws? Well they're just not true in this case. I really like his parents. They're very nice."

"I'm happy for you, truly. It's just, how sure are you that he's given up his partying ways? "

"He told me he has and I trust him. He would never lie to me. He's not like that." I shook my head. "You just don't know him."

Alyssa smoothed the napkin on her lap before looking at me. "Justin and Pamela have begun talking about marriage too."

"Oh? Well, that's great. I'm happy for them."

"Yeah. It's good he's moved on."

"So will you be able to come to my wedding?" I asked. "I want you to be my maid of honor."

"You do? I'd love to. I'll make sure I can come."

I smiled in relief. "Oh, I'm so glad. You'll be the only person there from my side of the family, so to speak." Even as I said the words, I had to swallow over the lump that formed in my throat as I thought of my father and how much I wished he could be part of my wedding day.

"Of course I'll be there, Lily," Alyssa said.

I smiled. "Thanks."

We finished eating and paid the bill, and a few minutes later I stood. "Well, I'd better get going. I want to get my books for the new semester."

Alyssa stood as well. “Yeah, I need to get mine, too. But I'm waiting a few more days.”

“Thanks for inviting me to lunch. We should do it more often.” I slung my purse over my shoulder.

“Congratulations on your engagement to Trevor. I'm really happy for you.” She smiled warmly. “And if you need any help planning things let me know. I'd be happy to lend my expertise. I've helped my mother plan two weddings already.”

“Great. I'll probably take you up on that.”

Later that afternoon, after I'd purchased my books for the spring semester, I went home and played with my new eReader. I bought a few books with the gift card the Caldwell's had given me and then began reading one.

A while later I set the eReader aside and booted up my laptop, then clicked on the UNR web site and decided to check my student email account. I didn’t check very often—I had a personal account I used for all of my email correspondence—but I thought I should see if any of my professors had sent anything for the new semester.

A moment later I saw two email messages from the same address. Both emails had been sent before Christmas.

I clicked on the first one, and when I began reading it, I gasped.

You stupid girl! Don't you understand anything? I told you not to get involved with Trevor Caldwell, but from what I've observed you've been spending lots of time with him. I am very disappointed.

With a racing heart, I reread the message. I was scared to open the other message, but knew I had to see what it said.

I understand Trevor proposed to you. For your own safety I strongly recommend that you not accept.

I didn't understand why this person was so interested in my life with Trevor. Gathering my nerve, I hit the Reply button.

Who are you? Why do you care if I marry Trevor Caldwell? I don't understand.

I hit the Send button and exited the program, planning on checking back later to see if I'd received a response. My hands trembled as I closed my laptop.

I couldn't get the messages out of my mind and was only able to wait half an hour before checking to see if the sender had replied. I signed on and was half disappointed and half relieved to find no messages waiting.

Trevor arrived before I tried to check again, and I debated whether to tell him about the strange messages. On the one hand, I didn't want to keep any secrets from him, but on the other, the messages were about him.

I'll wait until I receive a reply. Besides, he didn't seem too concerned about the other strange things that happened.

"How's my favorite girl?" he asked, enveloping me in a hug.

In his arms, I felt safe. "Now that you're here, I'm great."

He pulled back. "What'd you do today? Anything exciting?"

I smiled as I gazed into his blue eyes. "I went to lunch with Alyssa, bought my books and then played with my new eReader."

"Oh, so you liked my present. I'm glad." He smiled, obviously pleased that his gift was a hit.

"I love it," I said. "Let's sit, Trevor, and you can tell me about your day."

He followed me to the couch. "Just a boring work day." He held my hand. "Have you thought any more about a wedding date?"

My stomach tightened at his words. After the ominous messages I'd received, I was reluctant to make such a definite commitment. "I don't know," I hedged. "Do you have any suggestions?"

"Tomorrow?" he said, laughing. "Really though, I want to get married right away. How long would it take you to get ready?"

"I . . . I don't know. I don't even know what needs doing. Alyssa offered to help. She said she's helped plan weddings before."

His face lit up. "That's great. Call her right now and find out what we need to do to get ready."

"Right now?"

He jumped to his feet. "Yes, now." Trevor went into the kitchen and grabbed the notepad and pen from the counter and brought them back to me. "Here. You can write down what she says." He glanced around. "Where's your phone?"

"It's in my purse."

Jumping up again, he picked up my purse and handed it to me. I dug around and pulled out my phone, but I didn't know why I felt so hesitant.

I'm not going to allow some anonymous person to spook me from marrying the man I love.

Determined to move forward with my plans, I dialed Alyssa's number.

After explaining my reason for calling, I listened as Alyssa told me what needed to be planned and I wrote it all down on the notepad. I hung up a short time later.

Trevor took the notepad from my lap. "Okay. So what do we need to do first?"

Trevor's excitement was contagious, and I began to feel more energized about planning our wedding. "It sounds like I need to find a dress right away. That way if any fittings need to be done there will be time for that. And then we need to order a cake and flowers. And of course we need to make arrangements for a place to get married and someone to do it."

"What's the procedure on finding a wedding dress?" Trevor asked. "Am I allowed to help you find one or is that against the rules?"

I laughed at his question. "I think it's best if Alyssa helps me find one. But thanks for the offer. We could pick out the cake together though. Which brings me to the reception. Where should we have it? I don't know that many people here."

"Hmm. Yeah, same here."

"Did your parents say anything to you about hosting a reception?" I asked, thinking that would solve a lot of my anxiety.

"No, but if you want me to, I could ask them."

"Would you? If we could let them be in charge of it that would be one less thing for us to worry about." I paused. "What about the cost? How are we going to pay for everything?"

"Hmm. I think we should split the costs up. Like, you pay for your wedding dress and the flowers. I'll pay for the photographer and the cake. How does that sound?"

"That sounds fair. What about any other reception costs?"

"I think my parents might cover the rest." He paused. "There's still the matter of the date. Now that you've talked to Alyssa, do you have any idea?"

"If I find a dress off the rack, which would be much cheaper, we'd only need a month or so."

His face brightened. "Only a month? That would be great."

I smiled at his enthusiasm—it made me feel incredibly loved and wanted to know Trevor was so anxious to have me become his wife. I grabbed my calendar, and together we looked at the dates in January and February.

"How about Valentine's day?" I suggested, thinking it would be romantic.

"That's not for at least six weeks. I don't know if I can wait that long." His eyebrows rose as he smiled.

I smiled in return then turned back to the open calendar. "Okay, you choose."

He pointed to a date. "How about right here? The fourth Saturday in January?"

"All right. That sounds fine."

Trevor set the calendar on the coffee table and pulled me into his arms. "Only four and half weeks. I can hardly wait."

I snuggled against him and let myself be enveloped in his body heat, not allowing any worries to press on my mind.

Chapter Twenty-Eight

Alyssa and I flipped through the racks at the bridal store, searching for the perfect bridal gown. Shopping wasn't one of my favorite activities and I was already getting discouraged, but Alyssa showed no signs of slowing down. She had several gowns draped over one arm.

"Can I put those in a dressing room for you?" the saleslady asked Alyssa, reaching for the gowns.

"Thank you. That would be great." Alyssa handed the dresses over.

"When is your wedding?" the saleslady asked.

"Oh, it's not me that's getting married. It's Lily." Alyssa pointed to me as I looked for a chair to sit in.

"When is your wedding, dear?" the woman asked me.

I told her the date Trevor and I had chosen.

"That doesn't leave us much time now, does it?"

I tried to smile, knowing most weddings were planned many months in advance.

"I don't see anything else, Lily," Alyssa said. "Why don't you try on what we've gotten so far?"

"Sure, why not?" I followed the two women to a dressing room and allowed Alyssa to help me try on the first gown, then I walked out of the dressing room and stepped onto a raised platform to admire myself in a three-way mirror.

"Well?" Alyssa asked.

"It's okay I guess. Let me try on the others."

The third one I tried on was my favorite—the bodice hugged my curves, lacy sleeves reached halfway between my shoulder and elbow, and the skirt gathered in at the waist then flowed outward from there. It was simple but beautiful.

"This is it," I announced. "This is my wedding dress."

The saleslady brought over several different veils, and after choosing one, I slipped it onto my long hair. "That looks gorgeous," the saleslady assured me. "And the dress should only need minor adjustments." She looked at the dress from different angles. "Yes, I do believe we can have it done on time."

As I wrote the check for my wedding dress, it occurred to me that my funds were diminishing a lot more quickly than I'd anticipated. The concern was fleeting as the woman handed me the appointment card for my fitting.

I dropped Alyssa off at her apartment and drove home, then decided to check my student e-mail account. As of that morning I hadn't gotten a response to my reply, but I couldn't help myself—I was becoming obsessive about checking my e-mail.

I dropped my purse on the kitchen counter then went directly to my laptop and booted it up. I signed into my e-mail account and held my breath while I waited for it to open.

There was a message. I tried to control the shaking of my hands as I clicked on it, and my heart pounded as I waited for it to open. My breath came out in a whoosh when I saw it was junk mail.

It's not even the right address.

I signed off, upset that I hadn't gotten a response.

Two days later it was New Year's Eve. Trevor picked me up for a party one of his friends was throwing. Though I wasn't looking forward to the party—I was more of a homebody—the thought of spending the evening with Trevor would make it worthwhile.

By the time we arrived at the party it was in full swing. The crowd looked a little rougher than I was used to, but I tried not to make judgments about Trevor's friends. Music blared from a pair of speakers as Trevor pulled me onto the small dance floor. When a slow song started I clung to him, hardly believing he would be my husband in just a matter of weeks.

After we'd been dancing for a while, Trevor asked me if I was thirsty, then led me to a chair to wait while he got me a soda.

A few moments later Trevor handed me a Sprite, then sat on the ottoman next to my chair. “Are you having a good time?” he asked, then he took a large swallow of his drink.

I couldn’t tell what he was drinking since the glass was opaque, but I hoped he was keeping his word that his partying days were behind him.

I sipped at my soda. “It's okay. I don't really know anybody though.”

“It's getting close to midnight. Do you want to get out of here?”

Relieved he’d made the suggestion, I smiled. “Yes, please.”

He took my hand as we walked out to his car.

“Where should we go?” I asked as I put on my seatbelt.

“I know just the place.” He grinned as he started the engine.

We drove for a while, and when we stopped we were overlooking the valley. Even though it was cold outside, the view was spectacular.

Trevor left the car running so we could stay warm. Even so, I cuddled up to him.

He gazed at me, the black of his pupils enlarged in his blue eyes. “It's midnight, Lily.” His voice was husky as he cradled my face in his hands. I closed my eyes, ready to accept his kiss, and a moment later he pressed his lips against mine—gently at first, then more urgently.

“I don't think I can wait four more weeks,” he groaned. “We're practically married now. Do we really need to wait?”

I pulled back. “But we’re not *actually* married.”

He stared at me in the dim moonlight. “You’re one stubborn girl.”

Wanting to change the subject, I searched for something else to talk about. The messages I'd received popped into my head and they wouldn't leave. “Trevor, I got a weird e-mail the other day.”

“Oh, yeah?” He said without much enthusiasm.

“Yes. They were about you.”

That got his attention, and he sat up straighter. “Who sent them?”

“I don't know.”

“Okay. What did they say?”

“Basically, they told me not to marry you.”

"What?" He shifted in his seat to face me more squarely.

"That's right. This time I sent an e-mail back, though." I smiled, proud I'd taken some sort of action.

"And did you get a response?"

"Not yet."

His hand shot out and he grabbed me by the arm. "Tell me if you do. Will you promise me?"

Startled by his response, I said, "Okay, if that's what you want." He let go of my arm and I rubbed it where he'd squeezed.

"It's getting late. I'd better get you home." He put the car in gear and we drove toward my apartment.

His sudden change in attitude concerned me.

What does he know that he's not telling me?

Chapter Twenty-Nine

When the spring semester started a few days later, I was excited to begin my new classes. My first one was a course required of everyone —Humanities. When I walked into the classroom I was surprised to find Justin sitting at a desk. There was an empty seat beside him, so I sat next to him.

"What are you doing in this class?" I said.

"Oh, hey, Lily. How's it going?" His smile was warm and friendly.

"Great. How about you? I hear you and Pamela are getting serious."

"Yeah, but not as serious as you, I hear."

He seemed genuinely pleased to hear about my engagement, which surprised me.

I guess he's over me. That's good, I suppose.

"Yes," I said. "Three and a half more weeks." I paused. "Why are you in this class? I would've thought you'd be down to just a few last classes by now."

"That's just it. After I talked to my counselor I realized I'd never taken this class. It's required for graduation, you know."

"Yeah, I know. I thought I'd get it over with early." I grimaced.

"Good idea. I wish I'd done the same."

We chatted about our classes until the professor arrived, and as I walked to my next class I realized that I hadn't been uncomfortable around Justin like I'd been in the past.

Maybe it's because we both have other people we're interested in. I don't have to worry about hurting his feelings because I love Trevor.

I went to my other classes and got home shortly after lunch. Trevor was going to come over later so I wanted to get any reading done right away. First I checked my e-mail. Nothing.

Why hasn't he or she responded to my e-mail?

Frustrated at the silence, I sighed.

Maybe I've scared the person off.

My spirits surged at the thought.

One less thing to worry about, I guess.

Trevor showed up late that afternoon.

"Are you sure your parents don't mind hosting our reception?" I asked as we stood in the kitchen making dinner.

"They seemed fine with it." He hesitated. "There's only one catch."

I stopped stirring the meat and looked at Trevor. "What?"

He smiled self-consciously. "We'll have to have it there."

"There?"

"Yeah, in Vegas."

I began mixing the meat. "Oh. Well, I guess that's okay. I did tell you I don't really know many people here. And I suppose it makes sense for us to go to your family."

He laughed in apparent relief. "Yeah, it might be kind of a hardship for my brothers and their families to all come up here."

"This is all so complicated. Maybe we should just elope." I laughed as I looked up at Trevor's face.

He wasn't laughing. "That's it! We'll elope. Today!" His lips turned up into a broad smile. "You're a genius, Lily."

I backed up a bit. "I was just joking, Trevor. I mean, I already paid for my dress and everything."

"So? We'll go pick it up and take it with us. We can drive to Vegas." He lifted my chin with a finger. "How about it? We can be married by tomorrow." His face seemed to glow with the idea.

"I don't know, Trevor. I don't know. This is kind of sudden."

"Sudden? It's not like we weren't going to get married. We're just speeding things up."

The meat was starting to burn, so I turned away from him to stir it. "What's your hurry? It's only three more weeks."

Trevor threw his hands up and stormed into the living room. “Lily, why do you have to be so stubborn?”

Stung by his remark, my chest tightened, and I took a deep breath to keep the tears from starting, then I sprinkled salt and pepper into the pan and mixed it in. “I'm not stubborn,” I said under my breath. I grabbed a glass and filled it from the faucet before gulping down the water. After another deep breath, I went into the living room where Trevor was flipping through channels on my miniscule television.

“Why don't you get a better TV?” He grumbled.

“This one works just fine for me.” I stood next to the couch.

Trevor looked up at me. “See what I mean? You're even stubborn about the stupid TV.”

Insulted and embarrassed, I said, “I think you'd better leave now, Trevor.”

He stood and came to me. “I'm sorry, Lily. I didn't mean it. I'm just frustrated you won't see things my way.” He tried to put his arms around me but I pushed him away. “Fine, I'm outta here.”

I watched as he opened the door.

He turned before leaving. “I'm not sure when I'll be back.” Then he slammed the door.

I watched him walk past my window, then I ran into my bedroom and flung myself onto my bed. “Why does he have to be so difficult?” I cried out.

Chapter Thirty

Over the next two days I had trouble concentrating at school, and when I had my second class with Justin, he must have sensed something was bothering me.

"Is something wrong, Lily?" he asked as class ended.

"No." I had no intention of sharing my problems with him. "Why do you ask?" I gathered up my books and put them in my backpack.

He stared at me for a moment. "No reason. Never mind. Have a good weekend."

"Thanks. You, too." I watched him leave and thought about what was bothering me. I hadn't heard from Trevor since our fight two days before, and when I recalled his parting words—*I'm not sure when I'll be back*—worry pressed on my mind.

Maybe he meant something more permanent.

Anxious to see if there was a message from Trevor, I checked my phone for messages. There was a message, but it wasn't from Trevor.

"This is Rory's Bridal Shop for Lily," the message began. "I'm calling to remind you about your fitting appointment this afternoon."

"Oh, shoot," I said out loud. "I forgot all about that." I knew I'd have to hurry to make the appointment.

Forty-five minutes later I stood in front of a three-way mirror while a woman pinned the hem and waist of my wedding gown. I gazed at my reflection, thinking about Trevor and our fight.

Is this wedding even going to happen?

Blinking back tears, I had to look away from the mirror until I could get myself under control.

When the fitting was done, I changed back into my clothes.

"Your gown should be ready by next Friday," the sales lady said. "We'll have you try it on one last time, but I'm sure it will be a perfect fit."

"Thank you," I said as I took the appointment card.

I waited until I got home to call Trevor, but when I tried his cell, I got his voice mail. Wanting to speak to him face to face, I drove to his apartment, hopeful I'd find him there.

Bronson answered the door. "Hi, Lily." His voice was slurred. "How's it goin', sweetheart?"

"Fine. Is Trevor home?"

"No, but I'm here. Why don't you come in and spend time with me?"

"Do you know where he is?"

"Nope. Can't help you there."

"Okay. Well, thanks anyway." I turned and hurried away.

I guess he's getting an early start on his weekend partying. At least Trevor isn't there with him. Maybe he's at work.

A few minutes later I pulled up to *Rob's Auto Body*, and when I entered the shop, no one was in sight. I stood at the counter for several minutes before getting up the nerve to go through the door I'd seen Trevor come through the last time I'd been there.

Carefully stepping around the counter, I tried not to touch anything that looked greasy, then opened the door and peeked into the adjoining room. Two cars had their hoods open, and a number of car parts were strewn about.

No one seemed to be in the room and I wondered if they'd all left for a dinner break. But the main garage doors were open.

Someone must be here.

I walked toward the other side of the garage, careful to avoid the tools and parts on the floor.

"Hey!"

I spun around at the sharp voice.

"What are you doing in here?" It was Rob, the owner of the shop. He strode toward me. "You're not supposed to be back here."

"I'm sorry. I was looking for Trevor. Is he working today?"

His voice softened when he recognized me. "Oh, you're Trevor's fiancé, aren't you?"

I smiled tentatively. "Yes, Lily." I would have held out my hand if his weren't so dirty.

"Yeah. I remember you. Trevor isn't here right now. He's . . . uh . . . he's running an errand for me."

"Okay. Do you know how long he might be?"

Rob glanced to the side then back to me. "It could be a while. Sorry."

"Would you tell him I came by?"

"Yeah, sure."

I backed toward the open garage doors and out into the sunlight. "Thanks." When he nodded, I turned and hurried to my car.

Once home, I fixed myself dinner before flipping on the television to watch the news. I squinted at the TV.

Trevor's right. This set is too small. Maybe I should get a decent one for us before the wedding.

As I thought about Trevor and our engagement, I hoped he would come by so we could straighten everything out. I hated it when we were angry at each other.

At nine o'clock that night Trevor knocked on my door.

"Rob said you came by," he said, his expression serious.

I stood at the door. "I did. I wanted to talk to you." His stern look frightened me.

Maybe he's still angry from two days ago.

"Do you want to come in?" I asked.

"Yeah." He stepped into my apartment and I closed the door behind him.

"Come sit down, Trevor." He did, and I sat near him without touching him. I tried smiling but he didn't return the favor.

"What did you want to talk about, Lily?"

"Are you still mad at me?" A blush rose on my face. "I'm sorry, Trevor."

His expression softened and he gathered me into his arms. "I'm not mad anymore."

I pulled back. "Then what's wrong? You seem upset."

He frowned. "Rob really let me have it when I got back. He said I needed to make sure you knew never to go into the shop like you did." He looked at his hands. "He said he'd fire me if you did it again."

I was horrified. "That's not fair! It's not your fault I went in there. He shouldn't treat you like that. Why do you put up with that? Maybe you should find another job."

Trevor laughed at my outrage. "He won't fire me. That's just him letting off steam. Besides, I know things about his business that he wouldn't want getting out. Don't worry, my job's secure."

"Good. And what do you mean? What do you know about his business?"

He frowned. "Nothing you need to worry about." He stroked my hair and guided my head back against his chest.

Happy he wasn't angry with me, I decided not to press him for more information.

"Now, about our wedding," he said.

I sat up, smiling. "What about it?"

He grinned. "We never finished working out the details the other day."

"Oh. Well, if it's easier for your family I don't care if we're married there." An idea occurred to me. "What about blood tests?"

"I don't know. I didn't think of that. I guess we'll have to find out."

"We could go online right now and see if we can get any information."

"Okay. You're the expert."

He watched over my shoulder as I searched for the information, and in only a few minutes we had our answer. I turned to Trevor. "Looks like no blood test." I smiled. "Which is good since I hate needles."

He smiled. "And there's no waiting period to get the marriage license."

"That makes it easier." As we continued searching the web, we found a site that listed different places in Las Vegas to have the ceremony. "We could have it here," I said, pointing to an image of a botanical garden. "It looks really pretty."

"I'm fine with that," he said.

"And look at this. We can even have the reception there right after the ceremony. These prices are actually really reasonable."

"Yeah. And look, they'll provide the cake."

I turned to him with a bright smile, excited to discover planning our wedding wouldn't be so challenging. "Do you think it will be available on the date we need it?"

"I guess there's only one way to find out," he said. "Let's see if we can book it."

We pressed the button to book the wedding and were thrilled to see that our date was available. A moment later we'd booked the location.

"I guess we won't need your parents to host the wedding after all," I said. "Do you think your mom will be disappointed?"

"She'll get over it."

I hoped so. I didn't want to start off on the wrong foot with my future mother-in-law. "Maybe you'd better call her right now and let her know the change in plans." He agreed, and a moment later he had his mom on the phone. I listened to his side of the conversation and it sounded like his mom wasn't mad. He hung up a few moments later. "So?" I asked.

He grinned. "She's fine with it. You heard me tell her we're keeping it really small. She said she'd get us her guest list ASAP."

I smiled, pleased that everything was coming together so nicely.

"What else do we need to do?" Trevor asked.

"We should get our plane tickets."

"We can do it online."

I went to the airline website and we soon had the reservations made. "You know," I said, "we need to figure out the invitations right away."

"What do you mean by figure them out?"

"Well, I know a lot of people do online invitations. Since time is so short, that would probably be a good option for us."

"Can you take care of that?"

"Don't you want to choose them together?"

He shrugged. "I don't care what they look like, as long as they say you're going to marry me." He lifted my chin with two fingers and pressed his lips to mine.

His touch made me slightly dazed and I tried to collect myself. "Okay." I gazed at him for a moment.

"What?" he asked.

"I just can't believe you'll be my husband three weeks from tomorrow."

He grinned. "Pretty cool, huh? Hey, what about a honeymoon?"

My smile faded. "We'll have to wait until the semester's over. I don't want to miss any classes."

He nodded. "I thought you might say something like that. That's fine. I understand."

My smile returned, relieved he understood how important my education was to me. "When your mom gives you her guest list, let me know and I'll get the invitations out as soon as I can."

"I'm sorry to put all this on you when you have classes," he said.

"It's okay. School only started the other day. Things aren't too bad yet." I paused. "What about you? How do you think your classes are going to be?"

He looked away. "Fine." Then he smiled at me. "You know, the usual."

I nodded. "Great."

The following Friday I had the final fitting for my wedding gown, and just as the saleslady had promised, it fit perfectly. "Would it be possible for you to ship it to Vegas? That's where I'll be getting married," I said.

"Certainly. Just give me the address and I'll take care of it."

I gave her the information, then drove home, secure in the knowledge that my gown would be waiting for me when I arrived at the Caldwell's home in two weeks. And I'd received the list of guests from Marcy and had sent out the eVites, so there really wasn't anything left for me to do.

The next two weeks flew by as I went to school. I usually came home to eat so I hadn't met Trevor for lunch.

In fact, I haven't seen Trevor around campus at all.

That thought was quickly replaced with the mental list of things I needed to pack before we caught our flight first thing the next morning. Alyssa would fly in after Trevor and I had arrived.

The next morning as we settled into our seats on the airplane, I thought about how much my life was about to change.

I think I'm ready for it.

"Do you have the rings?" Trevor asked as he fastened his seatbelt.

"Yes, yours and mine both." I smiled a secret smile. "And you don't get to see yours until Saturday."

He reached for my hand. "That's fine with me, although it doesn't seem quite fair."

"What's not fair about it?" I squeezed his hand.

"Well, you got to see the wedding band that goes with your engagement ring."

I smiled in response. "Your mom said my gown arrived and is hanging in one of the closets. I have to admit, I was a little worried it wouldn't get there on time, but it did."

The plane started moving down the runway.

"I called the hotel we'll be staying in tomorrow night to make sure they didn't screw up our reservations or anything," he said. "By the way, my brother Chris will get us checked in and put our luggage in our room so we can bypass that when we get to the hotel."

"Okay. And then we fly home on Sunday." I sighed, ecstatic. "This is sure a quick trip."

He gazed into my eyes. "Yeah, but what a trip. We'll come home Mr. and Mrs. Trevor Caldwell."

"Mmmm. I like the sound of that." I leaned back in my seat, imagining how the next day would go.

Chapter Thirty-One

On my wedding day I woke before anyone else, took a long shower, went back into my room to finish getting dressed, then tiptoed into the room where Alyssa was staying.

"You're already dressed and everything," she said as she rubbed the sleep from her eyes. "You aren't excited by any chance?"

I laughed quietly. "Just a little. Now get up, sleepyhead. I want you to help me do my nails. Yours always look so good."

"Okay, okay. At least give me time to take a shower first."

I wandered into the kitchen and poured myself a glass of orange juice, and though I had no appetite, I forced myself to drink the juice. The sun was just starting to come up, and I could see it would be a beautiful, sunny day.

Only three hours until my wedding. I can't believe it.

I considered waking Trevor but decided to finish getting ready first. Normally I would have preferred that he not see me until the ceremony, but the wedding package we'd ordered included a limousine ride to the ceremony, so we'd be riding there together. Even so, I didn't want him to see the dress before the ceremony, so Alyssa and I had devised a way to cover the dress while we traveled.

Half an hour later, Alyssa joined me in my room. "Okay, where do you want to set up?" She held nail polish and other supplies in her hands.

I giggled. "I think in here will work."

She spread her things out on a table before closing the door. "Put your hand on this towel so we don't get anything on the Caldwell's table."

I did as instructed and watched my nails transform from plain to beautiful.

Alyssa admired her work, then looked at my face. "What about make-up? You don't usually wear much. Do you want me to get you all made up?"

"Sure, why not? It *is* my wedding day."

"Let me get my things. I'll be right back."

After she left, I admired my nails some more, and moments later she returned. She looked at me with raised eyebrows. "Your groom is awake."

My heart leapt.

My groom. My husband-to-be. I can hardly believe it.

I closed my eyes as Alyssa painted my face, and a short time later I looked in the hand mirror she held up. "Oooh! I love it. Thank you."

"Now we just need to do something about your hair," Alyssa said.

There was a knock at the door.

"Who is it?" I called out.

"It's me," Trevor said.

The sound of his voice brought a wide smile to my face.

"You can't come in," Alyssa shouted. "Lily's getting ready for her big day."

"Ahh. Come on," he said through the closed door.

"Nope. You're going to have to wait until it's time to go," Alyssa said.

"Okay, fine." We could hear Trevor walking away.

I smiled at my friend. "You sure are bossy."

Alyssa grinned. "Do you want your hair up or down?"

"Um, I guess up."

Alyssa fiddled with my long, dark hair. "How's this?"

I held the mirror up. "That looks good. And I think it will help the veil stay on."

"Great." Alyssa brushed my hair into a French twist, then clipped it into place. "Very sophisticated, I must say."

I stood and looked into a full-length mirror that had been placed in my room for the day. "Yes, I have to agree," I laughed. "Now what about you?"

"Don't worry about me. I'm not the star of this show, remember. I can get ready quickly."

I looked at the clock on my phone. "Oh my gosh. The limo will be here in thirty minutes!"

"Calm down. Don't get a case of nerves now."

Another knock came at the door."

"Yes?" Alyssa asked.

"It's Marcy," Trevor's mom said. "Is everything going all right?"

Alyssa opened the door. "Lily's pretty much ready."

"You look lovely, dear," Marcy said. "Is there anything I can do to help you?"

"No, but thank you. How's Trevor doing? Is he nervous?" I smiled at the thought.

"I think he's fine," she said. "But I wanted to see if you need any help getting your gown on."

"I think we can manage. But thank you."

"Okay then. I'll leave you girls alone."

Alyssa shut the door behind her. "She seems nice, Lily. Just like you said." Alyssa fussed with my hair, capturing stray pieces.

"She is. I'm really lucky." I watched in the mirror as Alyssa put the finishing touches on my hair. "Now remember, we need to put that cape over my gown so Trevor can't see my dress before the ceremony."

"Let me help you get the gown on and then I'll put on my dress." Alyssa said.

We struggled to get my gown over my head without mussing my hair or make-up. After several tries we succeeded. Next, Alyssa slipped the bridal veil onto my head and secured it in place.

"You look absolutely gorgeous," she said.

"Thank you. I'm so glad you could come. It wouldn't have been the same if Marcy were helping me."

Alyssa hugged me. "Okay. I'll get my dress on and then we'll throw on the cape."

Finally alone, I thought about Trevor and the life we were about to embark on together. I loved him and he loved me, and the future held endless possibilities.

Over the last week I'd made room in my closet for his things in preparation for him to move in when we got back to Reno.

It's going to be strange to not be by myself anymore. But I'm sure looking forward to it.

A short time later Alyssa was back. She helped me wrap the cape around my dress and secure it into place, and as soon as we were done, we went into the living room and found Trevor and his parents waiting. Trevor wore a tux with a blue bow tie and cummerbund, and as I looked at him, love for him overwhelmed me. He looked so handsome and the blue accented his eyes perfectly. And when he smiled at me, I could hardly believe my good fortune in marrying him.

"I like your cape," he said with a laugh.

At a loss for words, I smiled back.

"The limo's here," Trevor's dad said.

Trevor held out his arm for me and we led our group out to the limo. The driver held the door open and we all climbed in. It was a short drive to the lake where the ceremony and reception would be held, and once we arrived, we went straight to the ceremony area.

Trevor walked me to the rear where I would come out when it was my turn, then went to the front where he would wait for my arrival.

Alyssa smiled. "I think all of the guests are here. It should begin anytime."

She helped me remove the cape, then straightened my dress.

John Caldwell, who I'd asked to give me away, asked, "Are you ready?"

I nodded.

"You look beautiful, Lily," he said. "Trevor is lucky to have you."

I beamed at his words.

As the music started playing, I grabbed Alyssa's hand and held on tightly.

"It's okay. Be calm," she whispered. "I'll go in first with the best man. You just follow us."

I nodded wordlessly. I watched Alyssa and Scott, Trevor's brother and best man, as they began walking down the aisle. John stood next to me. A flower-covered arch stood at the front with the lake in the background. I glimpsed Trevor standing underneath the arch, his eyes searching for me. Heart pounding, I smiled, thrilled and nervous to be marrying the man I loved.

When Alyssa reached the front, I took John's arm and stepped onto the path. The music changed to the wedding march and everyone turned to look at me. The crowd stood as I appeared and all eyes shifted to me. I felt beautiful and loved.

When I reached Trevor's side, he had tears in his eyes. Touched by his show of emotion, tears filled my eyes. John took my hand and placed it in Trevor's, then sat beside Marcy on the front row.

I was afraid that if I made eye contact with Trevor I would break into tears, so I stared at the minister as he spoke. I hardly heard anything he said as the enormity of the ceremony pressed on my mind. Then I heard him ask me if I would take Trevor for my husband.

I turned toward Trevor and gazed into his eyes. "I will."

"Trevor Caldwell, will you take this woman, Lily, to be your wife?"

His hands held mine tightly. "I will."

As I watched his face my heart was so full I thought it might burst at any moment.

Then the minister asked for us to exchange the rings. Trevor turned to his best man, Scott, who reached into his pocket and handed Trevor my wedding band. Trevor lifted my left hand and slipped the wedding band on my finger, then looked deeply into my eyes.

To keep from weeping, I quickly turned toward Alyssa, who handed me Trevor's ring. I slid it onto Trevor's left ring finger.

"I now pronounce you husband and wife," the minister said. He looked at Trevor. "You may kiss your bride."

Trevor cradled my face in his hands and gently pressed his lips to mine. "I love you," he whispered as he pulled away.

I allowed the tears to fall as I clung to Trevor's hand.

The minister turned to the assembled group. "Allow me to present Mr. and Mrs. Trevor Caldwell."

Trevor and I glowed with happiness as we faced those who had come to share in our special day.

Trevor held out his arm. "Are you ready, Mrs. Caldwell?"

I giggled. "It's going to take a little while to get used to that."

We walked to the garden area and formed a reception line with the rest of the wedding party. I didn't know most of the people that came through the line, but felt their love as they shook my hand or gave me a quick hug.

Food was passed out butler-style and once we'd finished with the reception line, I tried to eat some of the food even though my appetite was still absent. Trevor had no difficulty eating, however. I walked around with Trevor to talk to the guests.

After a while Marcy announced, "I think it's time to cut the cake."

Trevor and I stood to the side of the wedding cake and smiled for the photographer before cutting a small slice, then carefully placed a piece of cake in each other's mouthes.

Finally it was time to leave, and I held tightly to Trevor's hand as we walked toward the limousine as the guests blew bubbles toward us. The driver opened the door and we climbed inside. A few minutes later we were on the road to the hotel Trevor had arranged for us to stay in.

"Can you believe we're married?" I asked, as we cuddled in the back of the limo.

He had a huge grin on his face. "No." He glanced at his wedding ring and held it up for me to see. "But I guess this proves it."

"Yes, I guess it does." My smile matched his.

When we stopped in front of the hotel, the limo driver helped us out, then we went into the lobby. This was our special day, the day I'd been anticipating for a long time. Trevor took my hand in his and led me onto the elevator. Once we were inside, he pressed the button for our floor.

We reached our room, and when he slid the electronic key into the slot, I heard the lock click free. Trevor pushed the door open and turned to me. "Come here, Mrs. Caldwell." He scooped me up effortlessly and carried me across the threshold, deposited me on the queen-sized bed, then hung the 'Do not disturb' sign on the door and locked the deadbolt.

Later that evening, when I finally had a chance to unpack my suitcase, I found an unopened bottle of vodka inside. I picked it up and held it out to Trevor. “Why is this in my suitcase?”

He smiled. “It was a gift from my parents.”

“Oh. But why is it in *my* suitcase?”

“I couldn’t fit it in mine.”

What a strange wedding gift. Even if they aren’t aware I don’t drink, I would have expected something more like champagne.

“Come back to bed, Lily,” Trevor said, patting the sheets next to him.

I moved in his direction, forgetting about the vodka.

Chapter Thirty-Two

Monday morning I awoke early to get ready for classes. I stared at Trevor, still asleep in our bed, stunned by how much more I loved him than even the previous week. Being joined as husband and wife was something special and I was grateful I'd insisted on waiting until marriage to become intimate.

"Trevor," I whispered, nudging him gently. "Trevor, wake up."

His left eye cracked open. "What time is it?"

"Eight thirty. Don't you have to get ready for school?"

"Not yet." He leaned up on one elbow. "Do you have to leave already? Come back to bed."

I smiled mischievously. "Now, now, Trevor. I have to get going."

He grinned. "Okay, but I don't know if I'll be here when you get back."

I gave him a quick kiss on the lips and dashed away as he lunged for me. "Bye, sweetie," I called over my shoulder as I headed out the door.

As I drove the short distance to school, I smiled, and when I was in class I found I had trouble paying attention as my mind was at home with Trevor. I wondered what time he would be done at school and hoped he would be home when I got back.

In my Humanities class I slid into the seat next to Justin.

"How was your weekend?" he asked, a smirk on his face. "I didn't really expect to see you here today, but I guess you're more dedicated to school than I would've been."

I smiled. "My weekend was fabulous, thank you very much."

"Everything went off without a hitch at your wedding then?"

"Yes, as a matter of fact it did. Thanks for asking." I smiled, pleased with the way Justin and I had become friends in the last few weeks. We always sat next to each other in class and I really enjoyed talking to him. He was such a sweet man—his girlfriend was lucky to have him.

That night as I chopped vegetables for dinner, I watched Trevor brown the meat.

He glanced at me. "Yes?"

"Yes, what?"

"You were staring at me," he said.

I smiled. "You caught me. It's still hard for me to believe you're my husband."

Trevor set the spoon on the counter, then drew me into his arms. "Believe it, Lily. I'm so glad you married me. I can't believe how lucky I am."

Warmth filled my heart. "I'm the lucky one." Then I burrowed against his chest. We stood that way until I noticed the meat sizzling. "Trevor, the meat."

"Oops!" he grabbed the spoon and quickly mixed the well-done beef with the uncooked meat.

I went back to chopping the vegetables. "By the way, do you have much homework tonight?"

"Not really."

"You're lucky. I have a ton." I set the knife down and took some carrots out of the refrigerator. "You never told me what classes you're taking this semester. Maybe I should make a note of which professors you have so I can have less homework," I said with a laugh as I began peeling the carrots.

Trevor abruptly turned off the heat under the pan he was stirring. "Lily, I need to tell you something."

I set the knife on the cutting board and turned toward him. "What's the matter?"

"You need to know that I'm not taking any classes this semester."

"What?" I was confused. "You mean you dropped your classes?"

"No, I mean I never registered this semester." He gazed into my eyes as he spoke.

The dazzling blue of his eyes distracted me and I had to look away. "Wait a minute," I said, then turned back to him. "What are you telling me? Are you just taking the semester off?"

He shook his head. "I'm dropping out."

My head jerked back. "Since when?"

His jaw clenched. "Since I decided to. What's the big deal?"

I folded my arms and walked to the couch before sitting down. Trevor followed me and stood on the opposite side of the coffee table. "The big deal is," I began, "you were supposed to finish school so you could get a good job to support our family."

"I'm making good money at Rob's place," he said. "And I was really starting to hate school."

"You might think you're making good money, but is it enough to support a family?"

I can't believe this. I thought we shared the same goals.

Clearly insulted, he said, "I do make good money, Lily." He straightened. "Besides, you've got some money saved up. We can always draw on that."

Is my inheritance going to be an issue?

"It's probably not as much as you think," I said. "Plus I've had to use a lot of it these past six months. I don't know how long it will hold out."

"How much did you inherit anyway?"

I hesitated, not sure if I wanted him to know.

But we're married now. Doesn't he have a right to know?

"The life insurance policy was for one hundred thousand dollars." I watched Trevor's face as he digested the information.

"Okay. And how much do you have left?"

"About eighty-five thousand."

His nostril flared. "You already spent fifteen thousand dollars? What have you been spending it on?"

"Excuse me! My father left it for me for my education." Hot tears pushed into my eyes. "Not to support my husband." Dinner forgotten, I fled the room and slammed and locked the bedroom door behind me.

Trevor was at the door seconds later, knocking. “I'm sorry, Lily. Let me come in so we can talk.”

Even though I knew he couldn't see me behind the closed door, I shook my head. “No,” I shouted. “I don't want to talk to you.” When Trevor started pounding on the door I sat up, blinking rapidly.

“I said to let me in!”

Confused by his behavior, I was unsure what to do, but certain of his love for me, I opened the door.

The veins on his neck stood out, and his face was flushed. Instinctively, I took a step back, but he grabbed my upper arms and squeezed.

“You're hurting me, Trevor,” I cried as the tears started anew, but he didn't seem to hear me.

“Don't you ever lock me out again!” His face was inches from mine, and spittle hit my skin. “Is that clear?”

“Yes,” I whispered. A moment later he let go of my arms and I gently rubbed where he’d squeezed.

Eventually he seemed to notice how upset I was, and tears sprang into his eyes. “Oh, Lily, I'm so sorry.” When he reached toward me, I didn't resist, afraid of his reaction. “Please forgive me,” he said. “I didn't mean to hurt you.” He lifted my sleeve and looked at the red marks where his fingers had been. An injured look came into his eyes. “Lily, my sweet Lily. Please, please, don't ever make me do that again.”

It was then that I knew I'd made a terrible mistake.

Chapter Thirty-Three

As I pulled my sweater over my head, I couldn't miss the bruises that had formed on my upper arms. I was grateful the weather was still cold—that way it wouldn't seem odd that I was wearing long-sleeved shirts all the time.

Trevor had been very solicitous and kind to me ever since the incident several days before, and the idea that I'd made a mistake in marrying him had faded. I knew he loved me as I loved him.

I'll just have to make sure I don't lock him out again. I mean, how would I have felt if he'd locked me out when I was trying to talk to him?

I brushed my hair before leaving the bathroom, and when I watched Trevor sleeping, my heart blossomed with love. He was my husband and I wouldn't give up on our marriage.

I know his heart. He's a good man. He's not perfect, but neither am I.

I tiptoed to his side and kissed him.

He stirred and opened his eyes. "Oh, Lily. Are you leaving already?"

"Yes. I have to get to class." I smiled down at him.

He gazed up at me, his blue eyes sleepy.

"What time do you have to be at work?" I asked.

Glancing at the bedside clock, he groaned. "In half an hour. I guess I'd better get up."

I bent toward him to give him another kiss, and when he dragged me down on top of him, I laughed. "Trevor, not now. I have to go."

"I'm sorry I couldn't be as dedicated to school as you are," he said as he gazed into my eyes.

Love filled my heart as I stared into his eyes. “That's okay. You have to do what makes you happy.”

He wrapped his arms around me, nuzzling my neck. “The planets must have been lined up just right when you came into my life. I love you so much.”

I pressed my lips against his. “I love you, too.” I smiled. “Do you remember the day we met?”

“You mean when you nearly knocked me over?” He laughed. “How could I forget? And you looked so lost that morning.”

“You showed me where to go.” My eyes brightened in remembrance. “I think I fell in love with you that very day.”

His eyebrows shot up. “Really? Even after I stood you up?”

“Yeah,” I paused. “Why did you do that, anyway?”

“I think Rob needed me to do something for him at the shop.”

“You stood me up for him?” I asked in mock outrage. “How dare you!”

“Ah, come on. I didn't even know you yet. I had obligations.”

“Yeah, sure,” I said with a smile, then pushed myself off of his chest. “I really do have to go now. I'll see you tonight?”

He smiled. “Yes, you certainly will.”

As I walked to class, I thought about Trevor and his decision to drop out of school. Obviously getting an education wasn't as important to him as it was to me. But it was important to me that he was happy, and if that meant working at Rob's shop, then that was all right with me.

“Marriage must agree with you,” Alyssa said as I sat across from her at lunch. “You look great.”

“Thanks.” I put a French fry in my mouth. “I'm so glad you were able to be there for our wedding. Did the Caldwell's take good care of you after I left?”

“Of course. They're very nice.”

"How are classes going?" I asked.

Alyssa picked up her fork. "Good. How about yours and Trevor's?"

I bit my lip. "Mine are fine. But Trevor . . ."

Her eyebrows drew together. "What about him?"

Frowning, I went on. "He's not taking any classes." I watched her face. "He dropped out of college."

Alyssa set her fork down. "When did this happen? Why didn't you tell me before?"

"I . . . I only found out myself the other day." I unconsciously rubbed the places on my arms where the bruises were.

"You mean he didn't tell you before the wedding?" She shook her head.

"Come on." I wanted to improve Alyssa's opinion of Trevor. "I'm okay with it. He's happy working at the auto body shop. I want him to be happy."

"But, Lily, don't you see? He should have talked it over with you first."

I had my own frustration with Trevor's decision and didn't want to hear my thoughts echoed in Alyssa's words. "He's my husband now and I don't feel comfortable with you saying those things about him."

She sighed. "Fine. I'll keep my thoughts to myself." She picked up her fork again and began eating her salad.

I watched my friend and felt bad for censoring her, but I wasn't up to hearing bad things about Trevor. I had my own conflicting feelings to deal with.

The apartment was empty when I got home, and I knew Trevor would be at work until late that afternoon.

At least he's bringing in a regular paycheck.

I booted up my computer, preparing to work on a programming assignment I'd been given, but decided to check my e-mail first as my professor had said he might be sending some information to the students.

I recognized my professor's e-mail address.

Yes, there it is.

There were a couple of other e-mail messages there as well—one was a mass mailing to all students, and the other email address was one I didn't recognize. I clicked on the unknown one first.

The moment I started reading it, I realized it was from the sender of the anonymous notes, e-mails and picture.

I'm sorry if I frightened you. That was my intent at first. I wanted to scare you away from Trevor Caldwell because he's not a nice man. You wouldn't listen. I heard you and Trevor are getting married. I hope it's not too late to call it off.

Adrenaline surged through my veins, and I took a deep breath to calm myself as I read the message again. It was unsigned and I had no idea who'd sent it. The incident that had occurred a few days earlier blazed into my head, but as I contemplated whether to reply to the message, Trevor's key turned in the lock.

Terrified he'd see the message, I exited the email program—but didn't delete the message.

"Hi, honey. I'm home," he said as he closed the door behind him.

I looked up, hoping my face looked normal. "Hi. How was work?"

He came over and kissed me fervently on the mouth. "Mmmm. It's much nicer being home with you."

I kissed him back, squeezing my eyes closed as I tried to push the message out of my mind.

"What's for dinner?" he asked, flopping on the couch. "I'm starved."

"I was going to make a casserole. Do you want to help me?"

Eyes closed, he rested his head against the cushions. "I'm too tired." He lifted his head and smiled. "Do you mind doing it by yourself? I just want to veg for a while."

"No problem, Trevor." As I went into the kitchen and began pulling out pots and pans, the message went through my mind, but I shook my head, angry with myself for believing some anonymous person about my husband.

He's not a bad person. Not perfect, maybe. But certainly not bad.

I opened the refrigerator and took out the ingredients I'd need.

I have to trust myself. I know him better than most anyone. I can't let some stranger play with my mind like that. He loves me and I love him, and one day I want to have children with him.

I smiled at the last thought.

Or at least practice a lot.

I could hear him grumbling in the other room. “What's wrong, honey?” I called out.

He came into the kitchen, the remote control in his hand. “We really need a new TV. The screen is so small on that one that I have to sit right in front of it to see anything at all. And half the time the sound doesn't work.” He set the remote on the counter as a smile slowly formed on his mouth. “What do you say? Should we splurge and get a decent one?”

I considered the idea. “Sure, why not? Our first big purchase together.”

He grabbed me around the waist and spun me around. “Great. Let's go tonight.”

Laughing, I shook my head. “I can't. I have a programming project due tomorrow and I'm still having a lot of problems with it. What about Saturday?”

Trevor set me back down. “I could go get one tonight.”

I turned on the oven and started grating the cheese. “Don't you want to go together?”

“Of course I do, but I don't want to wait two more days. It's not a big deal. I'll just go pick one up.” He leaned against the counter.

“How much money do you plan on spending?” I asked, setting the chicken on the cutting board and reaching for a knife.

“Only a few hundred dollars, I guess.”

I looked at him. “That's a lot of money, don't you think?”

“Not really. Besides, Rob gave me a bonus today. That should cover it.” Trevor took out two plates and set them on the table.

I began slicing the chicken and dropping it into a pot of water. “What was the bonus for?”

Trevor dug through the silverware drawer. “You know, working extra hours, that type of thing.”

“Oh.” I was surprised to hear that Rob was such a generous person.

"That was nice of him."

Trevor looked at me as he pulled glasses out of the cupboard. "That's why I like working there. Rob takes good care of his employees. That's worth something, you know."

"I had no idea, but I'm glad to hear it."

"How long until that casserole will be ready?" he asked as he placed the glasses on the table.

"I don't know. Forty-five minutes or so." I scrubbed the cutting board with hot soapy water before putting it back in the cupboard. "Why?"

He smiled mischievously. "I thought if there was time I could run over to the electronics store right now and get that TV."

"Trevor," I laughed. "You're just like a little kid. At least wait until we eat."

"Okay, okay," he laughed. "You win. But I'm going as soon as we're done eating."

True to his word, Trevor was out the door the minute we finished cleaning up. I immediately went to work on my programming project, and I was so immersed in it that I didn't realize how long Trevor had been gone until he walked through the door and I looked at the clock. "It's a good thing you didn't go while dinner was cooking," I said. "It's been two hours. You would've missed dinner."

He smiled happily. "Yeah, it took a little longer than I thought it would."

I watched his face. "Well? Where is it?"

He grinned. "You'll see it in a few minutes. It wouldn't fit in my car so I got them to deliver it."

"I'm impressed you got them to deliver it tonight."

"I told the salesman that I'd only buy it if they promised to deliver it tonight."

I laughed. "You drive a hard bargain." My eyes narrowed. "How much did you spend? I can't imagine they'd make such a bargain for a TV that costs only a couple hundred dollars."

Trevor seemed to avoid my eyes. "Just wait. You'll be able to see for yourself. I'm sure you'll approve."

The doorbell rang and Trevor dashed to open it. I couldn't see the men on the doorstep, but was quite astonished at the size of the box they carried in.

They were gone a short time later, and as I watched him excitedly open the box, I ground my teeth together. “We never agreed to you buying a big screen TV, Trevor.”

His obvious joy faded. “I don't have to ask your permission. It's my money. I worked very hard for it, too, I might add.”

Too tired to argue, I said, “Fine, whatever. I'm going to bed.” I shut down my computer and went to bed, falling asleep long before Trevor finally joined me.

Chapter Thirty-Four

All Saturday afternoon Trevor sat in front of his new television and watched sports. I had a lot of homework and also wanted to get the apartment cleaned, and as I scrubbed the toilet I heard him yelling at the announcer on the TV. Frustrated that he was just sitting around when I had a million things to do, I stewed, but didn't say anything.

I finished the bathroom and brought my laptop into the bedroom to get a head start on the next week's programming project, and while my computer booted up, I gathered the papers that explained the assignment and spread them out on the bed around me.

Knowing Trevor was occupied with the TV, I decided to open my student email account and reread the awful email I'd received.

I'm sorry if I frightened you. That was my intent at first. I wanted to scare you away from Trevor Caldwell because he's not a nice man. You wouldn't listen. I heard you and Trevor are getting married. I hope it's not too late to call it off.

With a glance toward the living room, I pressed the Reply button.

I don't know who you are or what your agenda is, but Trevor and I are already married. I love him with all my heart and I would appreciate it if you wouldn't contact me again.

I clicked Send and prayed that would be the end of it, and as I contemplated my new marriage, I thought about the fact that the first year could sometimes be difficult as the spouses got used to living together and got used to each other's habits.

We'll get through it. I know we will.

The thought cheered me immensely as I signed off my email

account and started on my assignment.

Over the next two weeks I kept busy with schoolwork, and as the first anniversary of my father's death approached, I was grateful for the distraction. I didn't know how I would react to that important date, and I considered just staying home in bed, but knew that would be a bad idea.

It would be better to keep busy and act as if things are all right.

I'd told Alyssa about the anniversary and she had agreed that it would be best if I went to classes, even if concentrating would be difficult.

On the morning of the anniversary of my father's death I woke early and couldn't fall back asleep. I snuggled up to Trevor and thought about how much my life had changed in the last year. I'd gone from being orphaned to being a happily married woman. It was amazing to me that my life could change so drastically in such a short period of time.

I lay in bed and stared at the ceiling until the sun came up and it was time to get ready for the day. As usual, Trevor was still asleep by the time I was ready to walk out the door, and when I woke him, I felt much sadder than I'd thought I would.

"Is it time to get up already?" he asked as he rolled onto his back.

On the verge of tears, I reconsidered whether I should go to school. What I really wanted was for Trevor to gather me in his arms and tell me everything would be all right. "It's seven-thirty, Trevor." I spoke softly and had to control my voice to keep it from shaking. "Don't you need to get ready for work?"

"Yeah, I do." He sat on the side of the bed and looked at me. "Is something wrong?"

I nodded, tears close to the surface.

"Well, what is it? I can't read your mind." He shook his head.

His reaction was not what I'd hoped for and the tears started leaking out. I was afraid to speak for fear my voice would crack.

"Lily, come on. You know how much I hate these guessing games." He stared at me. "Are you going to tell me what the problem is or not?"

"Don't you remember?" The notion that he'd forgotten a day that was so important to me was stunning.

He looked completely clueless. "I can't keep track of everything."

My sadness was being replaced by anger. "My dad . . . died . . . one year ago."

Remembrance dawned. "Oh, yeah. Now I remember you telling me." He reached toward me. "I'm sorry, Lily. I'm such an idiot. Please forgive me."

When he finally drew me into his arms and held me while I let the tears fall, relief that he cared swept over me.

"Are you sure you should go to school today?" he asked when my tears slowed.

I shrugged, then pulled back to look at him. "Can you stay with me today if I decide not to go?"

He grimaced. "Sorry, but I have to work."

"Can't you call in sick or something? Take a personal day?" I really didn't want to stay home by myself.

"I can't do that to Rob. He's counting on me to show up today. We have a lot to do."

"What about me? I'm your wife. Don't you know I'm counting on you, too?"

I can't believe he's putting Rob before me.

His arms went up in surrender. "Hey, don't put me in that kind of position, Lily. I have a responsibility to support this family and I can't just decide I don't want to go to work." His arms came down and he gave me a patronizing look. "As long as I'm the only one bringing in the money I have to take my commitment seriously."

Stung, I said, "What are you saying? That I'm a drain on your income?"

He rubbed my back. "No, not at all. You're doing what you should by getting your education. I'm just saying I don't have the luxury of taking a day off whenever I don't feel up to it."

"Don't feel up to it?" My anger was replaced by outrage. "Is that what you call it? My father *died* one year ago today! When's the last time you lost someone close to you?" Hot tears fell from my eyes. "How dare you imply that it's a luxury for me to grieve!"

Trevor shook his head as he stalked to the bathroom, and when I heard the shower turn on, I went into the kitchen and blew my nose and splashed cold water on my face before grabbing my backpack and heading out the door.

My body was tense as my heart raced.

He doesn't understand anything.

When I got to Humanities class my anger hadn't abated at all, and when I didn't see Justin, I sat in an empty chair and lay my head on my arms on the table. A moment later someone tapped my shoulder. I looked up, and when I saw Justin holding a bouquet of flowers in one hand and a box of chocolates in the other, my anger evaporated, replaced with delight.

"Good morning, Lily," he said as he set the items on the table in front of me. His face became serious. "How are you doing?"

Fresh tears filled my eyes. "How did you know?"

He smiled warmly. "Alyssa told me. I thought you might be feeling sad today so I took it upon myself to get you a pick-me-up. I'm sure your husband's already done this, but I figured more wouldn't hurt."

My throat thickened with tears at at the mention of Trevor. I was embarrassed to admit that not only hadn't he thought to do anything like this, he had completely forgotten about the significance of the date and then sent me off to school feeling even worse than when I'd woken up. "Thank you, Justin. This was very thoughtful of you. You have no idea how much it means to me."

He smiled, then sat beside me.

As I studied at home that afternoon I glanced at the flowers in the vase every time I felt tears threaten. Seeing them on the kitchen table made me feel much better. I'd met Alyssa for lunch and had again felt blessed to have such caring friends. I didn't have a lot of friends, but the ones I had meant everything to me.

When Trevor came home in the early evening, I was pleasantly surprised by what he held in his hands.

"These are for you, Lily. Kind of a peace offering, I guess." He held out a beautiful arrangement of flowers and a handful of balloons.

I was in a forgiving mood and took them from him with a smile. "Thank you. That's very sweet of you."

He took the arrangement out of my hands and set it on the coffee table before pulling me into his arms. "I'm sorry I blew it so badly this morning. Can you forgive me?"

I nodded against his shoulder. "Of course I do. You know I do."

Trevor lifted my chin and kissed me gently on the lips. "I'm taking you out to dinner tonight. Wherever you want to go. How does that sound?"

"That sounds wonderful." Beyond pleased that he'd come through after all, I beamed.

"Grab your sweater and let's get out of here."

It wasn't until we got back that Trevor noticed the flowers on the kitchen table. He walked over to them and fingered a petal, then gazed at me. "Where'd you get these?"

Wariness cascaded over me. "A friend gave them to me at school today."

He smiled tentatively. "What friend?"

As much as I wanted to lie, it made me feel uncomfortable to do so. Instead I tried to avoid a direct answer. "Just a friend. Are you ready to go to bed? I'm tired."

He stepped in front of me, all traces of his smile gone. "Who?"

I rubbed the place where the bruises had been. They were faded now, but the memory was still fresh.

"Were they from Alyssa?"

I didn't meet his eyes as I nodded.

Trevor lifted my chin to force our eyes to meet. "That was nice of her." He smiled but it didn't reach his eyes. "Let's go to bed."

I followed him into our bedroom.

Chapter Thirty-Five

As the weeks went by there were many ups and downs in our marriage, but there weren't any more incidents, as I liked to think of them. There had been arguments over silly things, like leaving all the lights on or making a mess in the kitchen and not cleaning up, but mostly just small bumps we needed to get past.

Overall things had been wonderful and I felt happy. I was grateful I hadn't received any more anonymous e-mail messages, and my classes were going okay, although my programming class was a struggle. I even began to question if I should go into the Information Systems field.

"At least my Humanities class is going well," I said to Alyssa as we ate lunch one afternoon.

"That's the one you have with Justin, isn't it?"

"Yes, why?" I set my soda on the table.

"Have you noticed anything different about him lately?"

I shook my head. He'd seemed okay to me. Of course, I'd been pretty wrapped up in my own world lately. "Have you?"

Alyssa sighed. "Yeah, I have. I think he and Pamela are having problems." She shook her head. "I don't know."

"You guys are good friends." I rested my arms on the table as I spoke. "Why don't you ask him?"

"That's the thing," she said. "I have asked but he says everything's fine."

I leaned back in my chair. "Then maybe it is. Have you ever considered that?"

Alyssa raised her eyebrows. “My philosophy is, you never really know what’s going on behind someone else’s closed doors.”

A sharp pang sliced through me at the truthfulness of her words—she had no idea what kinds of things had gone on in my home. It's true that things had been good lately, but I was learning that I couldn't predict what would set Trevor off, and sometimes I felt like I was walking on eggshells.

Alyssa stared at me intently. “I have something I need to tell you, Lily.”

“What?” An abrupt feeling of foreboding washed over me as I looked at her face.

“Do you promise you won't get too upset?”

“I . . . I guess. You're scaring me.”

Alyssa leaned forward and took a deep breath. “This has been bothering me for a while now. Ever since your wedding.”

Somehow I knew I wasn't going to like whatever she had to say. “Go on.”

“Okay. When I was at your reception I overheard Trevor’s mother talking. It seems she’s under the impression that you have a drinking problem.”

“What?!” This was nothing like what I'd expected. “I don't understand.”

“Apparently Trevor gave her the idea that you’re hiding a drinking problem.”

I was uncertain what to believe. “You must've misunderstood. That just doesn’t make any sense.” I shook my head and adjusted the napkin in my lap.

Alyssa frowned. “I wish I had, but I know what I heard. Marcy Caldwell clearly stated that she was concerned that your problem would get in the way of your being a good mother to her grandchildren.”

“Where exactly did you hear this and what exactly did she say?”

“It was during the reception. I was in the bathroom, in a stall, when I heard some women come in. I guess they didn’t realize I was in there and they started talking about you. One woman said that you were hiding your problem really well. And then another woman, who I thought sounded like Marcy, said she was surprised when Trevor told her you were struggling with a drinking problem. She said she'd been shocked when you'd stolen from their liquor cabinet, but when she'd asked Trevor about it, he'd paid her for the liquor and asked her not to say anything."

Stunned at what Alyssa was telling me, I stared at her. Desperate to find a reasonable explanation, I said "Maybe it wasn't Marcy. Maybe it was someone else and they were talking about someone else."

Alyssa shook her head. "That's what I thought too, at first. Then the first woman said, and I quote, 'Marcy, what about when she has children?' Then Marcy said, 'I don't know. I'm actually really worried about what kind of mother she would be to my grandchildren if she has a drinking problem.' Lily, I about died when I heard that. I know how you feel about drinking, you know, since your mom was killed by a drunk driver. I didn't know what to do. I'm so sorry."

My stomach churned. "But why would Trevor tell her that?" The feeling of betrayal was so strong I thought I might vomit.

"I don't know, Lily."

Then like a bolt of lightning, it hit me. "Oh my gosh. I think I know what happened. When Trevor and I were on our honeymoon there was a bottle of vodka in my suitcase. When I asked him where it came from he said it was a gift from his parents. He must have taken it, and when they found out, he must have blamed it on me." Dizzy at Trevor's treachery, all I could do was whisper, "Thank you for telling me."

Trevor's parents think I have a drinking problem. And that I stole *from them.*

Mortified, I stared at the tabletop.

Alyssa reached across the table and squeezed my arm. "I'm sorry. I should have told you sooner. I wanted to tell you before, but I just couldn't bring myself to do it."

I lifted my gaze, then shook my head. "No, it's not your fault. But I . . . I'm glad you're telling me now."

Drawing her hand back across the table, she asked, "What are you going to do?"

I smiled wanly. "What can I do?"

"You could talk to Trevor about it. He obviously was afraid to tell his parents the truth about his own mistakes, so he projected them onto you."

"Yeah, I guess he did." I gathered my things, my appetite gone. "I'd better get going. I have a lot of homework to do."

Alyssa nodded. "All right."

I slung my backpack over my shoulder and left.

Chapter Thirty-Six

Once home, I contemplated how I should handle the information Alyssa had given me.

Maybe I should just forget it. It's in the past. I know the truth and that's what's really important.

But my self-respect wouldn't let me get away with that.

I thought about John and Marcy Caldwell.

Even though they believed I had a drinking problem they showed me nothing but love and kindness. I am so lucky to have them as my in-laws. But they deserve to know the truth.

Somehow the idea of calling my in-laws sounded easier than talking to my husband.

I'll call the Caldwell's and then *talk to Trevor.*

The phone rang on the Caldwell's end, and when I heard Marcy's voice, I almost hung up without speaking, but I took a deep breath and pressed on. "Hi, Marcy. It's Lily."

"Oh, hello, dear. How are you?"

I'd spoken to my mother-in-law a few times since Trevor and I'd married, but this was the first time I'd initiated the call.

"Is everything all right?" she asked.

A fine bead of sweat broke out on my forehead as I gathered the courage to tell her the truth. "Actually, I believe there's been a misunderstanding about something and I felt the need to clear it up."

"Oh?"

My throat went dry and I had to swallow several times to moisten it. "Yes. It's about . . . uh." I didn't know how to go on.

"Yes, dear? About what?" Marcy's voice sounded concerned now.

"Well, about something Trevor told you about me."

"Oh." She sounded like she knew what was coming.

"It's not true!" I said, a pleading tone in my voice.

"I don't think I understand. Would you mind explaining it to me?"

I took a deep breath, then slowly released it. "Trevor told you I have a drinking problem and that I stole that vodka from you and it's just not true!"

There was a brief silence. "I thought that's what you were referring to and I understand that you're overcoming your problem, Lily. But it does no good to deny it. Admitting you have a problem is the first step toward healing."

She doesn't get it. I'm going to have to explain it more clearly.

Horrified at the realization, I said, "Marcy, I don't have a drinking problem now nor have I ever had one. I don't even drink. Do you understand what I'm saying to you?"

This time the silence was longer. "I'm not sure that I do."

I knew I would have to be very specific, and I dreaded it. "Trevor told you a lie about me, Marcy."

"But why? Why would he do such a thing?"

Closing my eyes, I went on. "Because *he* is the one who took the vodka. He was afraid to admit it to you, that's all." When Marcy continued to be silent, I went on in a rush. "I know he's trying to cut back on his drinking and he's doing really well."

Marcy's voice went cold. "I think that's just about enough, Lily. I won't listen to any more lies about my boy. I know my son and that just doesn't sound like him. Good-bye."

I held the phone in my hand, stunned by Marcy's inability to see the truth about her beloved youngest child. Gently setting the phone down, I realized that telling Marcy Caldwell about Trevor had been a grave mistake.

I glanced around the room—the room that had started off as such a sanctuary but was now becoming a frightening place for me to be. My gaze landed on the flowers that Justin had given me.

It's almost time to throw them out.

I pictured his friendly face.

I'll bet it would never occur to him to tell such a horrid lie about Pamela. He has too much integrity.

Heat rushed to my face.

What are you saying? What are you implying about your husband?

I mentally scolded myself for comparing Trevor to Justin

He is who he is and I know that my love can mold him into who he has the potential to be.

I tried to push from my mind all negative thoughts about my husband.

He loves me and I love him. He's a good person.

He's not a nice man. The message from the e-mail came to my mind unbidden.

Yes he is! He's just an imperfect man as I'm an imperfect woman. I know the first year of marriage is never easy—I've read it in magazines. But we'll get through it and then we'll be happier than we could ever have imagined.

When Trevor came home that night my stomach churned. I knew I needed to talk to him about what he'd told his parents, but I had no idea how he would react. Would he deny it? Would he be angry? My stomach roiled in anticipation of the conversation.

"I'm going to take a shower," he said as he headed toward the bathroom.

"Okay," I said softly.

Maybe I can put it off for a while.

The shower turned on and I relaxed. Then Trevor's phone rang. I rushed to read the Caller ID.

Marcy Caldwell.

I realized there would be no procrastinating talking to Trevor.

If I don't speak to him about it right away, his mother will. And there's no telling how her displeasure with me will impact Trevor.

I sat on the couch and twisted my hands in my lap as I waited for Trevor to emerge from our bedroom.

Chapter Thirty-Seven

"I thought I heard my phone," Trevor said as he came out of the bedroom, toweling his hair dry.

My fingers trembled slightly. "Yes, it was ringing."

"Oh." He stepped into the bedroom and tossed the towel onto the bed, then came back out, pulling a clean shirt over his head. He picked up his phone and looked at the screen. "It looks like it was my mom. I wonder what she wanted."

"I don't know," I lied.

He dropped his phone into his pocket and walked over to me, pulling me up to face him. "How was your day?"

I gazed into his blue eyes and felt his good mood.

Maybe I should tell him now.

I tilted my face up for a kiss and he pressed his lips to mine. "It was good. What about yours?"

"Great." He pulled me against him and held me tight. "Mmm. You smell so good. Much better than that shop."

I pulled back and laughed. "I should hope so."

Yes, this is the right time.

I held his hand as I moved to sit on the couch, and he followed my lead. "Trevor, I need to talk to you about something."

"What is it?" His blue eyes sparkled as he watched me.

I glanced at our intertwined hands then back to his face. "I found something out today that really upset me."

His eyebrows drew together and he watched me intently. "Yeah?"

My mouth had gone dry. "I found out that your parents think I have a drinking problem."

He slowly smiled. "Oh, is that all?"

I was confused. He didn't seem to understand the severity of the problem. "What do you mean, 'is that all'?"

He shook his head and stroked my back. "No, that's not what I meant. I thought it was something really serious is all."

Dumbfounded by his attitude, I said, "But this is serious. It's serious to me."

"Don't go all crazy on me, Lily," he said with a smile.

I took several deep breaths to calm myself. "How do you think your parents got this ridiculous idea?" Even though I knew he was the source of the information, I wanted to see if he would admit what he'd done.

He stood and began pacing in front of the coffee table. "I have no idea. How should I know?"

I closed my eyes in frustration. "Trevor, don't you think it's odd that the very thing that you've been struggling with has been placed upon me? I mean, I really don't think your parents would have come up with that all on their own."

He stopped his pacing and faced me. "What are you saying, Lily? Are you calling me a liar?"

His good humor seemed to be evaporating. "No. I would never call you that. I'm just wondering how your parents would get the idea that I drink. Especially when you know how strongly I feel about not drinking."

He shook his head. "I don't know, and quite frankly, I don't care."

I stared at my hands, my frustration mounting. Trevor came to my side a moment later.

"Don't you see?" he said, then his voice dropped. "It doesn't matter what lies other people believe. As long as we know the truth." He paused. "I know you're a good person and that's really all that matters."

I didn't look up, just listened in disbelief to his deluded view of the world. Finally I gazed at his face, and in a soft voice, I said, "But it matters to me. These are your parents, Trevor. I want them to like me. Why can't you tell them the truth?"

"Tell me this. If someone told you horrible things about me, would you believe them?"

The messages I'd received flooded my mind.

Do I believe them? Words from a complete stranger? No, of course not.

"No, Trevor, I wouldn't."

He smiled in triumph. "There, you see? It only matters what we think about each other. We know each other better than anyone else knows us."

I looked at him with pleading in my eyes. "Won't you please do me this one favor? Please tell your mother that I don't have a drinking problem. Will you promise me?"

He lifted my hand and kissed my palm. "Yes, m'lady. I promise."

I smiled in relief.

Trevor went into the bedroom and shut the door. I stared after him, worried about what he was going to tell Marcy. The fact that he wasn't going to have the conversation in front of me made me suspicious, so I tiptoed to the door and pressed my ear against it. He was speaking rather quietly and I could only hear snippets of conversation.

"No. . . fine. . . truth . . . yes. . . pretend . . . promise."

When it sounded like the discussion had ended, I hurried back to the couch and picked up a book, pretending to be immersed in it. I looked up when Trevor came out of the bedroom with a smile on his face.

"Well?" I asked.

He slipped his phone back in his pocket and walked toward me. "Well, what?"

I let out a sigh. "Well, what did they say?"

"Not much." He avoided my eyes as he walked around the coffee table to sit beside me. "Mom felt bad about the misunderstanding. She might be calling you later."

I briefly closed my eyes, relieved that things had been cleared up. "Thank you, Trevor. It really means a lot to me."

"Sure. Hey, what do you have planned for dinner?"

After the turmoil of the afternoon I hadn't even though about it. "I could cook up some pork chops that we have in the fridge. Does that sound okay?"

"Yeah, that works for me." He looked at me steadily. "After dinner Rob needs me to go back over to the shop for a while."

"What for?"

Trevor stood and walked to the TV, then picked up the remote. "He just has some work he needs me to do. I shouldn't be home too late."

I stared at my husband's back, disappointed he would have to leave for the evening. "All right. Do you want me to wait up?"

He spun around. "No, no. That's okay. I might be late."

I watched his face.

He walked over and smiled down at me. "I wouldn't want you to be too tired for your classes." He pulled me into a warm embrace, pressing his face into my hair. "I'm sorry, Lily. I'd much rather stay here with you."

"You would?" I asked, pulling back.

"Of course. I didn't marry you to take off all the time. I want to be with you whenever I can."

His words comforted me. "Me too, Trevor."

After he left for work, my cell phone rang. "Hello?"

"Hello, Lily. It's Marcy." Her voice was warm, although subdued.

I smiled. "I'm so glad you called."

"Yes, well, I felt I should. Trevor explained things to me and I just . . . uh . . . I want to apologize."

Pleased that Marcy was making the gesture, warmth toward her rushed through me. "That's all right. It was just a misunderstanding. No harm done."

Marcy hesitated. "Yes, that's what Trevor said. Anyway, let's just pretend it never happened."

Though curious to know exactly what Trevor had said, I was too shy to come right out and ask. "That's fine with me, Marcy."

"Well, have a nice evening, dear."

I hung up the phone feeling much better about things.

Trevor cleared things up with his mother and she called to apologize. Yes, I feel much better now.

Chapter Thirty-Eight

"Can I borrow your notes?" Justin asked me as we waited for class to begin. "The professor moved on before I was able to get it all down."

I laughed. "I know what you mean. Good thing I write fast." I pulled out my notes from the previous class and handed them to him.

"I'll get these back to you before the test."

At home that afternoon I was working on a new programming project when there was a knock at the door. It was Justin. He held the borrowed notes. "I'm getting these back to you before the test, just like I promised."

I took the notes and thanked him. "Do you know Java by any chance?" I knew he would be graduating with a degree in computer science.

"I sure do. Why? Do you need some help?"

"Yes. This program is due in a couple of days and I just can't get it to work." I opened the door wider for him to enter.

He stepped inside and followed me to the desk where my laptop was set up. "Let me see the assignment."

I handed him the paper that told what the program was required to do.

He looked at it before sitting in front of my computer and looking over my work, then he glanced up at me and pointed to the screen. "You need to move this line down here, and then put this one inside the loop."

I nodded, beginning to see what I'd done wrong. "Thank you, Justin. I've been staring at that screen for so long that I couldn't see what I was doing wrong."

Justin glanced at his watch. "I'd better get going. I have a study group in a few minutes." He stood and walked to the door. "Thanks again for the notes."

I smiled. "Anytime. And thank you so much for your help." I shut the door behind him and immediately went back to my program. I made the changes Justin had suggested and ran the program. It worked perfectly.

Trevor came home later that afternoon, and after greeting me, headed straight to the shower. I finished up some assignments, then went into our bedroom to wait for him to emerge from the bathroom.

"How's school going?" he asked, his freshly washed hair sticking up in places.

I laughed. "I think you missed a spot." I reached up and smoothed his hair into place.

Trevor grabbed my hand, a grin on his face, and held me close. "Do you have any plans tonight?"

"No," I said, returning his smile.

"Neither do I," he said, his voice husky, then his lips met mine. We kissed deeply for several moments before he pushed me onto the bed and began unbuttoning my blouse.

My cell phone rang, breaking the mood. "I'll get it," he said, then he grabbed my phone off the bedside table before I could respond. "Hello?" Frowning intensely, he held the phone out to me. "It's for you, Lily."

Surprised by Trevor's disapproving look, I took the phone from his hand. "Hello?"

"Hi," the voice announced cheerfully. "It's Justin."

"Hi, Justin." I felt extremely uncomfortable having my husband watch me, and when I glanced at the expression on his face, it had turned from disapproval to open fury. My heart pounded, and trying to keep my voice steady, I said, "What can I do for you?"

"I was just wondering if you got your program to work. I didn't have time to stay and make sure my suggestions were correct." His voice sounded friendly and natural, a sharp contrast to how I was feeling.

"Yes, it worked perfectly. Thanks again for your help." I was terrified to look at Trevor's face. "I've got to go now, but thanks for calling."

"Okay. I'll see you in class."

I hung up, my face flushed as I turned toward my husband.

His jaw clenched and unclenched. "Why is Justin Radford calling you, Lily?"

I knew the best course of action would be to tell the truth, but as little of it as possible. "He . . . he . . . uh . . . helped me with one of my programs today. I was having trouble getting it to work and he told me what I'd done wrong. It works fine now," I finished weakly.

"Well, gee, I'm so glad he could help out my *wife*." His lips had pulled away from his bared teeth.

Angry at his unreasonable response, yet terrified, I tried to put a positive spin on it. "Think of it this way, Trevor. Since I finished my program I have more time to spend with you." I tried to laugh. "I mean, it could've taken me hours to figure out what I'd done wrong."

He seemed slightly mollified, but then his eyebrows drew together. "I thought you weren't going to spend time in the computer lab. You said you were only going to work on your programs on your own computer."

Trapped by a circumstance that was not of my doing, I scrambled for an explanation.

If I admit I was working on my computer he'll know Justin has been in our home.

My mouth went dry as I tried to form the lie I knew I had to tell. I tried to maintain eye contact as I spoke, knowing that would help convince him that I was being honest. "You're right, Trevor," I started.

His fury was instant. "What?!"

"Wait, wait," I quickly went on, my heart racing and my arms waving in self-defense. "Let me finish."

He stared at me, his blue eyes like ice.

"I *was* planning on only working on my computer, but I was having so much trouble that I decided to take it to the lab and see if one of the lab assistants could help me out."

The ice in his eyes melted a little. "So now Justin works in the lab?"

"Not exactly." I wiped my sweaty palms on my jeans. "He just happened to be in there when I went in. All the lab assistants were busy so I asked him to help me." I smiled tentatively.

Please believe me, please believe me.

He smiled and reached for my hands and I placed them within his larger ones, hopeful he was okay with my story. His smile vanished. "I seem to recall telling you to stay away from him." His grip tightened and my hands began to ache.

"You're hurting me, Trevor." I tried to pull my hands out of his stronger ones. "Please let go." Tears of pain filled my eyes and streamed down my cheeks. "Please, Trevor," I whispered.

He let go abruptly and my hands fell to my lap. I massaged them, trying to relieve the pain. He lifted my chin with one finger, making me look into his eyes. "Do I make myself clear?"

I nodded.

There was no way I would tell him that Justin and I had a class together.

Chapter Thirty-Nine

When I woke the next morning my hands were still sore. I gently massaged them before slinging my backpack over my shoulder and leaving for school.

On the drive over I thought about Trevor's anger over Justin.

Why did he react that way? Does he think I would be unfaithful with Justin? If he does, then he doesn't know me at all. Justin's a good friend, that's all.

Though I knew the truth about my feelings, I wasn't sure if Trevor would believe it.

Maybe he lacks confidence. Maybe if I could somehow give him more attention he would be sure of my love for him and only him.

Regardless, I knew it was imperative to convey to Justin the importance of never calling or stopping by again. *Ever*. I had class with him that morning. I would tell him then.

As I entered the classroom I saw Justin and slid into the seat beside him, then I spoke in a near whisper. "I need to talk to you, Justin."

"What's wrong, Lily?" He looked at my face closely.

"Nothing's wrong," I said, then I cleared my throat, uncomfortable with the message I needed to deliver. "I . . . uh . . . please don't call me again." I looked at him with pleading eyes, praying he would understand the importance of my message and not question it.

"Why not?"

"Please, don't ask. Just don't call again." At the hurt in his eyes, I inwardly winced.

"I suppose you don't want me stopping by either."

I smiled in relief at his statement. "Yes. Especially don't come over."

"Boy, Lily, you really know how to make a guy feel wanted." He shoved his books into his backpack. "I thought we were becoming friends. I guess I assumed too much."

Though I'd hoped he wouldn't be offended by my request, I wasn't about to explain that my husband, the man I'd chosen over him, was the cause of the appeal. I was too ashamed at the way Trevor had reacted the previous evening.

It's my own fault. I never should have allowed Justin to come in when Trevor wasn't there. It just wasn't right.

Justin stood and tossed the backpack over his shoulder, then moved to a seat in the back of the room. I glanced at the few other students who were there and saw them watching Justin and me with questioning looks on their faces. I ignored them and tried to swallow over the lump that had formed in my throat.

It's for the best. It's not right for me to become friends with another man now that I'm married.

"Did you see Justin today?" Trevor asked that evening.

I shook my head, trying to avoid his eyes.

"That's my girl." He drew me into his arms and held me tight, then he nuzzled my neck before looking in my eyes. "Try to understand, Lily."

I watched him, listening.

"I just love you so much. I can't stand the thought of you spending even one minute with another man." He laughed, but it didn't sound natural. "Even thinking about it makes me crazy. Can you understand that?"

I tried to put myself in Trevor's shoes—I wanted desperately to understand him and the way he reacted to things. I pictured him with Amanda from our Sociology class and felt a flash of jealousy so strong that I had to briefly close my eyes. I nodded. "Yes, Trevor. I think so."

"Good." He pulled me back against him.

The next morning I was surprised to see that Trevor was already up and dressed as I was just waking up.

"Good morning, sleepyhead," he said as he leaned over me.

I smiled up at him. "Why are you up so early today?"

He gazed down at me, his blue eyes sparkling. "Rob needs me to come in early today."

"Oh." I tossed the covers off and sat on the side of the bed.

Half an hour later, while I was eating a breakfast of toast and orange juice, Trevor kissed me good-bye and walked out the door.

As I left the class I had with Justin, I glanced to the left and did a double-take as I saw the back of a student who looked suspiciously like Trevor. I almost called out, but then wondered if he'd been spying on me. Panic washed over me as I realized he would have seen that I had a class with Justin. But partial relief followed when I visualized the distance between where Justin had been sitting and where I'd sat.

Surely Trevor will know it's not my fault that Justin's in my class.

When I walked into the apartment after my classes had finished, I was exhausted. I'd had two mid-terms that day and was planning on taking a nap to rejuvenate before Trevor got home. I assumed he would be home early since he'd gone in earlier than normal, although I wondered how much time he'd taken to spy on me, if indeed that had been him I'd seen.

By four o'clock I'd finished my nap but Trevor still hadn't gotten home.

He sure is putting in a long day.

The thought made me feel guilty that I was just waking up from a long nap.

My phone rang a short time later.

"What's going on with you and Justin?" Alyssa asked without preamble.

"It's nice to hear from you, too," I said, a frown on my face.

"I'm sorry. I didn't mean to be so abrupt, but I saw Justin today and he is really down in the dumps."

My eyebrows furrowed. "Why would that have anything to do with me? I'm not the one dating him. Maybe you should be talking to Pamela." Irritated that Alyssa was blaming me for Justin's demeanor, I frowned.

Alyssa sighed. "He said you basically blew him off the other day. He said you made it clear you didn't want to have anything to do with him."

Oh, boy. How am I going to explain this to Alyssa without telling her about Trevor's jealous reaction? Maybe I should just tell her the truth.

That thought was immediately squelched when I thought about how much Alyssa already didn't like Trevor. I didn't want to give her any more reasons to dislike him. "I didn't mean to blow him off. That wasn't my intention."

"Intention or not, that's how he feels. He said you told him not to contact you in any way. What's up with that, Lily? Does Trevor have anything to do with this?"

Though I hadn't liked Trevor's reaction, after imagining how he'd felt, I'd decided I didn't want to feel that way. "No, he doesn't. It was my decision." And that was true. It had been my decision to tell Justin not to contact me anymore.

"Well, okay. I guess it's certainly your prerogative. I just hope Justin gets over it. He seemed pretty devastated."

I squeezed my eyes closed, guilt crashing over me in waves. I hated the idea that something I'd done had caused another person pain. Opening my eyes, I glanced around the room I shared with Trevor.

I have to keep him *forefront in my mind.* He's *the one whose feelings I need to place first.*

"Look, Alyssa, I'd better go. I just wasted half the afternoon napping and now I need to get some homework done."

"All right. I'll talk to you later."

I hung up the phone, forcing all thoughts of Justin Radford out of my mind.

Later that evening I looked up from the textbook I was reading as Trevor walked in the front door. I marked my place and set the book on the coffee table, then I stretched my arms over my head and smiled at Trevor as he came over and planted a kiss on my lips.

"You must be tired, Trevor. Sit on the floor and I'll massage your shoulders."

He did as I asked and moaned with pleasure. "That feels so good."

I moved my hands over his shoulders and back, squeezing and rubbing the spots I thought might be sore. "How's that?"

He smiled over his shoulder. "It feels great."

"Do you want to go out to eat tonight?" I wasn't in the mood to do any cooking and hoped Trevor would say yes.

"I would, but I'm only here for a quick bite to eat, then I need to get back to the shop."

My hands stopped moving. "What? You've been there all day. I think you deserve some time home with me."

He twisted around to face me. "I know. But Rob's really getting behind."

"Why doesn't he hire some more people then? It's not fair that you have to do all the work."

Trevor got up from the floor to sit beside me on the couch. "It's not that often he needs me to come in at night. Besides, he pays me very well for my time." Trevor smiled. "Doesn't that make it worth it?"

I tried not to frown. "I'd rather have you home."

Trevor sighed. "I don't want to listen to your whining, Lily. I'm working my tail off and you don't seem to appreciate that."

Hurt by his words, I stared at him.

He stood and walked toward the door. "I'll just grab something on my way back there. Don't wait up."

The moment the front door slammed shut, tears filled my eyes. Though I knew it wasn't my fault he was mad, I still felt terrible that he'd left when he was angry with me.

I'll give him some time to cool down and then I'll stop by the shop with a treat for him.

Chapter Forty

I drove away from the donut shop and headed toward *Rob's Auto Body*.

Trevor loves these donuts. I hope he'll be pleased by my surprise visit.

The moment I pulled up in front of the shop I knew something wasn't right—the place was dark and seemed to be deserted, and I couldn't see Trevor's car anywhere. Gathering my courage, I climbed out of my Honda and walked toward the door of the darkened shop. I tugged on the door, but it was locked. Peering through the glass, I tried to see if there was any movement at all.

As I stood at the door I thought I heard a sound coming from somewhere behind me. Heart pounding, I raced back to my car, got inside, and locked the doors. It was creepy there in the dark.

Where's Trevor? Could he be home already?

I called his cell phone, but it went to voice mail. I hung up and drove home, hopeful I would find him there, but as I parked at the curb in front of our apartment it was obvious that Trevor wasn't back yet. His car was nowhere to be seen.

I grabbed the box of donuts and went into the apartment, then set the box on the kitchen counter. Concerned about Trevor's whereabouts, I sat on the couch to wait for him to return.

Could he be out drinking?

The thought made me even more worried. I lay on the couch, determined to know the moment he got home.

Forty-five minutes later I heard a key in the lock. I flew to the door and pulled it open. Trevor stood there, looking like he always did when he got home from work. I was confused. If he'd been working all this time, why had the shop looked so empty?

"What are you doing up, Lily?" He smiled, obviously pleased to find his wife greeting him at the door.

I flung myself into his arms, thrilled to see him home safe, and in a good mood as well. "I've been so worried, Trevor."

"Why? I told you I was going to work." He closed the front door behind him, then wrapped his arms around me.

I let go of him. "I wanted to surprise you so I bought some donuts and brought them to Rob's shop." I motioned toward the kitchen where the donuts sat on the counter.

Trevor walked into the kitchen and opened the box, then stared at the donuts for a moment before lifting one out and taking a large bite. Keeping his back to me, he said, "You must've come by right when I'd left to pick up a part." He turned toward me, a smile on his face. "But thanks for thinking of me."

With a tentative smile, I said, "When you left you were upset with me. I felt bad and I wanted to cheer you up."

Trevor wiped his fingers on a napkin, then walked over to me. "That was very thoughtful of you." He kissed me and stroked my face. "I'm going to take a quick shower, then I think I'll be ready to hit the sack."

I smiled again, glad I'd thought to get the donuts for him. "Okay. I'm ready, too."

On Saturday I spent the morning finishing up assignments, and when I was done I asked Trevor, who was watching TV, if he would help me clean the house. Pleased that he agreed, we spent the next hour making the place spotless. Trevor had just finished dusting, and I was bent over the bed tucking in some fresh sheets, when I felt something hit my bottom.

Startled, I turned around to see Trevor grinning at me, a dust rag in his hand. He flicked it at me again and I grabbed it and pulled, drawing Trevor closer to me. He wrapped the dust rag around my waist and hauled me against him, then pressed his lips to mine. His kissing became more passionate and he pulled me onto the bed.

Two hours later I woke up from an afternoon nap and went into the living room to find Trevor gone. There was a note on the kitchen table.

Had to go into work. Be back later. Love, Trevor

Disappointed that we wouldn't be able to spend the afternoon together, I sat at my desk, but I'd already finished all my homework and didn't really have anything else I needed to do. Trevor hadn't given any indication of when he would be back. I felt lonely and discouraged.

Maybe a visit with Alyssa would make me feel better. I'll just drop by, and if she's not home I'll just drive around a bit. I don't care. I just need to get out of the house for a while.

I freshened up before leaving a note for Trevor telling him I went to Alyssa's, then I headed out the door.

As I climbed out of my car and began walking toward Alyssa's apartment, I hoped she would be home. I really didn't want to drive around by myself. What I wanted was to visit with a friend.

When I knocked on the apartment door I thought I heard noises coming from inside and hoped that meant Alyssa was home. The door swung open and I smiled at Alyssa.

"Lily! What are you doing here? Is everything okay?" She stepped back to let me enter.

"Yes, everything's fine. I just thought it would be nice to come over for a visit." I saw several people in the living room. "Is this a bad time?"

Alyssa laughed. "No, not at all. We're just all hanging out. You're welcome to join us."

I smiled. "Okay." She and I sat on empty chairs.

"Where's Trevor this afternoon?"

"He had to work. That's why I decided to come over. It was too quiet at our place."

Alyssa nodded. "Well, you're welcome to come over anytime. You know that, don't you?"

"Thank you. That means a lot to me."

Someone in the group took out a game and we all began playing. A short time later the doorbell rang. I looked up as someone went to answer it, thinking it might be Trevor coming to find me.

Justin stood on the landing. "Am I too late for all the fun?" he asked.

Oh no. What should I do? What would Trevor do if he showed up and saw me here with Justin?

I was sitting on the floor and knew Justin hadn't seen me yet, and I hoped it would stay that way.

A moment later he stood in front of me. "Hey, Lily."

I looked up. "Oh, hi, Justin. I didn't see you come in."

"What are you doing here?" he asked, his voice friendly as he sat beside me.

I tried to smile, but my heart pounded as terror ripped through me that Trevor would show up at any moment. "I, uh, came to see Alyssa. I hadn't realized there would be a party going on."

"Naw. Not a party. Sometimes we like to get together on Saturday and just hang out."

That's when I remembered that it was at the dance that I'd first met Justin. He'd been with this same group of people. *I* was the intruder here, not him.

He leaned towards me and spoke softly. "Can I talk to you, Lily?"

I pictured what this scene would look like to Trevor if he were to appear right now, and I knew he would be absolutely furious.

The doorbell rang. I jumped, frightened beyond all measure, but frozen to the spot. Justin put his hand on my arm. "Are you okay?"

I ignored him, my gaze riveted to the front door. Someone reached toward the doorknob and pulled the door open, and I held my breath, terrified it would be Trevor.

"Hey, Cathy. Come on in," the person who had answered the door said to the blond woman standing on the landing.

My breath came out in a rush. "I've gotta go, Justin." I stood abruptly.

He jumped up to stand beside me. "I really need to talk to you."

I shook my head from side to side. “I can't. Tell Alyssa good-bye for me.” I dashed out the door before Justin had a chance to respond. Once I was several yards from Alyssa's apartment, I stopped to catch my breath, then stood there until my heart rate had returned to normal.

I walked toward my car and as I turned a corner I ran right into someone. “Trevor!” I said, stunned to see him there at just that moment.

If I hadn't left when I did . . .

I didn’t want to complete the thought.

Trevor smiled broadly. “Hi, honey. I just got your note and thought I'd come by and tell you I'm back.”

I forced a smile to my lips and took Trevor’s hand. “You could've called.”

“I thought it would be nice to say hi to Alyssa.” He turned me back toward Alyssa's apartment. “I came all this way, I might as well finish the trip.”

Panic gripped my mind.

He can’t know Justin is at Alyssa’s apartment.

Thinking quickly, I said, “She’s not feeling very well. That's why I was leaving. I don't think she’s up to having company just now.”

Trevor stopped walking. “Are you sure? It would only take a minute to say hello.”

I tried to steer him in the opposite direction. “Really. I think she might be coming down with the flu. You don't want to take a chance catching that, do you?”

“No, you're right. That would be bad.”

We walked to the parking lot together, and Trevor opened my door for me before going to his car.

My hand shook as I tried to put my key in the ignition, and my stomach churned so violently I thought I might vomit.

I drove home slowly, trying to collect myself before facing Trevor again.

Chapter Forty-One

Once home, I went straight into the kitchen to distract myself with the work of preparing our dinner. Trevor took a shower then came into the kitchen.

"Did you get the things done you needed to?" I asked, feeling calmer.

Trevor pulled out a chair and sat facing me. "Pretty much. But you know how it is—there's always more coming in."

I smiled. "It sounds like Rob's shop gets a lot of business. That's good, I suppose."

"Yeah, it is. He always has plenty to keep me busy, that's for sure." We were silent for a moment, then he asked, "Is Justin Radford in any of your classes?"

My hand froze over the bowl and my heart pounded as I used all of my self-control not to whip my head in Trevor's direction. Instead I turned toward him slowly, trying to act casual. "Yes, as a matter of fact he is. In my Humanities class."

So that was Trevor I saw.

Trevor's jaw clenched then relaxed.

"Why do you ask?" Then I wondered if he knew Justin had been at Alyssa's apartment.

What if he saw Justin coming in and then just pretended to show up later?

The thought left me breathless with fear.

"I was just wondering," he said. "But I'm wondering why you never told me." He stared at me, his eyes cold.

I set the spoon down and walked over to him, remembering my thought that I needed to make it clear that it was *him* I loved. I knelt in front of him and held his hands, then gazed up at him. His eyes seemed to warm. "What does it matter, Trevor? *You* are the man I love. *You* are my husband. Please don't ever forget that. I've never given you a reason to think I don't love you, have I?"

His face softened and he pulled me onto his lap. "You're right. I'm sorry." He nuzzled my neck. "I get so jealous sometimes. I hate feeling that way."

I cradled his face and gazed into his eyes. "I love you, Trevor. I want to be with you forever."

He groaned as he pulled me close, and we stayed that way for several minutes. Finally I pulled back. "I need to finish making dinner, okay?"

He smiled as I stood and walked into the kitchen, and I watched him go into the living room and turn on the TV. Pleased with the way our conversation had gone, I hoped his fears were beginning to be put to rest. I knew I had no interest in Justin. Trevor just needed to be convinced.

The next morning I arrived to class before Justin, and when he finally came in he ignored me and sat in the back of the room where he'd gone each class period since I'd asked him not to call or come over.

Though I felt bad at the hurt I'd seemed to have caused him, I didn't know what else I could do. I had to put my marriage and Trevor's feelings before Justin's.

I thought about being at Alyssa's apartment when Justin had asked to speak to me. I assumed it was about me asking him not to contact me and I didn't want to discuss it with him. There was no way I would explain to him the reason for my request. I didn't feel right in sharing Trevor's feelings with Justin—that was a private matter between Trevor and me.

Justin will just have to take my word for it that it's best for us to not have any contact.

Once class was over I gathered my books and glanced at the back of the room, but Justin wasn't there. After threading my arms through the straps of my backpack, I walked toward the door in the back of the room, then stepped out into the hall and turned right.

"Lily?"

I turned around to find Justin waiting for me. Dread washed over me as I knew I would have to talk to him. "Hi, Justin." I put a friendly smile on my face. "How are you?"

"Good. Which I would've told you Saturday if you'd given me a chance."

Terrified someone had overheard Justin's comment, I looked around, my gaze darting in all directions.

"What's wrong?"

"Nothing," I said. "I just need to get to my next class."

"Look, I don't know what's going on with you, but you don't seem like yourself." He waited for me to respond.

I tried to smile. "I don't know what you're talking about. I'm still my same old self."

Justin shook his head. "Fine. I'll see you around." He turned and stalked off in the opposite direction.

I watched him go, feeling terrible for the way I was treating him, but I didn't know what else to do.

After my last class I went out to the parking lot and climbed into my car. Worn out after my confrontation with Justin, and then having to take a major test, I was ready to go home. I put the key in the ignition and turned. Nothing happened. I tried again, but still it wouldn't work. I called Trevor to see if he could help me, but he said he couldn't get away from work just then. Sighing heavily, I grabbed my backpack, locked the door, then slammed it shut. It was going to take at least twenty minutes for me to walk home, but I didn't have any other choice.

As I walked along the sidewalk, a car pulled up beside me.

"Need a ride?" a male voice called out.

I recognized Justin's voice right away. I turned toward his car, which had pulled over next to me, and smiled. "Thanks, but I'm fine."

"Are you sure? You've got a little ways to go yet."

I glanced up at the sky. "It's a beautiful day, but thanks anyway."

"Suit yourself," he called out his window, then he stepped on the gas and sped away.

I watched him go, irritated at Trevor that I didn't feel comfortable accepting a ride from a friend. It was a beautiful day, but my backpack was heavy and the sun was beating down on my head. I would have much preferred the ride.

Twenty minutes later I unlocked the door to my apartment, then dropped my backpack on the floor and flopped onto the couch, too tired to do any homework. I turned on the television and flipped through the channels.

Nothing but garbage on.

A moment later I turned it off.

My phone rang a short time later. It was Trevor.

"I just wanted to make sure you got home okay," he said.

Pleased that he'd taken the time to check on me, I smiled. "Yes. It was a long walk, but I'm home."

"When I get home from work you can show me where your car is parked and I'll see what I can do."

"Thank you, sweetheart." I hung up the phone, grateful to have a husband who could take care of the car problems. I hoped he could just take it to work and fix it there.

Maybe it won't even cost us anything besides the cost of any parts we might need.

Trevor came home a short time later and the two of us drove to the school parking lot.

"There it is," I said.

Trevor pulled up behind my car and we got out. He tried to start the car but it still wouldn't start. He lifted the hood and looked inside, made a few adjustments, but when he tried to start the car again, it didn't respond.

"It looks like I'll need to take it to the shop." He shut the hood and locked the car before opening the passenger door on his car for me. "I'll take you home then come back with a tow truck to tow it to the shop."

I squeezed his arm. “I'm so glad you can take care of this for me. Thank you, honey.”

He smiled half-heartedly. “At least I'm good for something.”

I leaned over and gave him a kiss. “You’re good for lots of things and I love you.”

He kissed me. “I love you too.”

Chapter Forty-Two

"I'll bring your car home tonight," Trevor said the next morning as he sat at the kitchen table eating a bowl of cereal.

"Are you sure? I could have Alyssa drop me by to get it." I stood poised in the kitchen doorway, my ever present backpack over one shoulder.

Trevor smiled in my direction. "Don't worry about it. I don't want you to have to make a special trip."

I smiled in return, then walked over and kissed him.

"Are you sure you don't want me to drop you off at school before I go to work?" he asked.

"That's okay. It's nice out this morning and I could use some exercise."

Trevor pushed his chair back and gathered me into his arms. "From where I stand you don't look like you need any exercise." He nuzzled my neck, working his way up to my mouth.

I laughed as his unshaven whiskers tickled my neck. "Stop, Trevor. You're going to make me late."

He let me go and I went out the front door, a joyful smile on my face. Things between the two of us had been good lately—it almost seemed too good to be true.

I shook my head, annoyed at myself for doubting our relationship.

It is possible to have a good marriage. A few incidents of anger aren't a cause for ending anything.

Then I began to argue with myself.

Don't you think it was a little more than anger?

It's not his fault. If I hadn't upset him, he never would have done those things.

Don't kid yourself, Lily. It wasn't your fault.

I tried to ignore the voice in my mind, not wanting to believe that anything was so far out of my control.

About half a mile from the school a car pulled up beside me.

"Do you need a lift?" Justin asked, a smile on his face.

My back was starting to ache from carrying my backpack and I longed to accept the ride. Half-expecting Trevor to be watching me, I glanced over my shoulder before approaching the passenger window of Justin's car.

Annoyance briefly flickered inside me when I thought about how such a simple and innocent decision like accepting a ride from a friend could be affected by my husband's disapproval. I reached for the door handle, trying to slow my racing heart, and pulled. The door swung open and Justin smiled.

"Thanks, Justin. I appreciate it." I slid into the seat and dropped my backpack onto the floor. "So much better," I said, resting my head against the headrest.

Justin pressed the gas and glanced in my direction. "Where's your car?"

I sat up straighter. "It's in the shop. I should get it back tonight." I rubbed my aching shoulders.

"Why didn't your husband give you a ride?"

I heard the irritation in his voice and was touched by his concern. "He offered but I decided I'd rather walk." I laughed. "It seemed like a good idea at the time." I smiled in Justin's direction, trying to show that all was well in my marriage.

"Oh," he said. "Okay then."

He pulled into a parking space and turned off the engine, then he turned toward me, a questioning expression on his face. "Since we have a minute, I was hoping you'd explain to me what's going on with you."

I felt trapped. There were no excuses for me to rush off, but I didn't feel comfortable talking to Justin about anything personal. Trying my best to look bewildered, I asked, "What are you talking about?"

Justin sighed. “You know exactly what I'm talking about. I thought we were becoming friends and then suddenly you say you don't want me to contact you at all.” He peered at me closely. “Does this have anything to do with your husband?”

A lump formed in my throat as Justin voiced the correct answer, yet I couldn't admit that Trevor was so tyrannical that he would keep me from choosing my friends. I searched for a suitable answer, but nothing came to mind. “Please, Justin. Don't do this.” Tears threatened as I reached for the door handle.

“Lily,” Justin said in a gentle voice. He reached out and touched my arm. “I don't understand what's happening with you.”

I decided to be as honest as I could without saying anything that would hurt Trevor. “Justin, it’s just that now that I’m married, things are different.”

He stared at me, apparently waiting for me to explain.

“I just think it would be better if we didn’t associate outside of class,” I said. “Okay?”

“Fine. Whatever.”

We got out of the car, and as we began walking toward campus, I had to force myself not to look around in a panic to make sure Trevor wasn’t lurking behind the parked cars, spying on me again.

Once we reached the building, I thanked Justin for the ride, then went into the ladies room and closed myself into an empty stall. He’d been accurate when he’d asked if Trevor was the reason behind our friendship coming to an abrupt end. Trevor had physically hurt me when Justin had called me on the phone. His reaction had terrified me.

And it wasn't the first time he hurt me.

I nodded, admitting to myself for the first time that Trevor’s reaction had been unreasonable.

But what about me? Don't I have some responsibility in this as well?

I closed my eyes, confused about what to believe. Could I have done something different to prevent Trevor’s outbursts? I mentally catalogued the incidents that had occurred. If I hadn't locked him out of our bedroom he wouldn't have gotten so angry. And I shouldn't have let

Justin come into our home when Trevor wasn't there.

What about the lie Trevor told his parents about you?

I wasn't sure how to respond to that one just yet, but I believed I had some responsibility in Trevor's actions.

I unlocked the door, left the stall, then went to the sink and splashed cool water on my face. After patting my skin dry, I checked the time and gasped. I hated to be late for anything, but really hated to be late for class.

Hurrying out of the bathroom, I rushed to class, hoping I hadn't missed too much.

When I reached the classroom for my Humanities class, the only seat left was in the back—next to Justin. Trying to act natural, I slid into the seat, unzipped my backpack, and pulled out my notebook and pen. The professor was lecturing and I tried to concentrate on what he was saying.

I sensed Justin watching me but forced myself not to turn in his direction. It was pure torture sitting there with Justin beside me, knowing he was wondering what was wrong with me. Even so, I managed to partially concentrate on the lecture, and when it seemed the professor was wrapping things up, I put my books away—I wanted to be able to leave quickly once class finished.

"Don't forget there will be a quiz next time," the professor announced. "Have a good day."

At the professor's words, I stood quickly, then left the room without speaking to Justin.

By the time my last class was over, I was dreading the walk home. My backpack was full and it didn't take long for the weight of it to feel oppressive.

Too bad Alyssa's in class right now, or I'd ask her for a ride.

I sighed.

I can hardly wait to get my car back. It had better be ready tonight like Trevor promised.

Resigned to the long walk, I bought a soda from the cafeteria and began the walk home. Once home, I dropped my backpack on the floor and sat on the couch. My gaze drifted to a photo from my wedding day and I thought about my life since I'd met Trevor, wondering if it really had become more difficult since marrying him or if it was just my imagination.

I thought back over the last couple of months, remembering the times Trevor had gotten angry with me and physically hurt me. I thought about the fact that one of my very few friendships had to abruptly end because of Trevor's insecurity. I considered the feeling that I was always walking on eggshells around Trevor because of his unpredictability. I thought about the fact that not only was Trevor working long hours, but that something seemed just a bit off about his employment.

Yes, things have definitely gotten more challenging in my life since I married Trevor. Was it a mistake?

I tried to be honest with myself.

Did I think about marrying him hard enough to know if it was the right thing to do? Or did I just want to be with him so badly that I didn't want to know whether he was a good match for me?

I didn't know the answer to that question. All I knew was that I'd made a commitment to Trevor to be his wife and that I would do everything in my power to fulfill that promise.

But where do you draw the line? At what point do you walk away?

I shook my head, too confused to consider that right now. I couldn't even contemplate such a drastic step.

We've only been married two months. How can I even consider ending it? It would break Trevor's heart. I don't know if I could do that to him.

What about your heart?

Squeezing my eyes closed and pushing that thought aside, I tried to think of other things before I drifted to sleep and had a dream.

Cars surrounded me. I called Trevor's name but there was no reply. My head twisted left and right, searching in the fog for my husband. He was nowhere to be seen. Only cars, endless rows of cannibalized cars, their parts strewn about the ground.

Despair began to overcome me as my chin fell to my chest. A hand clamped on my shoulder and a faceless voice whispered in my ear,

"You don't want to be here."

My head whipped up and swung to the side to see who was speaking to me. No one was there—only a whisper of a breeze coming from the large doorway behind me.

A shiver of fear raced up my spine, and just as I turned to escape the creepy place, Trevor appeared.

At first he didn't notice me and I smiled to see him approach, but my joy was squelched when his eyes met mine and his face became a mask of rage.

"What are you doing here?" he demanded.

I began to tremble as a strong sense of foreboding engulfed me and my mind screamed a warning.

Get out now! Get out!

I woke in a cold sweat, a vague feeling of warning washing over me. Bits and pieces of the dream floated into my mind but I had trouble grasping them and putting them together to form a coherent whole.

Not liking the feeling of confusion that hovered over me, I pushed myself to a sitting position, then made my way to the bathroom where I splashed cold water onto my face. I patted my face dry then flopped onto my bed and called Alyssa.

"What's up?" she asked.

I fingered the comforter as I spoke. "I just want to get out of the house for a while."

"Sure. Let's go out and do something."

I swung my legs over the side of the bed. "That sounds great. But you'll have to drive. My car's in the shop."

"Yeah, that's what Justin said."

Reminded of the episode with Justin, I squeezed my eyes closed again. I didn't like to think of Justin—it only made me feel bad. I opened my eyes and glanced at the clock. "When do you want to go? I don't know when Trevor's getting home so I'm ready to go whenever."

"You don't think he'll mind coming home to an empty house?" Alyssa voice was tinged with sarcasm.

"Actually, he might. But it'll do him good. Make him appreciate me more." I hoped that was true.

Or he might be furious and wonder where I am. I'll just leave him a note.

"Okay. I'll be there in a few minutes. We can go get some dinner and do some shopping."

After I hung up, I went to the desk and penned a note to Trevor telling him I'd gone out with Alyssa and didn't know when I'd be back.

Chapter Forty-Three

As we pulled out of the mall parking lot, I turned toward Alyssa. “Thanks for driving.”

“Anytime. I know it's hard to be without a car once you get used to having one.” She glanced at me. “When’s yours going to be back?”

“Hopefully tonight. Trevor was supposed to bring it home with him after work.” I stared out my window at the darkness before turning to Alyssa. “I have an idea. Let's stop by Rob's shop and see if the car's ready.” I glanced at the time on my phone as Alyssa turned at a stop light. “It's nearly six-thirty. It should be ready by now.”

When we pulled into the parking lot I didn't see my car anywhere.

“It looks like they're closed,” Alyssa said as we parked near the front door.

“Yeah, it does.” I got out of the car and tried the door, but it was locked. I peered through the glass but wasn't able to see anything, so I climbed back into Alyssa's car and snapped my seatbelt on. “Hopefully that means Trevor already brought it home.”

“I don't see Trevor’s car either,” Alyssa said.

“That's strange.” I twisted in my seat but couldn't see Trevor’s blue Camaro anywhere. “I guess I'll just go on home then.”

Alyssa put the car in gear and headed toward my apartment. A few minutes later we parked behind my Honda, although I didn’t see Trevor’s car.

I smiled in relief. “I guess Trevor got it done on time.”

“Great,” she said. “Thanks for going shopping with me.”

I opened my door and stepped out before leaning down to speak through the open door. "It was fun. And Alyssa?"

"Yeah?"

"Thanks for being my friend." I was so grateful to have her in my life. I didn't know what I would do without her.

She smiled back. "You keep life interesting. I'm glad we're friends too."

I shut the door and waved as she drove off, then went inside where I found a note from Trevor.

Lily, Rob took me back to the shop. I'll see you later tonight. Love, Trevor.

I frowned.

That's strange. If he's at the shop, why wasn't his car there when Alyssa and I stopped by?

Deciding to check out his story for myself, I grabbed a warm jacket and headed out to my car. The engine started up right away and I smiled as I thought about Trevor and his ability to repair my car.

Maybe I should leave well-enough alone.

Guilt swept over me for not believing Trevor, but something just didn't seem right. I turned on my headlights and pulled away from the curb.

A short time later I found myself in the parking lot of *Rob's Auto Body*. I turned off the engine and walked toward the front of the shop, which still looked deserted. Feeling a little spooked by the dark and silent night, I looked around, trying to see if Trevor had parked somewhere out of sight.

Not seeing his car anywhere, I decided to wait a while.

Maybe they went to get a bite to eat.

I turned up the heat against the cold night air, but half an hour later I decided I was wasting too much gas running the engine and just waiting. I decided to head home.

Half expecting to see Trevor's blue Camaro parked at the curb in front of our house, I was half-disappointed and half-relieved that he wasn't there—half-relieved because I didn't think he would be happy to know I'd been staking out his workplace.

After waiting up a while longer, I finally went to bed, tossing and turning for an hour before falling asleep.

When I woke the next morning I was relieved to find Trevor sleeping on his side of the bed. I got ready for school, then sat on the bed next to him and lightly kissed his cheek.

His eyes cracked open and he smiled, then he reached up and pulled my face down to his. “Hey, beautiful.”

I smiled at him and tried to push away my feelings of concern. “Thank you for taking care of my car.”

He propped himself up on one elbow. “I'd do anything for you.”

“I missed you last night. Will you be home tonight?”

“I hope so, but no promises.”

I took a deep breath. “What time did you get home last night? I waited up quite a while.”

He looked away. “I don't know. I didn't really pay attention.” He gazed at me with his piercing blue eyes. “I'll try to be home tonight. I promise.”

Feeling unsatisfied with his answer, but knowing I wasn’t going to get a better answer, I stood. “Okay. I'll see you later then.” I gave him a quick kiss before grabbing my backpack and heading out to my car.

Chapter Forty-Four

Later that afternoon, after a grueling day of tests, I arrived home and had a quick snack before starting on another programming assignment. I knew it could be hours before I got it to work, so I settled in for the duration. Now that the semester was more than halfway over the assignments were getting harder.

I wish I could ask Justin for help, but that's one argument I don't want to start. With Trevor or Justin.

Instead I worked on my assignment for three hours before quitting for the day. I shut down my laptop, went to the couch and picked up my eReader, then started reading the novel I'd been trying to get through.

Immersed in the story, I was startled to hear a key turning in the front door. I smiled as Trevor entered, but my happiness quickly died at the scowl on his face. "Hi, honey," I said as I stood and walked toward him. "How was your day?"

"Busy. I didn't even have time to eat lunch." He tossed his coat on the couch and walked into the kitchen. "What's for dinner?"

Annoyed that he was ignoring me, I said, "I'm kind of tired myself. I don't really feel like making dinner. Why don't we go out?"

He turned to me, his nostrils flaring. "Go out? That costs money. Don't be so stinkin' lazy. Why can't you fix us something to eat?"

"Why can't you?" I nearly shouted, hurt by his name-calling.

He gripped my wrists, twisting them. "Don't talk to me like that. You need to learn to show me some respect."

"Trevor! You're hurting me! Let go!" Tears filled my eyes.

He dropped my wrists as quickly as he'd grabbed them. "Maybe if you actually had to work you'd understand what being tired is."

Fearful of angering him, I stayed silent. Not wanting him to see the distress he'd caused, I tried to blink away the wetness in my eyes.

"Well?" he asked.

"Well, what?" I nearly whispered.

"When are you going to start pulling your weight around here? You know, get a job?"

Baffled by his sudden desire for me to go to work, I said, "You know how important it is to me that I do well in my classes. If I got a job I wouldn't be able to spend as much time studying."

"Lots of people work while they go to school and do just fine. I don't see what makes you so special."

My chin trembled, but I tried to control my voice. "The money my father left me covers my schooling, and—" I hesitated. "And it covered my living expenses pretty well before you came along." My heart pounded as I waited for his reaction.

His lips flattened. "How long do you think you could've lived like this without getting a job?" His head tilted. "And that's another thing. Why do you keep that money in a separate account? Don't you trust me?"

In truth, I *didn't* trust him with my inheritance. "It's not that. It's just that it's earmarked for my schooling. I need to keep it separate so it doesn't get spent on anything else."

"Don't you think I should at least have my name on the account too? I am your husband, after all."

I wanted to smooth over this argument and steer him away from the topic of my savings. I stepped toward him and rubbed his arm. "Yes, you are my husband and I love you. Can't we stop fighting?"

His expression softened slightly. "I guess so."

"I'll make us some dinner," I said as I walked toward the kitchen.

He followed me and leaned against the counter. "It really would be nice if you could make dinner more often."

I set some vegetables on the cutting board and pulled out a knife.

"You've been home for hours," he said. "How could you be tired?"

I stared at him. "Excuse me?"

"You heard me."

Frustrated at the undeserved criticism, my voice rose in volume. "I may have 'been home for hours', but I've been doing homework. You remember what that is, don't you?"

He straightened and stared at me with narrowed eyes. "What's that supposed to mean?"

"You know exactly what I mean. You should be in school too, working toward something better."

Trevor's jaw clenched, and as he gazed at me, his expression hardened. "One of us needs to earn a living, and since you obviously have no intention of doing that, it looks like it's up to me."

I flinched, hurt by his charges. "Are you saying I'm holding you back?"

"No. But it would be nice if you could earn some money too."

Fixing my gaze on the vegetables, I picked up the knife and began slicing the carrots, then softly said, "Maybe I am holding you back. Maybe this marriage was a mistake."

"What did you say?" His voice had gone cold.

I lifted my eyes to meet his, and forced my voice to remain steady. "I said maybe we shouldn't have gotten married."

His hand shot out and grabbed my arm, the one holding the knife. He forced the blade to point in my direction, and when he spoke, his voice was unnaturally quiet and calm. "I don't ever want to hear you say that again. Do I make myself clear?"

Nausea rose in my throat. "Yes, Trevor," I whispered.

"Good." He let go of my wrist. "I'm going to watch TV. Let me know when dinner's ready."

Though my appetite had vanished, I managed to finish making dinner, and at the dinner table I picked at my food while Trevor ate two helpings.

When he reached for my arm and gently stroked it, I tried to keep from flinching.

"I'm sorry about earlier, Lily. It's just that the thought of you leaving me makes me crazy. I love you so much. I can't live without you." He gazed at me. "Can't you understand?"

Swallowing my revulsion, I nodded.

He didn't seem to notice my hesitation. “Do you remember when you moved here and you didn't tell me where you'd gone?” He stopped stroking my arm and just rested his hand there.

“Yes,” I said, beginning to wish I’d broken up with him then.

“You should have seen me.” He laughed. “I think I scared my roommate. I was freaking out when I couldn't find you. I was so relieved when you called me.”

His grip on my arm subtly tightened. “At first I thought you'd run off with someone else. Maybe Justin Radford. But then I realized you really didn't have anywhere to go, what with your family gone and everything.”

Glancing at his hand on my arm, I tried to keep my expression neutral.

Is this the same man I fell in love with?

I remembered comments Alyssa had made, about not knowing him very long or very well, and realized it was true. I didn't know him at all.

He let go of my arm and sat back in his chair. “I don't know what I was so worried about. I mean, here you are, married to me. You're not going anywhere.”

That was the moment I started planning my escape.

Chapter Forty-Five

The next day after my last class finished I filled up my gas tank and went for a long drive. I needed time to think. Conflicted about whether to leave Trevor or give him one more chance, I wanted to stay long enough to finish the semester. There were only a few weeks until finals and I was determined to complete my classes. However, I did allow myself to think about where I would go if I decided to leave.

That evening I made a nice dinner for Trevor and put a candle on the table to set a softer mood—before I'd left for school that morning he'd promised he'd be home by six o'clock. I was pleased when he actually arrived home on time.

"Mmmm. It smells good in here." He wrapped his arms around me and kissed my neck.

It felt good to be in his arms and I hoped the previous evening had just been a mistake, that it wouldn't happen again.

"The table looks great too." He pulled out his chair and sat. "What's the occasion?"

"No occasion. I just wanted to make dinner nice for you." I set the casserole dish on the table and poured water from a pitcher into both of our glasses.

"Thank you, honey."

As we chatted and ate, I began to relax and enjoy Trevor's company.

"Where did you go today?" he asked, a pleasant smile on his face.

My stomach tightened. "What do you mean?"

"Well, I was getting something out of your car and I noticed you'd put about two hundred miles on it since yesterday."

My mouth fell open. "You were checking my miles?"

"You didn't answer my question," he said, still smiling.

"I just went on a drive. Nowhere special." I sipped my water, nervous now that he was keeping tabs on my whereabouts.

"Do you do that very often?" His smile had faded.

"No. This was the first time, as a matter of fact." I hesitated. "Is there something wrong with taking a drive?"

"That depends. Were you by yourself?"

"Of course. Who would I be with?"

"I don't know. You tell me." The earlier warmth had left his eyes.

"I wouldn't be with anyone." I wasn't sure what else to tell him—I didn't want him to suspect my possible plans.

"So what made you decide to take a drive today?"

"I guess I've just been stressed about my classes and I needed to go somewhere and not think about school for a while."

Nodding, he said, "Okay. I guess that makes sense." He paused. "I expect you'll take the cost of the gas out of your little school account and not out of our regular budget then."

"Of course, Trevor."

He smiled again as he picked up his fork and continued eating. "I've enjoyed eating dinner with you, Lily. We should do this more often." He wiped his mouth with his napkin. "I'll make a deal with you. If you have dinner ready at six o'clock every night, I'll make sure I'm home to eat with you." He gazed at me. "How does that sound?"

After what had happened tonight and the night before, I was beginning to think I preferred eating dinner alone.

But if he's willing to make an effort, I should too.

"Okay." I forced a smile on my face.

I went to bed early, leaving Trevor in front of the television. I hadn't felt well at dinner and hoped I wasn't coming down with the flu.

Over the next week Trevor was home by the promised time every night and I began enjoying our meals and actually looked forward to him coming home each night. However, by the end of the second week, Trevor's old habit of coming home whenever he felt like it, which was usually late, returned, and I stopped making an effort at dinner. I figured he wouldn't notice since he was never there.

Then one evening he came home early and in a bad mood. He slammed the front door, tossed his keys on the counter, and flopped onto the couch before picking up the remote and flipping through the channels.

I'd been napping in the bedroom and was startled by the sound of the front door slamming. Groggy, I rubbed my eyes and pushed myself into a sitting position, then glanced at the clock and saw it was six-thirty. Slightly panicked, I tried to force myself to wake completely.

"Lily!"

"I'm right here," I said, walking into the front room.

"Where's dinner? I'm starved."

It's nice to see you too.

"In case you haven't noticed," I said, "you haven't held up your part of the deal."

"So?" He looked at the TV as he continued channel surfing.

"So I've stopped having dinner ready for you."

He set the remote down and stared at me. "You must be fixing something to eat. You're getting fat."

I blanched. I knew I hadn't gained any weight. If anything, I'd lost a few pounds. "You might want to take a look in the mirror when you're saying that."

Trevor sat up straighter, glanced at his stomach, and said with sarcasm, "I don't think so, sweetie."

"I've already eaten. You can fix yourself something to eat." I turned and walked back to the bedroom, closing the door behind me, careful to leave it unlocked.

A moment later Trevor stood in the doorway. "What were you doing in here when I got home? Sleeping?"

Sitting on the bed, I glanced at the blankets, noting the evidence of recent use.

"See what I mean?" Trevor said, a mean look on his face. "You're getting fat and lazy."

Hurt by his words, I turned my back and gazed toward the night stand at a picture of the two of us on our wedding day.

A few minutes later the front door closed. I ran to look out the front window and saw Trevor driving away. Despair overwhelmed me and I sunk onto the couch cushions.

I don't think he even loves me.

Self-pity blossomed inside me.

How did this happen? Was I so lonely that I fell for the first man to cross my path?

I thought back to the first day of school only seven months before when I'd literally bumped into Trevor and fallen for him right then.

A short while later, exhausted, I went to bed, no closer to a decision then when the day had begun.

Chapter Forty-Six

All the next day at school I felt sick. Unsure if it was from stress or if it could be something more, I decided to buy a pregnancy test. When I got home from the store I was glad Trevor wasn't home.

Carefully following the instructions, I stared at the stick, waiting for the results to appear, and uncertain what I wanted those results to be.

We'd been using birth control, but I knew no birth control method was one hundred percent effective.

A pregnancy would certainly complicate things. But a baby! Someone to love and hold who would love me back.

My thoughts drifted to the mother I barely remembered, and sadness washed over me. Trying to push the feeling away, my gaze shifted to the pregnancy test. The result was in, and I blinked, trying to clear my vision and verify what I thought I saw. Picking up the stick, I stared at the plus sign.

I'm pregnant.

I gently stroked my abdomen.

There's a baby inside me.

Warmth cascaded over me as I pictured the child Trevor and I had created.

Trevor. How will he react? Is this a sign? Telling me to try to make it work?

As I thought about the best way to break the news to Trevor I tried to imagine his reaction and had no idea how he would feel. When we'd discussed having children before we'd gotten married, he'd been vague about his interest. I'd taken it to mean children would be okay with him—although this was a little sooner than I'd planned.

I'll make a special dinner for him. It's two o'clock now, so that gives me four hours to create a gourmet meal.

Knowing there was a possibility that Trevor wouldn't be home at the right time, I decided to call him and let him know I had something special planned. I called his cell phone and was pleased when he answered right away.

“Hi. It's Lily.” I hesitated, wondering how he would react to me calling him—he’d told me once not to call while he was at work.

“Is something wrong? Why are you calling me?” Irritation was clear in his voice.

“I just wanted to let you know I have a special dinner planned. Do you think you can be here by six?”

He paused. “Yeah, I guess so.”

“Okay. I'll see you then.”

Trying not to let his gruff response spoil my happiness, I took out my one recipe book and pored over the recipes, searching for the perfect choice. After I found one I thought Trevor would like, and that I could make successfully, I wrote down the ingredients and went to the store.

Humming as I prepared the meal, I only felt nauseated enough to run to the bathroom once. I set the table with my mother's china, then stepped back and surveyed my work. Pleased with the result, I placed a pair of candles on the table and went into the kitchen to check on dinner.

The clock said I had only fifteen minutes until Trevor would be home. Excited at the news I was going to share with him, I could hardly keep the smile from my face as I changed into an outfit I knew Trevor liked.

At exactly six o'clock I set all the food on the table and went to the window, watching for Trevor’s arrival. As the minutes ticked by, I worried my fancy meal would get cold before he got home. At six-thirty I began pacing, wondering if he’d forgotten. At seven I sat at the table and ate a few bites before running to the bathroom and throwing it all up.

Furious at Trevor for having skipped this important night, I didn't even bother to clean up and left the food on the table. I considered trying to get in touch with him but decided if I wasn't important enough for him to remember on his own, I wasn't going to be a nag and remind him to come home.

By ten o'clock my anger had built to the point that I wanted to confront him about his thoughtlessness. Though exhausted, I stayed on the couch, forcing myself to stay awake for his return. I turned on the news to keep myself occupied, then turned up the volume as the news anchor started speaking.

"Tonight's top story is the recent rash of car thefts here in Reno. We first reported several months ago that the rate of car thefts had increased dramatically and then seemed to drop off. However, the problem has started to grow once again."

I began falling asleep as the news anchor droned on. Curled up on the couch, I drifted in and out of sleep as I listened for Trevor's key in the lock. When I finally heard it, I jerked awake and looked at the clock on my cell phone. It was nearly one o'clock in the morning.

Quickly turning off the TV, I sat up on the couch and tried to collect my thoughts as I watched Trevor step into the room. He didn't notice me as he closed the front door, and I watched him as he stepped toward the table, which was still covered with the food I'd prepared that evening. He picked up a serving spoon and scooped up some of the entrée. Taking a small bite, he quickly pulled the spoon away and muttered, "Cold."

"It was hot at six o'clock," I said as I stood next to the couch.

Trevor spun around, dropping the spoon. "What are you doing up?"

"Waiting for you. Did you forget about the special meal I'd planned?"

He blinked quickly. "What are you talking about?"

"Did you or did you not tell me you would be home at six tonight?"

"When did I supposedly tell you that?"

Exasperated, I shook my head. “When I spoke to you at two o'clock. I said I was making a special meal and you agreed you'd be home by six. Does that ring any bells?”

A light came on in his eyes. “Oh yeah. I guess I got busy and forgot.” He walked toward me. “What was so special about this meal?”

As he came close to me, the odor of alcohol emanated from him. I recoiled. “Have you been drinking?”

He wiped his hand across his mouth as if he could wipe away the smell, but he didn't answer me.

“I asked you a question,” I said, my happiness at my pregnancy forgotten.

“You're not my mother,” he spat in my direction. “I don't have to answer to you.”

Disappointment that he obviously had no intention of cutting back on his drinking stabbed at my heart, and my hope that we could make this marriage work diminished.

But what about the baby? Doesn't our baby deserve a mother and a father?

Conflicted, I tried to reason with him. “No, you don't have to answer to me, but do you really want to live your life this way?”

“What 'way'? I like my life just fine. It's only you that makes things difficult. You're always nagging me.”

“Maybe if you acted like an adult I wouldn't have to nag you.”

He stepped right in front of me and glowered at me. “I think you'd better watch what you say, Lily, before you say something you regret.”

Fear rolled up my spine, but I didn't let it stop me from speaking. I later wondered if it had been some kind of test to see how far Trevor would go. “Maybe I should call your parents and break the news to them that their golden boy is tarnished.”

He shoved me so hard that I fell backward over the coffee table and twisted my back as I landed against the side of the couch.

“You're useless,” he snarled as he left me lying on the ground and went into the bedroom, closing the door behind him.

My first thought was for my baby. I pressed my hand against my flat stomach as a fierce protectiveness replaced the fear I’d felt before.

I absolutely will not raise my child around that man.

I dragged my aching body onto the couch, then dropped my face into my hands and forced the tears to stay away. A moment later I gingerly stood and reached for the pair of shoes I'd left near the side of the couch. Slipping them on, I glanced toward the desk and was grateful to see my purse there.

I looked through it to make sure my wallet, keys, and cell phone were there, then I unplugged my laptop and put it in its carrying bag. I grabbed my coat from the hall closet, snaked my arms through the sleeves, then put the computer bag and purse over my shoulder, and walked out the front door.

It was one thirty in the morning and I didn't know where I should go. I considered going to Alyssa's house but didn't want to wake her. Instead I drove to a hotel far from my house and checked in, then lay awake most of the night, wondering what I should do next.

Chapter Forty-Seven

I rubbed my neck as I finished nibbling on some crackers—my body was still sore from my fall the night before. Now, as I sat on the bed in my hotel room, I played through the confrontation I'd had with Trevor.

I knew I'd pushed his buttons—maybe I'd wanted to see how far he would go. His reaction hadn't surprised me, though I wondered if that was his limit. I doubted it.

Yet I was pregnant with his child. Did he have a right to know? Would that change anything? I resolved to give him one last chance. I would go to the apartment and tell him about our child and give him the opportunity to make a choice—either change his behavior or lose me forever.

At seven o'clock, the time was right. The odds were high that he would be home from work, and as I left my hotel room, which I'd decided to keep for one more night, I trembled as I anticipated my conversation with him.

When I arrived at our apartment I wasn't surprised that his car wasn't out front. On impulse, I parked out of sight around the corner and walked back to the apartment.

As I opened the door my nose and eyes were assaulted with the biggest show of destruction I had ever seen. The food I'd prepared the night before was smeared on the table and floor, stinking up the whole apartment. But worse than that, every dish which had been on the table had been smashed—thrown to the floor or against the wall.

My heart sank as I surveyed what Trevor had done. My mother's china, one of the few things of my mother's that I owned, had been mostly destroyed. I looked toward the bedroom door and hesitated as I imagined what I might find there. Gathering my courage, I walked into the room I'd slept in so recently, and when I saw what Trevor had done, the blood drained from my face.

Every one of my belongings was on the floor, most of them torn and shredded. Something crunched under my foot and I looked down to see my jewelry mostly destroyed. I looked toward my nightstand and wasn't surprised when the wedding picture was not there.

Walking around the room, I looked for anything that could be salvaged. There wasn't much. I gathered all the undamaged pieces of jewelry from the floor and placed them in my pocket, then picked up a few pieces of clothing, finding some that were still intact. As I tossed the pieces of clothing on the bed, I heard the front door open and recognized Trevor's voice.

Panic sliced through me as I imagined how he would react to seeing me there. My gaze darted around the room as I searched for a place to hide. When I dashed into the bathroom I heard an unfamiliar male voice comment on the mess in the kitchen and Trevor respond that I was a bad housekeeper. The other man laughed and Trevor said he'd be right back.

I climbed into the bathtub and silently slid the shower curtain closed, then curled up on the cold floor of the tub. As I listened to Trevor enter the bedroom I prayed he wouldn't notice the few pieces of clothing I'd placed on the bed.

When he entered the bathroom, I squeezed my eyes closed, terrified he would discover me. I breathed as quietly as I could as Trevor stood right next to the bathtub, using the toilet and then washing his hands.

As he dried his hands on the towel, a piece of jewelry slipped out of my pocket. The moment it hit the floor of the bathtub my eyes shot open, but I managed to stop its progress, silencing the barely audible tinkling sound. I held my breath and hoped Trevor hadn't heard the noise.

It sounded as if Trevor had stopped drying his hands and then paused, listening. My heart pounded and tears sprang to my eyes as abject terror drenched me.

Please, please don't let him find me.

A moment later he left the bathroom and I nearly wept with relief. I heard him and his friend talking—they seemed to be discussing something work-related—and I realized Trevor's companion was his boss, Rob.

"We need to cool it for a while," Rob said. "The cops are getting closer and I'm having some trouble moving the merchandise. Our contact is getting nervous and he's stopped buying from me."

"That's fine with me," Trevor said. "I could use some down time." Then his voice became dark with anger. "Besides, I need some time to find my wife."

I trembled as I listened to the rage in Trevor's voice. In silence, I prayed the men would leave so I could make my escape.

Rob laughed at Trevor's comment, then said, "I'd hate to be her when you show up." I couldn't make out Trevor's reply. Then Rob said, "Let's get out of this pigsty and go grab a beer."

A moment later the front door closed and all was quiet. Frozen in place, I waited a full minute before standing and peeking out from behind the shower curtain. Gingerly, I stepped onto the bathroom floor and tiptoed to the door, peering into the bedroom. I silently checked the rest of the small apartment, then looked out the window to make sure Trevor's car was not out front, then I raced into the bedroom, grabbed a small suitcase that was relatively undamaged, and shoved in anything I could. Heart pounding, I zipped the suitcase closed, hurried to the front door, and stopped, listening for any sign of Trevor's presence.

All was still.

I opened the front door and slipped out, thankful for the darkness. As I ran to my car, I was even more grateful I'd impulsively parked around the corner. I could only imagine how the evening would have gone if Trevor had come home and found my car parked at the curb. He would have torn the house apart looking for me—if it was possible to tear it apart any more than it was.

On the drive back to my small hotel room despair flooded me.

What a mess I'd made of my life. When I'd left my small hometown and headed to Reno I'd had such high hopes for my future—my whole life had been spread out before me, the possibilities endless.

Then I'd made a tremendous mistake and gotten involved with Trevor. I recognized that I'd been lonely and had been thrilled when Trevor had showered me with such intense interest. Something about him had attracted me and I'd ignored the warning signs, certain I could change anything about him that didn't fit my ideals.

As I entered my hotel room and locked the door behind me, I tried to focus on the good things and realized things could be much worse. I was getting out before I'd become trapped in an abusive marriage. It would be difficult raising a child on my own, but I was confident I could do it.

At least Trevor doesn't know about the baby. That will give me an advantage.

Then I thought about the inheritance my father had left me. I'd planned on using it to finance my education—now it would be critical to my survival. I could get a job until the baby was born, but I knew that would only be temporary.

What about this semester? Finals are in a couple of weeks. Is it possible to finish? Is Trevor really going to be searching for me? Will it be safe to go to class?

I'll think it about it overnight before I decide.

I got ready for bed and quickly fell asleep with my hands resting on my abdomen.

Chapter Forty-Eight

When I woke the next morning I felt unbearably sick. Already I'd made several trips to the bathroom. Now, as I lay in bed staring at the ceiling, I realized this pregnancy was going to complicate things more than I'd anticipated.

Drifting in and out of sleep, I nibbled on soda crackers when waking, then tried to keep them down, but found myself dashing for the bathroom more and more.

Over the next two days, as my energy continued to drain, my pride in my independence faded as I realized I needed help. Picking up my cell phone, I found the battery had died and I didn't have my charger. Instead I reached for the phone next to my bedside, but in my weakened state, I struggled to remember Alyssa's phone number. Punching in the number that hovered in my brain, I listened as it rang.

"Hello?" a male voice answered.

Confused to hear my husband's voice answering Alyssa's phone, I whispered, "Trevor?"

"Lily? Is this Lily? Where are you?"

Quickly hanging up, I didn't understand what had happened. Then in a moment of stunning clarity I realized I'd dialed Trevor's cell phone by mistake.

And he had Caller ID.

My foggy brain began to clear and I knew I would need to pack up and get out as quickly as I could. My weakened body wouldn't cooperate. Pushing myself to a sitting position, I slowly shook my head until the dizziness passed. Then I tested the strength of my legs, finally able to stand without collapsing.

Looking down at myself, I knew I wasn’t in any shape to step outside my hotel room, let alone rush out to my car. I wasn't even certain if I could drive without passing out. Forcing myself to move to the bathroom, I took a quick shower, hoping that would revive me, then found a clean set of clothes to put on.

Feeling better, I packed up my few belongings, took one last look in the mirror, then opened the door.

“Hello, Lily,” Trevor said.

The blood drained from my face and my heart stopped beating before it went into a gallop. “Trevor,” I choked out. Then I tried to close the door.

Blocking the door with his foot, he said, “Please don't do that. I'm here to help you.”

I stared at him, my eyes wide with fear.

“I've already settled up your bill and I'm here to take you home.”

“What if I don't want to go with you?”

“I know I made a mistake, Lily. I'm sorry, okay? I want you to come home with me where I can take care of you and our baby.”

Shocked he knew my secret, I gasped. “Our baby?”

His eyes softened. “Yes, our baby. I found your pregnancy test.” He stroked my cheek. “You look like you don't feel well. You're pale.”

I closed my eyes at his touch. I was so tired. If I had many more days like the ones I'd just experienced I knew I couldn't take care of myself for long. Who else could I turn to? Alyssa had roommates—she couldn't very well take me in.

“I'm your husband. I love you. Let me take care of you.”

Not knowing where else to turn, I allowed him to take my hand and lead me down the hall, then out to my car. We drove to our apartment in silence.

As Trevor opened the front door, he turned to me. “I'll make it up to you. I promise.”

The first thing I noticed was that the apartment had been completely cleaned up. If I hadn't seen the mess for myself I wouldn't have believed it had ever existed. I wondered if Trevor knew I'd seen it.

He escorted me to our bedroom. “I'll leave you alone so you can sleep.”

I smiled tentatively. “Thank you.”

A short time later I was curled up in my bed. Though I was uncertain if being here was a good idea, it felt good to be back in my own bed. I pictured the expression on Trevor’s face as he'd spoken of our baby.

Is it possible he's changed?

Glancing at the place where our wedding picture used to stand, I remembered the shape the house had been in only a few days before and the anger I'd heard in Trevor’s voice.

He’s like two people—one minute loving and caring, and the next minute angry over nothing and taking it out on me.

My father had had such an even temperament that this was a new experience for me and I wasn't sure what to do.

Maybe I should give him another chance.

I drifted off to sleep before I could think it through, and when I woke an hour later I had to blink to clear my vision and force my mind to acknowledge what I saw.

It was our wedding picture, sitting in the same spot I'd kept it before. It was as if Trevor had gone out and bought a new frame and then printed off a new copy of the picture, then put it in our bedroom and assumed I would never notice the difference.

Fine. I'll play along. If Trevor wants to make an effort to be the person I know he can be, I'm not going to do anything to stop it.

When Trevor fixed me a bowl of chicken soup and placed it in front of me on the kitchen table, I was pleased.

“It's not homemade or anything,” he said. “But it's hot.”

I smiled as I lifted a spoonful to my mouth. “Thank you, Trevor. This is very thoughtful.” With him watching my every move, I felt self-conscious as I ate. “Don't you have to work?”

He shook his head. “Rob said I can take off as much time as I need.”

“Oh.” I ate the rest of my soup. “You can work while I'm at class, at least.”

He shook his head again. “Come on, Lily. You and I both know you're not going back to school. Your place is at home now.”

Alarmed at his pronouncement, my mouth fell open. “But the semester's almost over. It’s almost time for finals.”

He stood, a grave expression on his face. “You're not going anywhere.”

“What do you mean?”

“I mean, I want you here. At home. And that’s where I intend to keep you.”

I tried to control the shaking in my voice. “What about doctor's appointments?”

He smiled. “I'll take you to those, of course.”

My home has become a prison. He hasn't changed. He'll never change. I should never have agreed to come back with him.

Helplessness and despair battled for dominance as I watched Trevor clear my dishes from the table.

That night, after he’d fallen asleep, I tiptoed out of our room, planning to leave. But when I went to get my purse, it wasn’t in its usual place. I quietly searched the apartment but couldn’t find it anywhere. I slipped back into bed to consider my options, but a wave of nausea forced me to run into the bathroom.

After brushing my teeth, I climbed into bed, exhausted and in no condition to plan my escape.

Over the next few days I heard people come to the door. I thought I heard Alyssa's voice at the door once, but Trevor never let anyone in, and my cell phone was with my missing purse. I heard him tell people that I wasn't feeling well and wasn't up to company. By the end of the week no one stopped by. It was as if they’d given up. That's how I felt. I'd nearly given up, too.

One afternoon when I was straightening the kitchen, Trevor’s phone rang. He’d left his phone on the counter and I saw that the caller ID said it was *Rob's Auto Body*. Trevor glanced at me as he picked it up and answered the call.

After he greeted the caller, who I assumed was Rob, he went into the bedroom and closed the door. Curious what Trevor’s boss was calling about, I pressed my ear to the bedroom door. I could hear Trevor's end of the conversation.

"When?" he asked. Then after a pause he said, "You know I can't leave Lily by herself." A pause. "I don't know. But I don't want to take the chance." A longer pause. "Fine. I'll figure something out."

It sounded like they'd finished their call, so I hurried into the kitchen. As I thought about Trevor's side of the conversation I wondered if Rob wanted him to come to work tonight, and if so, why at night? Why not during the day?

Isn't that when most shops like Rob's do their business?

Then I remembered the conversation I'd overheard that day I'd hidden in the bathtub. I tried to recall exactly what they'd said.

I'd been so frightened that it had been hard to concentrate on what they were saying. All I could remember was Rob talking about the police getting closer and having trouble with some merchandise.

Is Trevor doing something illegal?

I considered the implications.

If the police catch him, he could go to jail.

The thought saddened me, but I also recognized it as my possible ticket to freedom.

He'll never leave me unattended as long as he fears I'll run. I've got to convince him that I won't leave. How else can I discover what he's up to?

It had been two weeks since he'd brought me home from the hotel and I couldn't recall anything I'd done that would make him think I'd want to leave. Of course I'd felt pretty awful the whole time and hadn't done much more than sleep and try to eat.

I looked up as Trevor came out of the bedroom, putting a bright smile on my face.

He smiled back. "Are you feeling better?"

"Somewhat." In truth I was tired all the time and became nauseated at the thought of most food.

"Good, because we're going somewhere." He held out his hand. "Ready?"

"Where are we going?" I tried to steady my breathing as I

reminded myself that I needed to convince him that he didn't need to fear I would run.

He smiled. “It's a surprise.”

Trying to show enthusiasm, I took his hand. “Great. I'm ready to get out of the house for a change.”

Chapter Forty-Nine

As we drove through the dark streets I wondered where he was taking me. A short while later we pulled up in front of his old apartment building.

"What's going on Trevor? Why are we here?"

He just grinned as he walked around to my side of the car and held the door open for me.

I stared at him but didn't move. "I'm not getting out of the car until you tell me what's going on."

His smile faded. "Just get out, Lily."

"No." I crossed my arms, put my head against the headrest, then closed my eyes. When Trevor's hand clamped around my upper arm and yanked me out of the car, I gasped. "Trevor, let go! You're hurting me."

"Knock it off," he said through clenched teeth. Then he nearly dragged me toward the door of his old apartment.

Dizzy with pain, I could only struggle to keep up. A moment later Trevor knocked twice then opened the door to his old apartment. He shoved me in ahead of him and I fell to the floor. Humiliated at the treatment, I looked up to see Bronson, Trevor's old roommate, staring down at me.

"Hi there, sweetie," Bronson said, grinning. Then he looked at Trevor. "How long are you going to be?"

"A couple of hours at the most."

I pushed myself to my feet and sat on the couch, furious at the treatment I was receiving. "Where are you going?" I demanded.

Trevor gazed at me. "I have to work and you'd better be here when I get back."

"Don't worry, dude. She's not leaving on my watch." Bronson winked at me. "Right, sweetie?"

Frightened at the thought of being left alone with Bronson, I stepped toward Trevor, a pleading expression on my face. "Why did you bring me here? I'd be fine at home." I forced a tender smile on my face. "Our home."

Trevor smiled and stroked my cheek. "You'll be fine here, too. And this way I can work without worrying about you." He looked over my shoulder, then back at me. "Bronson will take good care of you."

Trevor pulled me close and I had to force myself not to go rigid at his touch. Instead, I lay my head against his chest in a show of pretended affection. "Don't be long," I whispered.

Tilting his head away from mine, he bent down and kissed me softly. "I won't be. I promise."

A moment later he was gone and I was left staring at the closed door.

"I have to go to the bathroom," I announced as I headed down the hall. I wrinkled my nose as I stepped into the less than clean room, then locked the door behind me.

Leaning against the bathroom counter, I stared at the windowless room.

I can't believe Trevor's doing this to me. He's treating me like a wayward child, not his wife.

Though I recognized that Trevor had good reason to fear I'd run if I had the chance, I was still incensed that I had no control over my own life.

"Are you okay in there?" Bronson called through the closed door.

I ignored him and turned toward the mirror. I splashed my face with cool water, then looked for a clean towel with which to dry it. Seeing none, I grabbed a handful of toilet paper and dabbed at my damp skin.

"If you don't answer me, I'll come in," Bronson shouted, pounding on the door.

“I'm fine!” I yelled back. “Leave me alone!”

“Sorry, sweetie. Can't do that. I promised your husband that I wouldn't let you out of my sight.” He paused. “Well, you're out of my sight right now.”

I yanked the door open, then pushed past him and walked toward the front door. “This is ridiculous,” I muttered as I reached for the doorknob.

Just as I was about to turn the handle, Bronson's hand clamped down on my shoulder. “I'm going to have to report this to Trevor,” he breathed in my ear.

His breath reeked of alcohol, and I inwardly cringed as I imagined spending the next two hours with him. Disgusted as I was with Bronson, I didn't want him to 'report' anything to Trevor. I still needed to gain his trust so he would leave me on my own. “I was just going to get some fresh air,” I said as I let go of the doorknob. I turned in his direction. “You can come with me if you want.”

“Naw. We'll stay here and watch TV. There's a ball game I want to watch.”

Never letting go of my shoulder, he steered me to the couch.

“You can sit right next to me.” He pushed me onto the couch and sat close enough that our legs touched.

I tried to scoot away but there was nowhere to go. “I'm thirsty,” I said as I stood.

“Me too.” Bronson stood alongside me and walked with me into the kitchen. He opened the door to the refrigerator. “Help yourself, sweetie.”

Letting out a sigh, I leaned toward the cold interior and looked at the offerings. I saw a few sodas and a lot of beers. Taking the first soda I saw, I straightened.

“Grab me a beer,” Bronson said.

“Get your own,” I spat out, then walked toward the living room. Glancing over my shoulder, I saw Bronson hurriedly choosing a beer and slamming the refrigerator door. He was by my side before I had a chance to dash for the front door.

As we sat on the couch, I wondered if Bronson knew what Trevor was really up to.

Maybe if I'm careful in the way I ask him, he won't get suspicious.

I waited until he finished three beers before I began my questioning. “Hey, Bronson.”

He looked at me, his eyes slightly glazed. “Yeah?”

“Shouldn't Trevor be back by now? It's been more than two hours.”

He smiled. “He'll get here when he gets here.”

“I guess someone needed their car pretty bad for him to have to work so late.”

Laughing, Bronson said, “Yeah. Something like that.”

“What do you mean?”

“Grab me another beer, sweetie,” he said.

I brought back two, hoping he would drink them both and pass out so I could leave.

He opened the first one and took a large swallow before belching.

“So Bronson, have you ever worked in the auto-body business?”

He gazed at me. “Naw. The only thing I like to do with cars is drive 'em.”

“What kind of car do you have?”

“Just a junker right now.” He leaned toward me conspiratorially. “But at least I don't have to worry about it getting stolen, right?” He laughed at his own joke.

I smiled in response. “Now that you mention it, I remember seeing something on the news about a lot of cars getting stolen recently. I hope mine's okay. Aren't Hondas pretty popular?”

He belched again and leaned toward me, closer this time. “Don't you worry. Trevor will make sure that doesn't happen.”

“I don't know how Trevor could have any control over that.”

Bronson just grinned and downed the rest of the beer he was holding before opening the next one.

What does he mean by that? Is Trevor involved in the thefts? Wow. His crimes could be more serious than I thought.

Twenty minutes later Bronson had fallen asleep and was snoring peacefully. I stood, careful not to disturb him, then walked toward the door, my heart racing. I placed my hand on the doorknob, then hesitated, wondering if Trevor would be standing on the other side waiting for me.

Where am I going to go? I have nothing. Not even my purse. If I really want to end it with Trevor I need to turn him into the police. If he's in jail he can't hurt me anymore.

I released the doorknob, walked back to the couch, sat down, and put my head in my hands. Just then the door sprang open and Trevor stood in the doorway. My head snapped in his direction, relief flooding me that I hadn't opened the door only a moment before.

I stood. He looked at me and then at the snoring Bronson. An expression of disgust crossed his face before he walked up to Bronson and smacked him in the back of the head. Hard. “Wake up, loser,” Trevor nearly shouted.

Bronson opened his eyes.

“I'm impressed, Lily,” Trevor said. “Even though he fell asleep, you're still here. Maybe I was wrong about you.”

I smiled and snaked my arms around his neck, then gazed at him with forced adoration. “I told you I would be fine at home.”

“Dude. You're back,” Bronson said, rubbing his eyes.

Trevor shook his head. “See ya later.” Then he held my hand and led me toward the door.

I glanced back at Bronson, glad he was too out of it to tell Trevor I'd tried to escape.

Chapter Fifty

As we drove back to our apartment I chewed on my lip, wondering if I should question Trevor about his evening. Deciding to push my luck, I turned in my seat to face him. “So, did you get a lot done tonight?”

“Huh?” he said, glancing my way.

“At work. Did you get a lot done?”

“Yeah. It was . . . productive.”

“Was it just one certain car that you had to do tonight? Is that why Rob needed you to come in so late?” I twisted my wedding ring on my finger as I waited for his reply.

Trevor shifted his eyes in my direction, then faced the road again. “Why all the questions?” He paused. “The only thing you need to worry about is whether my check clears.”

I turned away from him, realizing he wasn't going to give up information so easily. “Forget it. I was just trying to make conversation.”

His hand stroked my neck. “Look. I really don't want to talk about work. Okay?”

“Fine.”

Once home, Trevor sat with me on the couch. “Rob needs me to start working more.” He paused. “That means I’m going to have to start trusting you to not take off.”

Hope surged through me. “Of course you can trust me, Trevor.”

Smiling, he nodded. “Good. That’s what I want to hear.” He gazed at me, his eyes locked on mine. “Because if I have to track you down again there are going to be some serious consequences."

A shiver of dread crawled up my spine. "What do you mean?"

All warmth fled his eyes. "It doesn't look good when my wife takes off for days without telling me anything. Especially in your condition."

As I thought about the evening I'd just endured, and the way Trevor had treated me in the past, fresh anger coursed through me, fueling my words. "How do you think it makes you look when you push your pregnant wife to the floor and leave her with a drunk for hours?"

He clenched his jaw as he glowered. "You'd better watch it or you'll find yourself getting babysat by Bronson on a nightly basis."

I stood abruptly. "I'm tired. I'm going to bed." Then I walked into our bedroom and closed the door. As I got ready for bed, I heard sounds coming from the TV.

As soon as he leaves for work, I'm out of here.

By the time I'd fallen asleep, Trevor still hadn't come to bed.

The next morning I woke early and was surprised to see Trevor's side of the bed empty. Elated, I checked the bathroom, then quickly checked the rest of the house.

I was on my own.

Fresh optimism flooded me. This was the first time in over two weeks that Trevor hadn't been constantly hovering over me. After throwing on some clothes, I began a more thorough search for my purse, but didn't find it anywhere.

Trevor must've taken it with him. I can't get far without my car keys and my money.

Alarm pounded inside me. I sat on the bed, taking several deep breaths as I tried to think clearly.

I can use a neighbor's phone.

Relief cascaded over me as I ran to the front door. But once I reached it, my mouth fell open, and I stared, dumbstruck.

Trevor had changed the deadbolt. He'd replaced the lock with a deadbolt that had to be unlocked with a key from both the inside and the outside.

And I didn't have the key.

Tears filled my eyes as I realized the mistake I'd made in arguing with him the night before.

I should've kept my mouth shut.

Angry with myself for letting my outrage get the best of me, my shoulders slumped.

If I hadn't said anything to him, maybe be wouldn't have locked me in.

Then panic set in.

What if there's a fire? How would I get out?

Frantic for a way to escape, I looked around the room, my gaze darting in all directions.

The window!

I rushed to the window and pressed my hands against it. It was a plate glass window and didn't open—there was no screen to simply push out. I'd have to break it to escape. Then I thought about the one other window in the small apartment. It was in the bedroom.

Clawing at my last hope, I raced into the bedroom and over to the window. I slid it open and pushed and pulled at the screen until it popped out. Examining the edges, I didn't see any noticeable damage. Then, climbing into the window well, I stood, but was dismayed that the top of the window well was far above my shoulders. The house was on a steep slope and this window well was deep.

I tried to boost myself up, but to no avail. I climbed back into the bedroom, then went into the kitchen, grabbed a chair, and dragged it into the bedroom. I tried to push it through the small window opening but it was no use. The chair was too big.

Pushing myself back through the window, I yelled as loudly as I could, "Is anyone there? Can anyone hear me?"

Silence was the only reply. I continued yelling for fifteen minutes until my voice started cracking from the strain. Hauling myself back into the apartment, I fell onto the bed, defeated.

If Trevor's goal was to completely isolate me, he'd done an excellent job of it.

Picturing the front window, I knew I could smash through it, but I also knew if I did, there would be no hiding it from Trevor.

What if I break it and I have nowhere to go? I can't come back home and pretend I haven't tried to escape. What if I cut myself trying to crawl through and hurt the baby? What if I bleed to death? Will anyone care? I already know no one will answer my yells for help. I just spent fifteen minutes proving that.

Waves of despair crashed over me as I lay there and considered my options. Eventually I came to the conclusion that there was only one way to escape.

I'll just have to convince Trevor to trust me. I'll put on the act of my life persuading him that I love him and am devoted to him and would never consider leaving.

Optimism replaced the despair as I got up from the bed and went to work. I put the chair back in the kitchen, then showered. I spent the rest of the morning cleaning the house, organizing cupboards, and generally making the house look as perfect as I could make it.

I searched my cookbook for a recipe we already had the ingredients for and that Trevor would like, then spent a portion of the late afternoon preparing the meal. When it came time to set the table, I hesitated over whether to use my remaining china.

What if things go wrong and Trevor breaks what's left of my mother's china?

Pushing aside my worries, and committed to playing the part of the perfect housewife, I set the table with my good china and hoped for the best. When I heard Trevor's key turn in the lock, my heart pounded.

I hadn't decided if I should say anything about the new lock.

"Hi, honey," Trevor said as he locked the door behind him and dropped the key into his pocket. He glanced around the spotless rooms. "Wow! You've been busy."

I walked up to him and gave him a warm hug and kiss. "It's only because I love you. I want you to look forward to coming home at night." Smiling adoringly, I gestured toward the table. "I have dinner ready. Are you hungry?"

"I'm starved. Just let me wash up first, okay?"

I nodded and set the food on the table while he went into the bathroom. A moment later we sat at the table and I asked Trevor about his day.

"It was busy, which is always good. But I don't really want to talk about work."

"Okay," I said. "What do you want to talk about?"

He leaned over and touched my abdomen. "How's our baby doing?"

"Fine, as far as I can tell." I hesitated. "I need to choose a doctor soon so I can make my first appointment."

He smiled with confidence. "I've already taken care of it. One of the guys at work just had a kid with his wife and he gave me the name of her doctor. I made an appointment for next month."

I forced a smile on my face. "Well, thank you. That was very thoughtful." I reached my hand under the table and pinched my leg to keep from telling Trevor what I really thought.

The rest of the evening went smoothly and I hoped Trevor was starting to build a little trust in me.

Over the next few days Trevor treated me kindly and I began to hope that the change in my behavior had helped him to change his. One evening as we watched TV, I decided to bring up the subjects of the door and my absent purse.

"Trevor, I'm worried," I said, leaning against him.

"What's wrong?" he asked as he looked at me.

I sat up and faced him. "Well, I've been thinking. What if something goes wrong with my pregnancy? I won't have a way to get in touch with you."

He stared into my eyes for a moment before smiling. "I've been thinking about that too, so I decided to get us a land line." He gazed at me more intently. "But you have to promise you won't do anything to make me regret it."

"I won't. I just need a way to contact you." I smiled faintly. "That's all."

"I'll be right back."

He unlocked the front door, then headed outside. A moment later he was back, a phone in his hands. He took a cordless phone and plugged it into the kitchen outlet, then came into the living room and sat next to me.

"Happy now?" he asked.

I nodded. "Yes, thank you." I leaned against him as he put his arm around me, and we began to watch TV.

When the news came on, and a story about more cars being stolen began, Trevor turned the channel.

"Wait," I said. "I want to see that."

Trevor kept flipping through channels. "Why?"

"Bronson mentioned something about stolen cars and I want to see what the news is saying."

Going rigid, Trevor turned off the TV. "What did Bronson say?"

His reaction made me wonder again if he could be involved in the thefts. "Nothing."

"He must've said something. Now tell me what it was."

"He was just telling me that his car is old and whoever's been stealing the cars wouldn't want to take his."

Trevor seemed to relax. "Oh." He stood. "I'm tired. Let's go to bed."

"I'm not ready yet. I'm going to stay up a while longer."

Trevor pulled me up. "Come on. It's late."

His reaction didn't leave me any space for disagreement. I followed him to the bedroom, all the while wondering how I could find out what he was involved with.

Chapter Fifty-One

As soon as Trevor left for work, I picked up the phone to make sure there was a dial tone. Relieved to hear the hum of an active phone line, I decided to call Alyssa, but then I realized my cell phone held all my stored phone numbers, and I didn't know Alyssa's number.

While eating breakfast I thought about the car thefts. I wanted to learn more about them and decided to try accessing the Internet with my laptop, which Trevor hadn't taken away from me. After plugging in the network cable, I booted up my computer, then opened a browser. When I received an error I checked the network connection screen and, though disappointed, wasn't surprised to discover we had no Internet connection.

Trevor had discontinued the service.

I decided to call the phone company to have the service reinstated —Trevor wouldn't know about it until he received the bill, and I hoped by then I would be long gone.

After looking up the number in the yellow pages phone book that I'd left in the kitchen junk drawer, I called the phone company and was told the DSL service would be restored by the next day. I was glad Trevor had at least kept the modem, otherwise it would have taken a week before I could access the Internet.

Careful to unplug the network cable and tuck it back along the floor, I shut down my computer and went about the rest of my day, anxious to have access to the outside world through the Internet.

The next morning as Trevor left for work, I wondered where he was keeping my purse with my keys, wallet, and cell phone. I hoped he was getting tired of running all the errands and would be willing to give me back that responsibility, which would force him to give me back my purse.

As soon as it was safe, I checked to see if the Internet was available. I ended up checking three more times before it was finally up and running.

Elated to have Internet access and a way to communicate with the outside world, I checked my email and found several messages from Alyssa. They were dated starting several weeks before.

I immediately wrote back.

Alyssa,

I'm fine. Trevor has been keeping me all to himself, but it's okay. Don't worry about me. It will all work out. Have fun this summer and I'll see you in the fall.

Love, Lily

Though I was tempted to tell Alyssa everything, there was nothing she could do from her parents' house and I didn't want her to worry.

I went through the rest of my email, deleting most of it, but one message caught my eye. The subject said *Trevor is dangerous.*

I opened it, anxious to see what it said.

I know you asked me not to contact you, but there is something I need to tell you. I can't do it in an email. Will you meet with me?

I inhaled sharply.

Who is this person and what information do they have?

Anxious to know who this person was, especially now that the earlier warnings seemed to have come true, I determined to try and meet with this person. I clicked Reply and began typing.

I would like to meet with you, but I don't know when I'll be able to break away. Trevor is keeping a close watch on me and I can't come and go as I'd like. Pick a time and place and I'll see what I can do.

I hit Send, then tried not to think about the email. Next, I pulled up the website of the local newspaper and read all I could about the car thefts. There wasn't much to learn—it seemed the police knew very little, although there was a number to call in tips. I jotted down the number, then frowned, considering whether to call and point the police to Rob's shop.

What will the consequences be if I call? It would be anonymous, of course. But still, if I'm right about Trevor's involvement, what will the fallout be? Am I ready to deal with it?

Last, I checked my bank account and was stunned to see the balance had dropped to less than one thousand dollars. I'd had eighty-five thousand dollars in my account the last time I'd checked. The account showed no activity for the current month, so I looked at the previous month's activity. That's when I saw that a check had been drawn for nearly my entire balance.

Did Trevor forge a check to himself? How can I escape with no money?

Upset over this new problem, I nearly forgot to clear my browser history to hide any evidence that I'd been online. I shut down my computer and leaned back in my chair, thinking about how I could meet with the anonymous email sender without Trevor knowing.

As the day went on, I couldn't stop thinking about the person who wanted to meet with me. I checked my email several times, and when I found a reply to my earlier email, I was almost afraid to open it.

If you can get to Wal-Mart this evening, I'll be waiting in the ladies' room. I know what you look like and I'll be watching for you.

I replied that I would try, then after shutting down my laptop, I nervously waited for Trevor to get home from work.

As it turned out, it wasn't difficult to persuade him to take me shopping. I convinced him I needed to buy some maternity clothes and he agreed to take me to the nearby Wal-Mart.

As we browsed, I watched the other shoppers, wondering which one had been sending me the emails. Trying to hide my anxiety, I kept a close eye on Trevor, trying to gauge his mood, waiting for just the right moment to excuse myself to go to the ladies' room.

After we'd been shopping for nearly an hour, I guided him to the electronics section, then placed my hand on his arm. "I need to use the bathroom. I think something I ate at dinner disagreed with me."

Trevor's brow wrinkled. "Are you okay? Do you want to go home?"

"No." I shook my head. "I'll be all right. I just need to use the bathroom." I paused. "Do you want to wait here? It shouldn't take too long."

He glanced at all the video games, then back at me. "That's okay. I'll walk you over there and wait for you."

"Thank you." I smiled brightly to show I was glad he was coming with me.

As soon as I entered the ladies room, I saw a woman standing next to the sink, watching me. "Are you . . ?" I asked.

"The one who asked to meet with you? Yes. Thanks for coming."

"I don't think you ever mentioned your name."

"You can call me Tina."

I nodded. "Trevor's waiting for me. I don't have much time."

"I understand." Tina stepped away from the counter and glanced around before coming close to me. "I don't know how your relationship is with him, but I would suggest running far, far away."

What if Trevor set up this meeting to test me?

"How do you know Trevor?" I asked, wary.

"We dated on and off for over a year. We finally broke up last summer."

"Why did you break up?"

One eyebrow went up at the question.

"I think I have a right to know," I said. "I feel like I'm taking a chance meeting with you."

"You are."

Surprised at her comment, I waited for her to explain.

"If he's been treating you anything like the way he treated me, I think you know exactly why."

My face paled. "Is that why you wanted to meet with me? To tell me what I already know?"

"No. If it were only that." She closed her eyes and shook her head before meeting my gaze. "Trevor has involved himself in some dangerous activities."

"Like what?"

"Look, you seem like a nice girl, which is why I tried to scare you away from him in the first place."

"Just tell me what's going on."

As Tina opened her mouth to speak, a woman entered the bathroom and looked at the two of us, a question on her face. "Which one of you is Lily?"

"I am," I said.

"Some guy out there is waiting for you and he asked me to make sure you're okay."

"I'm fine," I said.

The woman nodded and went into a stall.

A loud knock sounded at the bathroom door. "Lily?" Trevor called out.

Panic swept over me.

What if he comes in and catches me talking to his old girlfriend?

"I'm sorry, Tina," I said. "I've got to go."

"Wait," she whispered urgently.

"I have to go. Please talk fast."

"All I know," she began, "is Trevor and Rob are running a chop shop out of that place of his—and they'll do anything to keep it going. Apparently it's very lucrative."

I was right. He is *involved in those car thefts.*

"Thanks for letting me know," I said.

She frowned. "Be careful."

I nodded, then hurried out of the bathroom.

Chapter Fifty-Two

The moment I walked through the door, Trevor stepped to my side. "It's about time," he said with a frown. "Do you feel better now?"

After the information I'd just learned, I was glad I'd told him I wasn't feeling well—a good excuse for my pale face. "I'm feeling worse. Can we go home now?"

"Yeah, sure."

That night I tossed and turned, anxious for the opportunity to report Trevor's involvement in the car thefts to the police. Later I realized I should have reported him for holding me prisoner, but at the time it didn't occur to me that he was doing something illegal in keeping me from leaving.

When Trevor left for work, I picked up the phone, ready to call the police, but then I hesitated.

Do I want to see Trevor in jail?

The thought made me sick, but the knowledge that it was my ticket to freedom pushed me to make the call. After a deep breath, I called the tip number and left a message, then hung up and desperately tried to put the whole thing out of my mind.

That night, as soon as Trevor got home, he went into the kitchen and picked up the phone. I lifted my gaze from the book I was reading as a tingle of worry fluttered inside me. It sounded like he'd pressed only one button on the phone—like he'd pressed the redial button

Is he checking up on who I called?

A moment later he came into the living room. "Why did you call Wal-Mart today?"

"Oh," I said as relief cascaded over me when I remembered I'd called them after I'd called the police tip line. "I was just seeing if they had a certain ingredient in stock." I smiled. "And they do."

He nodded. "Okay."

I went back to my book, but I watched him out of the corner of my eye as he turned on the TV.

Why did he check on my phone calls today? He didn't do it last night. Did something happen at work? Something that made him suspect I'd called the police?

When I woke the next morning and thought about Trevor checking up on my phone call, I had a fresh sense of urgency to free myself from the prison he'd created for me. After he left for work I waited half an hour before calling a local locksmith and explaining that I'd locked myself in my house and couldn't find the key.

He said he'd be over within the hour.

As I watched the locksmith work on the deadbolt, I anxiously glanced at the kitchen clock, terrified Trevor would show up and catch me. A short time later he was done. He unlocked the front door and handed me the new key.

"You might want to think about getting a regular deadbolt. Since this is your only exit, it's kind of dangerous to depend on a key to open the door."

I smiled and nodded, well aware of the dangers. "Thank you." I handed him payment for the job, glad I'd known where Trevor kept some extra cash.

I just hope he doesn't notice that some money is missing.

As soon as the locksmith left, I locked the door behind him and hid the key among my cleaning supplies.

Trevor will never stumble upon it there.

Elated to know I could leave whenever I wanted, I resolved to get my important belongings back first—my wallet, which held every form of identification I had, and the keys to my car. Without those things, it would be much harder to go anywhere.

As evening approached, then nightfall, I began to wonder where Trevor was. He'd been home most nights and I'd begun to expect him to be home by at least late evening, but after the late news finished I went to bed, anxious to know what was going on.

The next morning when I woke, I was surprised to find Trevor's side of the bed still smooth and unslept in. He'd never stayed out all night before.

Has he been arrested?

My heart stuttered at the thought.

At eight o'clock I called *Rob's Auto Body*, impatient to discover where Trevor was, but no one answered the phone. I tried calling several times throughout the day, but no one picked up.

At one point I dug out my new key and stared at it, considering whether to leave even though I didn't have my car keys or my wallet.

But where will I go?

As I tucked the key back into its hiding place, the phone rang. Startled, I looked at the caller ID screen, but it was blank—apparently Trevor hadn't gotten the Caller Id service.

I picked up the phone, and with a tentative voice, asked, "Hello?"

"Lily," Trevor said. "I need you to do something for me."

"Trevor? Where are you?"

"Don't worry about that now." His voice was sharp and impatient.

"Ok. What do you want me to do?"

He was silent.

"Trevor? Are you there?"

"Listen carefully. I need you to get something for me at Rob's shop and then come back to the apartment and wait for my call."

My thoughts went in all directions at once.

He's kept me prisoner for the last several weeks and suddenly he wants me to go out on my own? What's going on?

"But Trevor, how am I supposed to do that when I don't have a way to get out, or my purse or my car key?"

"Bronson is on his way over. I told him where to find your purse and I gave him a key to the apartment."

My muscles tensed.

That loser Bronson is going to be touching my purse, going through my things?

Though furious, I kept my voice calm. "Okay. What do you want me to get at the shop?"

Trevor was silent for a moment, then his voice dropped to a whisper. "After Bronson leaves, drive to Rob's shop and tell them you need to get into my locker. There's a safe in there. It's bolted to the floor so I have to give you the combination." He paused. "I can trust you, right?"

"Trevor, I'm your wife. If you can't trust me, who can you trust? I want you home with me." I almost gagged on the last words.

He told me the combination and I wrote it down.

"What am I going to find in there?" I asked.

"There's a gym bag. For your own safety, it's best if you don't open it."

"Why not? What's in it?"

"Don't ask any questions now. Just get over there, get the bag, and come back to the apartment to wait for further instructions."

I agreed to his strange request and watched for Bronson's arrival.

He showed up a few minutes later, unlocked the door, and walked in like he belonged there. With my purse in his hand, he said, "Here you go, sweetie. I don't know why your hubby wants to give this back to you all of a sudden, but here it is."

I took it from him, hiding my disgust at seeing him again. "Thank you."

He stood there a moment. "I guess I'll get going."

I forced a smile on my face and nodded slightly as I watched him walk out the door.

I stared at the purse in my hand. This was what I'd been working toward for weeks, but now that the opportunity for escape was right in front of me, fear tickled the back of my neck.

What is Trevor up to? If I run, where will I go? How will I take care of my baby? What will Trevor do when he finds that I've left?

I unzipped my purse and dumped the contents on the table, then looked through the items. Although my cash was gone, and my cell phone was missing, my driver's license was tucked into my wallet, and my car keys were there.

I placed everything back inside and walked to the front door, then stopped, my hand on the doorknob as alarm began to grow within me.

What if this is a test? What if Trevor's watching me to see if I run? He'll follow me, and then I don't know what he'd do. What if he's having Bronson watch me?

Heart pounding, I sank onto the couch as I tried to figure out what I should do.

I should at least see what he's hiding in his locker.

With fresh resolve, I walked out the front door, and as I slid behind the wheel of my Honda, I relished the feeling of having a small measure of control back in my life.

Chapter Fifty-Three

I tried to enjoy the short drive to Rob's shop—I hadn't been out on my own in quite a while. I took in the sight of all the people I saw, living their normal lives. I wanted to be one of them, not some cowed woman who was afraid of her husband, willing to do whatever he asked.

Do I have the courage to leave Trevor for good?

A wave of nausea reminded me that I had more than myself to think about now. Swallowing the sick feeling, I turned into the parking lot of *Rob's Auto Body* and pulled into a parking space. Gathering my courage, I climbed out of my car and strode toward the door, and as I entered the tiny lobby, I glanced around, looking for someone to show me to Trevor's locker.

"Can I help you?" an older man asked as he entered through a side door. He wore dirty coveralls and had a two-day growth of beard.

Suddenly nervous, I stammered out my answer. "I'm . . . uh . . . Trevor Caldwell's wife."

"He's not here."

"I know." My heart raced. "He sent me to get something out of his locker."

"What's your name?"

"Lily. Lily Caldwell.

"If you're his wife, how come I never heard of you?"

"I don't know. I guess he just never mentioned me."

What if he doesn't let me go to Trevor's locker? Then what?

"I think you'd better come back when Rob's here," he said before turning away.

"When will that be?"

He spun around and scowled. "Don't know. Haven't seen him in a couple of days." Then he went back through the side door.

Where's Rob? Could he be with Trevor? Is that why Trevor asked me *to open his safe and get whatever's inside? Because Rob can't?*

I walked to the door where the man had gone, then pulled it open and peered inside. The man was the only person around. I slipped through the door and stepped into the large shop, then started walking toward the man, who was now bent over a car.

"Excuse me," I began.

"What the . . ?" He straightened and looked at me, then started flailing his arms around. "You're not supposed to be in here. I told you you'll have to come back later."

Through another door at the other end of the room I saw a bank of lockers and knew I was too close to finishing my errand to allow failure. Drawing on all the courage I could muster, I said, "I'm sorry to bother you, but I'm going to have to insist that you let me into Trevor's locker."

He scowled again. "Look here, missy. No one tells me what to do. I'm in charge here today and I'm not going to allow a stranger off the street to be snooping around the employee lockers." He stood up straighter. "How do I know you're not one of them undercover cops?"

I narrowed my eyes. "Why? Do you have something to hide?"

His scowl was replaced by a look of complete innocence. "Absolutely not." He stared at me for a moment. "Do you have any proof that you're Trevor's wife? Some identification?"

My driver's license still showed my maiden name, and I didn't have anything else to link me to Trevor. "We just got married a few months ago. So no, I don't have any proof." I wondered if there was any way to call Trevor, but he had specifically said I was to wait to hear from him. Besides, I had no idea where he was.

"Then I'm going to have to ask you again to leave."

The opportunity to make my escape seemed to be slipping away. Fueled by desperation, I felt a surge of boldness. "And what if I refuse?"

The man's mouth fell open as if he wasn't used to being so blatantly disobeyed. "Then I guess I'll just have to call the police and have you arrested for trespassing."

I decided to call his bluff. "Then that's what you're going to have to do, because Trevor sent me here and I'm not leaving until I've gotten what he sent me for." At this, I rushed past him and toward the open door on the other side of the room.

"Hey," the man yelled from right behind me. "Hold on."

My heart jackhammered with fear, and just as I entered the room with the lockers, the man's hand clamped onto my shoulder. I cringed, waiting for him to harm me—after all, no one was around, and I didn't know what he was capable of.

What am I doing? I could get hurt or killed. This isn't worth it.

I spun around to face him, forcing his hand to drop from my shoulder. "I'm sorry. I was wrong to come in here uninvited." My voice shook as tears filled my eyes. "I'll leave now."

The man sighed as his eyes softened. "I know how Trevor is. If he sent you here and you came away empty-handed, it will be all my fault."

Fresh hope pulsed through me. "Are you saying you'll let me into his locker?"

"Yeah. Why not?" He stepped toward the locker on the far end. "It's this one."

Suddenly giddy, I grinned. "Thank you." I went to the locker, and as I pulled it open, the man stayed right next to me. Out of the corner of my eye I saw him perusing the items in Trevor's locker, including the safe bolted to the floor.

I can't open the safe with this guy watching me.

I smiled at him. "I think I can take it from here."

His scowl was back. "What if I want to see what old Trevor has in his locker?"

"How do you think Trevor would feel about that?"

The man looked thoughtful. "Yeah. I guess you're right."

I watched him walk away, and once he was out of sight, I squatted in front of the safe, pulled out the slip of paper on which I'd written the combination, and unlocked the door.

Glancing around to make sure the man wasn't lurking nearby, I pulled open the door of the safe and saw the gym bag Trevor had mentioned. I lifted it out, curious what was inside, but after taking one last look at the empty safe, I closed the door and spun the lock, then stood and closed the locker.

As I walked back through the shop, I smiled briefly in the direction of the man, who stared after me.

Once I was safely in my car, my curiosity got the better of me, and I slowly unzipped the bag, half expecting a snake to jump out and bite me. When I saw what was inside, I gasped.

It looked like Trevor had put every last dollar he had in the bag. Warmth rushed through me as I realized this was the inheritance money he'd taken from me. It was mine and it would finance my freedom.

Now I had to decide if I would go back to the apartment to wait to hear from Trevor.

Chapter Fifty-Four

Though tempted to flee with only the clothes on my back, I feared that Trevor was watching me to see what I would do.

I have to be extremely careful. This could just be an elaborate test —a test where failing could cost me my life.

A few minutes later I was back in my apartment, stuffing what I could into my suitcase, wanting to be ready to flee the moment that seemed right. After I'd packed the essentials, I looked in the closet for the box that held my school books. Gazing at the stack of partially read textbooks, despair washed over me.

What if Trevor catches me trying to sneak away? What will happen then?

Shaking my head with forced confidence, I unloaded the box and took it into the kitchen, then after carefully wrapping the few pieces of my mother's china, I placed them in the small box and closed the lid.

I set the box near the front door, then set my suitcase and laptop beside the box. I took several deep breaths before opening the front door and walking to the mailbox. Trying to pretend I was just out to check my mail, I surreptitiously glanced around, on the lookout for Trevor, Bronson, or anyone else who might be spying on me. I didn't see anyone, so I grabbed the mail and hurried inside.

A moment later I had my keys in one hand, my suitcase in the other, and my laptop bag slung over my shoulder. With a feeling of urgency, I strode to my car, placed the two items in the trunk, then closed it, not wanting someone to see that I was preparing to leave. I went back for the small box of china and the gym bag and placed them in the trunk as well.

Just a few more minutes.

I rushed back into the apartment to get my purse, but just as I shut the door, the phone rang.

With my heart banging against my ribs, I looked at the phone, uncertain what to do. My palms dampened with sweat.

What if I don't answer and he gets tipped off that I'm leaving? What if he's watching right now and saw me loading my car?

Frantic to make the right decision, I was paralyzed. I squeezed my eyes closed, trying to focus, then I opened them and grabbed the phone.

"Hello?" I tried to control the shaking in my voice.

"Lily?" Trevor asked. "Did you get it?"

Unable to speak, I nodded.

"Lily! Answer me!"

Snapped out of my stupor, I swallowed my fear. "Yes. I got it."

He exhaled audibly. "Did you open it?"

"No," I said, almost too quickly.

"Good girl." He paused. "Now, what I need you to do is bring the bag to the county jail."

I drew a sharp breath.

He is *in jail.*

"What happened, Trevor? Why are you in jail?"

"That doesn't matter now. What matters is that you come through for me, honey. Just like I came through for you when you were so sick. Remember that? Remember how I've cared for you all these weeks?"

More like kept me prisoner. "Of course I remember."

"You'll do this for me, won't you, honey?"

Freedom was so close I could feel it, and I tried to keep my voice steady. "I'll be there as soon as I can."

"Okay."

I was about to hang up and race for the door when Trevor made a statement that changed all my plans.

"I know how you can get lost, so Bronson is going to come over and make sure you get here safely."

"Right now?" I asked, glancing toward the door, despair once again crashing over me.

"Yeah. I called him a while ago. I'm surprised he's not there already. Now, he doesn't know about the gym bag, so keep it to yourself."

"What does he know?"

"Just that he's supposed to take you to the county jail to see me."

Pounding on the door made me jump.

"I guess he made it," Trevor said, obviously hearing the loud banging. "Let me talk to him."

"Sure. Hang on." I set the phone down and went to the door, cracking it open.

"Hi, sweetie." Bronson leaned against the door frame, then pushed through the door. "You ready to go?"

"Trevor wants to talk to you." I tried to keep a neutral expression on my face as I pointed to the phone on the kitchen counter.

He nodded and headed toward the phone.

The moment his back was turned, I walked to the open door, picked up my purse and hurried outside. As soon as I'd stepped onto the porch, I ran toward my car and yanked open the driver's door, but just as I was about to slide behind the wheel, Bronson appeared at my side and held onto my arm.

"You weren't going to leave without me, were you, sweetie?" he murmured in my ear.

Startled, I nearly screamed. "Of course not. I knew you were right behind me."

"Good. We wouldn't want to disappoint Trevor. He's looking forward to your visit."

Trying to force my breathing to return to normal, I started the car and glanced at Bronson, who watched me closely. Unnerved by the attention, I tried to distract him as I pulled away from the curb. "It's too bad about Trevor getting arrested, don't you think?"

He tilted his head. "I wouldn't want to be him."

"Why do you say that?"

"I just think he's landed himself in a whole lot of trouble." He turned toward the window and said almost to himself, "I tried to tell him crime doesn't pay."

Surprised by his comment, I wondered how much he knew about Trevor's crimes. "I've found he pretty much does what he wants."

Bronson looked at me with narrowed eyes. "What do you know about it?"

"I know he works late hours and that there have been a lot of cars stolen recently."

He didn't respond. After a moment he told me to turn right at the next light.

A moment later the county jail was in front of me and I still didn't know how I was going to get away.

Chapter Fifty-Five

The moment we pulled into the jail parking lot, Bronson became fidgety and nervous.

"Are you okay?"

"Yeah," he said. "This place just gives me the creeps."

"You've been here before then." I steered into a parking stall and turned off the engine.

"You could say that."

I pulled the key out of the ignition and placed it in my purse. "Were you an inmate here?"

Bronson shifted in his seat, clearly uncomfortable. "Look. You go and see Trevor. I'll wait in the car."

I felt like I'd just been handed a gift. "If you're sure." I reached for the door handle, then stopped. I pulled a twenty dollar bill out of my wallet—money I'd taken from the gym bag earlier— and held it out to Bronson. "This might take a while. Why don't you grab something to eat while I'm inside?"

He eyed the money and pressed his lips together. Suddenly snatching the money from me, he smiled. "Sure. Why not?"

"Just lock the car when you leave," I said with a smile. "I might be in there a while," I repeated for good measure.

I climbed out of the car, shut the door, and took a deep breath before walking to the entrance of the county jail. Controlling myself to not look at Bronson to make sure he was leaving, I walked steadily to the door and slipped inside. I waited thirty seconds, then walked toward the door and peeked outside.

Bronson was trotting away from my car and toward the street.

Taking several deep breaths to slow the pounding of my heart, I waited until Bronson was out of sight, then hurried out the doors and ran to my car. A moment later I sat behind the wheel. I jammed the key into the ignition and was relieved when the car started right up.

A moment later I pulled out of the parking lot, my gaze darting in every direction to make sure Bronson wasn't around. I got on the freeway at the first opportunity and headed west on I-80, having no idea where I would go, but feeling better than I had in a long time.

The longer I drove, the less afraid I felt, and the fear that had been a constant low hum, always on the verge of breaking into something more, was beginning to fade. Even as I put more distance between myself and Trevor, I couldn't help but wonder when he would get out and come after me. I didn't want to think about his reaction when he discovered I'd left him in jail and taken my money back.

Proud of myself for having the courage to leave, I also felt anxious —anxious about what the future held, anxious about having my baby, anxious about how I would support myself. But my overriding feeling was one of relief—relief in knowing I could move forward with my life. Though I would have to be cautious, I could at least choose what to do next.

It didn't take long before I'd crossed into California. I continued driving and passed Sacramento. After a while I turned south onto Highway 99.

As the evening turned to night, I pulled off the freeway and checked into a hotel. It felt strange, though exhilarating, to know no one knew where I was. After a good night's sleep I drove to a nearby drug store and bought a few supplies before coming back to my room.

I gazed at myself in the mirror, admiring my long black hair one last time. Sadness filled my eyes as I picked up the scissors and angled them toward the clump of hair I'd gathered in my left hand. My vision blurred and I had to set the scissors down to wipe my eyes.

I don't know if I'm ready to do this.

I hadn't cut my hair since before my mother had died.

Thinking of my mother led to thoughts of my father.

Dad, are you disappointed in me? I got married too soon and now I'm pregnant and on the run from Trevor. I'm afraid, Dad. Afraid he'll find me, afraid I'll fail.

Squeezing my eyes closed, I grabbed a handful of hair, then opened my eyes and picked up the scissors. Large hanks of shiny black hair fell to the floor as I wielded the scissors in controlled movements. When I was done I gathered the hair from the floor and threw it in the trash can.

"Not bad," I said out loud as I fluffed my new short hairstyle. Fresh hope in my future replaced the sadness I'd been feeling. "Now for the finishing touch."

I read the instructions on the box of hair dye before carefully going through each step. When I'd finished, I hardly recognized myself—my once long black hair was now auburn and a short pixy cut.

If I can't recognize myself, maybe Trevor won't recognize me either.

I checked out a short time later and pulled back onto the freeway. Overwhelming peace flooded me, telling me I was doing the right thing. As I continued driving south, my excitement grew as I pictured the possibilities for my new life.

I'll find a home and make it a place of refuge, a place where I want to be. Not a prison, but a sanctuary for myself and my child.

The thought brought warmth and comfort.

After a while I stopped to fill my gas tank, and as I stood next to my car pumping the gas, I noticed a cell phone store across the street

I need a new one to replace the one Trevor took from me.

A short time later I'd bought a pay-as-you-go phone with no contract. I didn't know what my future held and wasn't at all ready to commit to anything for two years, even a phone contract.

Back in my car, I angled my rear view mirror so I could check my new hair style again, blinking as I looked at my reflection. Every time I saw myself it was like looking at a completely different person. Though saddened by the circumstances that had forced me to so drastically change my look, I wasn't unpleased by the effect the new cut had on my face. The short style made my brown eyes more prominent on my heart-shaped face and accentuated the soft curve of my lips.

Moving the mirror back into position, I sighed before pulling away from the cell phone store and reentering Highway 99, heading south. With no idea where I wanted to go, I hoped that I would find a place where I would be safe and could make a life for myself and my baby.

Thinking of my baby, I rested my hand against my flat stomach and smiled. Difficult as it had been to leave my last home, I knew I was doing the right thing.

I drove through the San Joaquin valley until nausea made driving too uncomfortable. Seeing a motel not far off of the freeway, I took the exit and checked into a room.

I thought about the stops I'd made since leaving Reno and wondered if Trevor would be able to follow my trail.

Maybe I should change my name.

I plugged in my laptop, and using the motel's Wi-Fi, began researching what was involved in legally changing my name. It didn't take long to realize that was not a viable option. Not only would I have to provide the reason for wanting to change my name—which I had no desire to do—but as part of the process, I'd have to publish that information in one of the approved newspapers once a week for four weeks in a row.

No way was I going to do that.

As I thought about my options, I realized that even though legally changing my name was not feasible, I could still introduce myself as something other than Lily Jamison.

Kate. I'll go by Kate Jamison. That was Mom's nickname. Short for Katherine.

Feeling better, I checked my email, but there were no new messages.

I wonder if Trevor's still in jail.

I put my laptop away and turned on the TV, watching a movie until hunger forced me to get up and find some food. I drove to a nearby fast food place and brought the meal back to my room, then watched TV until I was too tired to stay awake.

When I woke the next morning, I thought it would be interesting to drive around the small town where I'd spent the night. Not yet sure what my next move would be, I didn't check out of the motel.

As I passed through different neighborhoods, I found myself on the outskirts of town, and with my poor sense of direction, I'd become turned around and wasn't sure where I was.

Pulling over to take a look at the map I'd purchased when I'd stopped to fill up my car earlier—my cell phone plan didn't include data, so I had no GPS—I glanced around, trying to figure out what street I was on. There were almond orchards all around me and I didn't see any street signs.

Sighing heavily, I climbed out of my car and leaned against the hood, trying to calm myself before choosing a direction to turn. As I gazed into the distance, I noticed a gravel road leading to a small house and decided to drive to it.

Maybe someone there can tell me how to get back to the motel.

I got back into my car and drove toward the gravel road, turning left up the unpaved drive to the house. No cars were around, and I wondered if anyone was home.

Hoping someone would be home, I turned off my engine, got out of the car, and approached the house. I immediately saw the For Rent sign in the front window. Taking a chance that someone still lived there, I followed the stone pavers to the front porch and knocked on the door. No one answered.

The curtain on the front window was open and I cupped my hand and pressed it to the glass as I peered inside. The place was vacant.

I stepped off the porch and stared at the house, taking in the blue shutters, the colorful pansies blooming in the flower garden, and the overall coziness of the house. Warmth rushed through me as I realized this was where I wanted to live.

I pictured myself living there with my baby, happy and safe, and as

I imagined myself sitting on the porch, my baby in my arms, I knew I could make a life for myself and my child—a life filled with joy. I knew there would be challenges, but I believed the good in my life would overcome any bad I might face.

A contented smile curved my lips.

Yes. This is where I need to be.

Lily's story continues in *Don't Look Back.*

About the Author

Christine has always loved to read, but enjoys writing suspenseful novels as well. She has her own eReader and is not embarrassed to admit that she is a book hoarder. One of Christine's favorite activities is to go camping with her family and read, read, read while enjoying the beauty of nature.

Please visit Christine's website: christinekersey.com

Made in the USA
Middletown, DE
14 August 2015